CANDLELIGHT
Ecstasy Supreme

"ARE YOU NICK DIAMOND?" ALEX ASKED.

Suddenly she felt very foolish. Of course, he was. The man standing before her was tall, arrogant, more masculine than handsome. A scar deepened the crease on one side of his face, but still he was appealing.

"Good guess," he replied with a lazy smile. "What can I do for you that seems so urgent?"

"I need your help to find a missing child."

"I'm not a private eye. Tourism is my business."

"But I was told that you could help me, if anyone in Hermosillo could. The police have given up. I don't know where else to turn!"

"I'm sorry, but you seem to have a misconception about me. I just run an aircraft tour service."

Alex's desperation turned to anger. "I had two misconceptions about you, Mr. Diamond. I thought you were something of a hero, and that in your heart there was at least a shred of compassion. But obviously I was wrong. You're just hard-hearted and down here to make a fast buck!"

CANDLELIGHT ECSTASY SUPREMES

MAN OF THE HOUR

Tate McKenna

A CANDLELIGHT ECSTASY SUPREME

Published by
Dell Publishing Co., Inc.
1 Dag Hammarskjold Plaza
New York, New York 10017

ISBN: 0-440-15457-X

Printed in the United States of America

First printing—September 1985

To Carol W., who encouraged and supported me through thick and thin; who is the best of friends. And to Jenny, the hope of the future.

To Our Readers:

Candlelight Ecstasy is delighted to announce the start of a brand-new series—Ecstasy Supremes! Now you can enjoy a romance series unlike all the others— longer and more exciting, filled with more passion, adventure, and intrigue—the stories you've been waiting for.

In months to come we look forward to presenting books by many of your favorite authors and the very finest work from new authors of romantic fiction as well. As always, we are striving to present the unique, absorbing love stories that you enjoy most—the very best love has to offer.

Breathtaking and unforgettable, Ecstasy Supremes will follow in the great romantic tradition you've come to expect *only* from Candlelight Ecstasy.

Your suggestions and comments are always welcome. Please let us hear from you.

Sincerely,

The Editors
Candlelight Romances
1 Dag Hammarskjold Plaza
New York, New York 10017

PROLOGUE

Hermosillo, Mexico
September

Dear Carol,

I just had a baby tonight! No, I haven't been keeping a secret from you. Actually, my housekeeper gave birth, but I almost feel as if I did. Anyway, I'm exhausted and exhilarated and far too excited to sleep right now. If the Mexican telephone system were more reliable, I'd call you, even though it's past midnight.

When the university sent Teresa to be my housekeeper a few months ago, no one knew she was pregnant. By the time I found out, I didn't have the heart to dismiss her. She's a good worker and needs the job desperately because she doesn't have a husband. She talks about going back to the States with me as if it were paradise. I've been so busy with my own job that I didn't give a second thought to how and where she would have this baby, just assuming she would go to the hospital. Imagine my surprise this afternoon when she asked me to send for the midwife! She was quite calm. I was a nervous wreck!

I'm sure I was slightly incoherent. I only remember saying "Don't you dare have that baby here, Teresa! You go to the hospital where you belong!" She just smiled and said, "No, señorita, in my room. Don't worry. It won't take long."

And sure enough, with the midwife attending, she had it! We sweated through ten hours of labor. I guess that's not too bad for a first baby. My God, Carol, Teresa is only a child herself, only eighteen! I tried to remember what the speaker from the Lamaze Method said, but it escaped me. I chanted things like "Breathe deeply," and "Try to relax," which, I'm sure, weren't highly appreciated at the time. My biggest contributions were to keep cool towels on her head and let her squeeze the hell out of my hand. By the time the baby's head appeared, we were all crying and laughing at the same time!

I will never, ever, forget the sound of her first squeaky cry! There are no words to describe what I was feeling at that moment.

Mother and daughter are doing fine. The midwife has completed her duty successfully. But la gringa assistant is going to have a tall glass of wine! Little did I realize when I accepted this Mexican assignment that I would become so involved in . . . life. Tonight, I've witnessed the awesome beginning!

A new Godmother,
Alex

P.S. The baby's name is Jennifer Teresa Alexis Portillo, and she's absolutely beautiful.

CHAPTER ONE

A million times after the accident, Alexis reconstructed the scene in her mind and attempted to place everyone and everything in the correct sequence of events. But it did no good. She couldn't visualize the moment of Jenni's disappearance.

She recalled every detail except the crucial one.

The sultry air was redolent with scents typical of a Mexican marketplace. Charcoal, grilling corn on the cob and *fajitas*, barbecued beef, only added to the steamy street. The strong aroma of garlic clashed with the perfumed fragrance of flowers. She walked past crates of live chickens and turned her nose away from the pungent odor of damp feathers. And the air smelled like rain. It was unseasonably hot for April.

She remembered the noise that day. It was nothing out of the ordinary, just the usual medley of sounds—the lilting Spanish phrases of vendors hawking their wares, children giggling, the occasional braying of a bored donkey.

Alex touched Teresa's shoulder in order to get

her attention. "I wish it would rain enough to cool things down, but not tonight. I want this party to be perfect."

"Si, señorita." Teresa grinned and shrugged. "So what can we do about it? If it rains, it rains. Do you want mangos for the fruit tray?"

Alex envied Teresa's nonchalant attitude. "Mangos? Ah, yes! My consuming passion! Be sure to get enough for all the guests."

"I'll get them." Teresa began to sort through the yellowish orbs and Alex watched, holding little Jenni's small hand tightly.

She heard the whining of tires but had no time to think, to react to the car that headed straight for them! She screamed at Teresa and tried to shield Jenni.

Jenni! Would she ever see the child again?

A green, partially rusted car appeared out of nowhere and rammed people and wagons in the open-air marketplace. The vehicle finally stopped when it crashed into a light post. The disaster replayed again and again in Alex's mind, sometimes in slow motion. She could see the events as they happened, the events that changed the direction of her life forever.

The light post toppled slowly against a building, and it lay like a matchstick that had been carelessly dropped amid a miniature Mexican street scene. Display wagons loaded with colorful fruits, vegetables, and flowers, fell like dominoes one on top of another, scattering their contents everywhere.

Vibrant colors flashed through Alex's mind—

14

yellow and orange and red flying in all directions. Then came the green object of destruction. It all happened so fast: the green car fishtailing toward them, then the cacophony. The screams of fright, perhaps of pain. The braying of donkeys, the yelping of dogs. Rapid chattering of Spanish, all filling the chaotic Mexican marketplace, echoing in her head.

There was a moment of nothing, a blank spot in her memory. Alex later realized she must have blacked out for a brief moment. She lay sprawled on the sidewalk, gathering her senses. *What happened?*

She struggled to a sitting position and her eyes fell on Teresa. That's when the inner panic flushed through every inch of her, coursing like hot liquid fire, threatening to explode in a frenzy of screaming terror.

Oblivious to her own scraped knees and elbows, Alex scrambled wildly over oranges and mangos to reach Teresa's still form. The young Mexican woman lay with her head nestled tranquilly against an adobe brick building, her eyes closed, her body slack.

Alex's head reeled. They'd been walking along the street, laughing and talking, selecting mangos for the party. What seemed so crucial moments ago now seemed ludicrous. It was like a horror movie, one you never believed because it just couldn't happen that way, certainly not to you. Yet here they were, Teresa unconscious with Alex hovering nearby, trying to retain some sense of control over her wildly racing emotions.

Teresa moaned and rolled her head away from the crumbling adobe brick. Her eyes remained closed, as if she were merely asleep. And yet, her usually-tanned face had an unnatural pallor. A lump the size of an egg marred the young woman's forehead, and was already turning deep blue-purple. For all the destruction and obvious harm, there was no blood. Teresa just looked like she was . . . asleep.

There was a moment of unnatural quiet while Alex tried to decide what to do. She wanted to scream, to cry, to shake Teresa awake. But she refrained, knowing instinctively none of that would help. Panic grew inside Alex, fueled by pumping adrenaline and revealed in her shaking hands which cradled and caressed Teresa's face. She was careful not to move her but yearned to wake Teresa and force those eyes open, to shake some life into her.

"Teresa . . . oh, my God, Teresa!" Alex's voice was oddly high-pitched and shaky. "Teresa, can you hear me? Wake up! Please, talk to me! Teresa! Everything's going to be all right. We'll get help."

She looked around frantically and later recalled the circle of stricken faces, all dark-skinned and dark-eyed. Before she could make an appeal for help, a man reluctantly shuffled forward from the crowd.

"How is she, señorita?" he asked in Spanish.

"She needs help. Call an ambulance," Alex ordered, also speaking in Spanish. Something clicked inside and she was filled with a sense of pseudo composure. Suddenly, her voice was sure and strong. She knew that Teresa needed help, not hysteria. That much was obvious and clear in her mind. "Quickly!"

"Si, señorita."

Alex turned back to Teresa's limp form and took her hand. She began to talk to the still, quiet face, muttering repeatedly in both Spanish and English, "Everything's going to be all right, Teresa. Help is on its way."

Then, and Alex didn't know what took her so long to think of it, she swung her head around frantically and demanded of a woman who stood helplessly nearby, *"La niña? Donde está la niña?* Where is she?"

The woman gazed over each shoulder and shrugged back at Alex. *"Yo no sé."*

"What do you mean you don't know? Get her for me! She's just a toddler!" Alex was filled with a sudden vexation. How could they stand around so ineptly when she needed assistance right now? She couldn't be everywhere at once. Here lay Teresa, unconscious, and Jenni was probably scared and—"Bring me the child, *por favor.* This is her mother." She patted Teresa's hand and felt as utterly helpless as she ever had in her life.

A siren pierced the air, and Alex shuttered with relief. The wail of a siren had always been an ominous, frightening sound. But now it was welcome. It heralded the reassuring arrival of assistance. The siren would bring clearheaded people who would help her. And take care of Teresa.

Alex rocked back on her knees and watched as a police car screeched to a stop, dividing the crowd. Immediately, another official car pulled up behind the first one and the place swarmed with uniformed men. Most of them descended on the green car, but one approached Alex and the prone form of Teresa.

He instructed the crowd to move back and knelt to feel Teresa's pulse. "Weak," he muttered, turning to Alex. "Do you know her?"

"Yes, she's my housekeeper," Alex responded frantically. "She needs an ambulance. Can you get help for her?"

"It will be here soon," he assured her, drawing out a pen and paper. "What is the name of the victim?"

Victim? Alex wrenched inside at the term. She answered numbly, "Teresa Marie Portillo."

"Address?"

"She lives with me. She's my housekeeper. On Linda Vista."

The policeman's eyes quickly assessed the slender, blond woman on her knees. "And your name, señorita?"

"Alexis Julian. I'm a professor at Sonoran University."

"The victim's age."

Alex swallowed. "Twenty."

"Can you tell me what happened here?"

Taking a deep breath, Alex explained, pointing in the direction of the horrible green Chevy. "A car, *that* car, came around the corner, skidded into all these fruit wagons, and crashed into that

18

pole. It knocked us—oh, my God, Jenni! Can you stay here with Teresa? I've got to get her baby!"

Alex sprang nimbly to her feet and began a frenzied search. Jenni was nowhere in sight! Alex shoved past vendors who stood helplessly beside their overturned wagons and stumbled over the scattered mess of fruit, flowers, and bread. Soon she was frantically throwing aside embroidered dresses and decorative shirts and rushing headlong from one side of the narrow street to the other, all the while calling "Jenni, Jenni!"

Finally, she turned to the crowd, her large indigo eyes brimming with tears. "Oh, please help me find the child. She's a little girl, eighteen months old. She belongs to the woman who is injured! She must be hurt too! Maybe under one of these wagons! Please look for her!"

A rumble of sympathy waved through the crowd and they began to scatter and do Alex's frantic biding. Two men helped her set one of the wagons upright and watched sadly as she dropped to her knees on the pebbled street. There was no child beneath it.

Undaunted, she scrambled to her feet and led them to another overturned wagon. "This one! Help me lift it. Maybe she's here!" With an inexhaustible energy, Alex searched, spurring the curious crowd to help her. "She's here! She has to be here! We had her with us before the crash!"

The sound of another siren reminded Alex of Teresa. She rushed back in time to murmur comforting words to the unconscious young woman before the medics lifted her onto the white-sheeted gurney. They closed the ambulance doors, and Alex turned frantically to a policeman.

"You must help me find her child. The three of us were right here. She's just a little girl, not quite two, with curly brown hair, wearing a pink sundress. And now I can't find her. Maybe she's hurt!" From the way the policeman looked at her, Alex wondered if she was making any sense.

He gave her a gentle smile. "We will find her, señorita. But, please—" He looked down and Alex followed his gaze. She was clutching his arm with white-knuckled fingers which dug into his forearm.

"Sorry." She released him and whimpered apologetically. "I'm just so scared. First, Teresa. Now, Jenni. Things are happening so fast. . . ."

"I understand, señorita. Don't worry. We will find her. Now, tell me more about this child that is missing." The siren from the ambulance taking Teresa away blotted out all possible conversation for a few minutes.

Nick Diamond heard the distant sirens and knew by the increasing swell, they were approaching his vicinity. Maybe there had been an incident at the neighborhood bar, a spot of constant turmoil, he thought. Then again, maybe not. What if there was some problem with their contact for the pickup tonight? What if someone had squealed? He always considered what might go wrong when the time grew close. It was his business to be a little paranoid.

Nick lurched instantly to his feet, moving rapidly for a man so large. Though lean, his legs were powerful, his body muscular, his chest broad. His deep umber eyes gleamed, alertly keened to his surroundings. There wasn't a speck of warmth in those eyes, though, for they were cagey, almost vicious, and dark. Those eyes had looked despair squarely in the face, and stared unflinchingly at all kinds of atrocities.

He had overcome the fear most men felt in dangerous situations, and anticipated his next risk with shrewd determination, almost an eagerness. It was the way he lived, on the edge of disaster and excitement. It was this edge that brought his lean body to a slightly crouched position, his taut muscles flexed like a coiled spring.

Although he was an American, Nick Diamond blended in with the dark-haired Mexican people around him. Purposely, he dressed in casual peasant-style clothing—white britches called *calzones* and a *camisa*, a shirt that hung outside his waistband. Beneath the loose clothes and behind the dark, bushy mustache was a man of tempered steel, a dangerous man. *Norteamericano*, some Mexicans called him. Those who knew him referred to the tall, commanding man as *El Capitán*. He definitely fit the title. His coarse, unfettered *camisa* sometimes concealed a small gun, which was almost completely hidden in his large hand when he held it. He wasn't reluctant to use the weapon; indeed, the cold steel had saved his life more than once. To those who'd seen him in action, he engendered fear. And respect. In a

21

time and place desperate for heroes, Nick Diamond was a reluctant proxy.

Before Nick could take another step, a short, stocky Mexican man in similar peasant attire appeared in the doorway. His muscular arms braced the arched portal, effectively blocking the exit.

"What the hell is that all about, Juancho?"

"It is nothing, Capitán. Listen." The burly man with the elaborate handlebar mustache held up a finger. It was almost a comical gesture coming from such a rough-looking man.

Nick paused as the siren's whine was cut short.

"See? They stop a couple of blocks away. Maybe two stubborn cars wouldn't give up their right of way. Didn't you hear the crash?"

"You make it sound like the cars down here have a mind of their own, Juancho. When, actually, you have the craziest drivers in the world! Might be trouble at Pancho's Bar again."

The first siren was followed closely by a second.

"Si." Juancho relaxed in the entryway and turned to look out into the street, still listening. "Or the marketplace."

"Maybe we should check it out."

"Not we, Capitán. Maybe I will go." Juancho shook his head and the carefully curled ends of his mustache jiggled. "It's probably just another fender bender. We don't earn our reputation for the highest number of car wrecks in the world for nothing."

"We need to make sure it's a wreck."

22

"No, Capitán. No more heroics, please. We're supposed to keep a low profile, remember? If you keep on saving lives, word about you will spread fast and everyone will be talking. We do not want that."

Nick relaxed his shoulders and leaned trim hips against the edge of an old wooden desk. "If you're referring to that incident last week, I merely performed basic CPR. Nothing fancy. The man was having a heart attack. I couldn't let him die in the street."

"And now everyone thinks you work miracles. It makes you some kind of hero." Juancho gestured with an expressive hand.

"Some hero," Nick grunted with a low laugh. "If they knew the truth about me, they'd swing me from the nearest mesquite tree."

Juancho grinned, his white teeth flashing beneath his handlebar mustache. "Si, Capitán. But they don't know the truth. They only know what they see. So you must lay low. Especially today. We cannot take a chance on messing up tonight's haul. Too much at stake."

"Ah, you're right, Juancho. I just need to know everything that's going on around me." Nick folded his muscular arms across his broad chest. "Anyway, the *policía* are there by now, and they can handle it. Probably."

His eyes flickered with sarcasm and Juancho sighed and looked away. He had worked with Nick Diamond long enough to know what he was thinking, how his shrewdly calculating mind worked. Nick's years of experience had left him wary and unyielding. No one or nothing could be trusted.

A third siren pierced the dead quiet.

Nick shifted uncomfortably and looked up, his unswerving umber eyes meeting his partner's in a mutual understanding.

Juancho nodded and began to move before the demand could even be made. "Si, señor, I'll go check it out."

"Good idea." Nick turned back to the shabby space he and Juancho called an office and picked up a paper from the desk.

Fifteen minutes later, Juancho returned with an account to relay. "A drunk driver crashed into a light pole and knocked over many wagons in the public marketplace. With the Saturday crowd in the market, they were damn lucky. Only a few people were injured."

"Badly?"

Juancho shrugged. "One woman. They took her away in an ambulance."

Nick's eyes narrowed. "You're sure it was an accident?"

Juancho nodded. "There was another young woman involved. A *norteamericana*, with blond hair. She was looking for a Mexican baby. Claimed the child was there before the accident."

"Injured?"

"They don't know. Couldn't find her."

"Hmmm." Nick looked back down at the sheet of paper in his hands. As soon as he'd memorized this information, the paper would be destroyed, leaving no evidence.

"The woman, she was very pretty, Capitán. Blond hair and blue eyes. *Muy bonita*. From the States—" Juancho halted.

Nick had already turned his back. He hadn't heard, nor did he care about any pretty, young woman. But it wasn't surprising to Juancho. In the year they'd worked together in Mexico, Nick had never shown anything more than lusty interest in any woman. Although his women were beautiful, Nick never bothered with anything more than a brief encounter.

The man was remarkable. Juancho knew his partner had blocked everything else out and now concentrated completely on the information before him, and the wrap-up of tonight's operation. It was just as well. He didn't need the complication of a woman in his line of business.

The policeman jotted down more information from Alex, then stuffed the pen and paper into his pocket and led her to his sergeant. The three conferred, then began a search in the streets which lasted until every cart had been set upright again and the wrecker had hauled away the ugly green hulk of a car. Its drunken driver had long since been whisked away to jail.

Even when the police gave up the search, Alex stayed. Hours later, after the mess in the streets was completely cleaned up and vendors were attempting to sell what wasn't destroyed by the crash, Alex was still there. Except for the light post resting against a building, the marketplace bore no trace of the tragedy that had darkened Alex's life.

But Alex couldn't give up. Jenni had to be here. If she wasn't injured, then someone had rescued her. Someone knew where she was, Alex was sure of it. One of the shopkeepers had to know where the child was, and Alexis was determined to find out. Tirelessly, she went from shop to shop, vendor to vendor, even to strangers on the street. "Have you seen a little girl? About two. Dark, curly hair . . ."

"Señorita?"

"Yes?" Alex halted wearily beside an open-front quick food shop.

"Señorita, please, come in. Have a seat." The shopkeeper gestured to a small round wrought-iron table near the wall. "Let me give you something to drink. To refresh you."

The small place looked like a welcome haven, and his voice was so kind that Alexis complied without a second thought. She slumped at the table and stared blankly, exhausted from the energy-draining events of the day. When he shuffled toward her with a blended fruit and ice drink in his hand, Alex recognized him as the same man who'd stepped forward to help her after the accident.

Alex smiled faintly, her mouth softening. "Thank you for helping me today." She spoke to him in fluent Spanish. "I was so scared."

"It was nothing." He shrugged and sat down

opposite her, sliding the tall glass across the table. "Here. Drink, please."

"Thanks." Alex sipped gratefully, not fully realizing how hot and thirsty she was until this minute.

"You must give up this search for the child," he said gently. "Let the police handle it."

"But the police have gone. Jenni has to be around here somewhere! If she wasn't injured, and obviously she wasn't, then maybe one of the shop keepers or street vendors saw her—"

"No, señorita. We know nothing."

"Nada, nada! That's all I've heard all day! I'm sick of it! Do you even believe we had a child with us this morning? The police don't! When we didn't find her right away, they questioned me about even having her along. Can you believe that?"

"Si, I think she was with you, señorita."

"Then where could she be now?"

He spread his palms. "She is not here, señorita. You will not find her here on this street."

"Then where—"

"I would say . . ." he paused and looked around. In a lower voice, he continued. "I would say that she has been taken."

"What? By whom? Why?"

"I cannot say. I do not know." He shrugged again. "I have told you too much already." He shuffled away to wait on another customer.

Alex sat stunned by what the shopkeeper had told her. Was it possible that Jenni had been snatched in the chaotic moments before anyone remembered to look for her? A thousand questions plagued Alex. Where was Jenni now? Was she safe? Was she being fed and cared for? Was she hurt? Was she scared and lonely and . . . crying?

Alex's indigo eyes softened as she recalled the child's dark tousled curls framing chubby, golden cheeks. She could almost feel the soft-skinned little girl sitting in her lap, listening to one more story before bedtime, and the gentle tug of Jenni's tight little arms hugging her neck. She could almost smell the baby-powdered fragrance and hear her high-pitched giggle of delight. *Mamacita! Mamacita! More cookies!*

Oh, dear God! Where was she?

Alex bolted away from the table, then stopped to dig for change.

"No, señorita. Please accept this small gift from me. You have been through a lot today."

Alex looked up and met the shopkeeper's honest, brown eyes. "Gracias, señor. For everything." *Even your dreadful opinion about what happened to Jenni.*

She hailed a cab and told the driver to take her to the hospital. First she had to check on Teresa, then she'd go to the police station. The situation was different now. If the child had been taken . . .

The ride to the hospital was quick, and Alex hurried into the Emergency entrance. A strong antiseptic smell and drab green walls accosted her senses.

Alex approached the dark-haired nurse at the

desk. "Where is Teresa Portillo? She was in an auto accident earlier today."

The nurse checked her clipboard, then looked up quickly. "You are looking for Teresa Marie Portillo?"

"Yes. Which room?"

"Do you know her?"

"Yes, yes," Alex answered impatiently. She had so much to do, to think about, and this nurse persisted with formalities. "I'm a teacher at the University. My name is Alexis Julian. Teresa is my housekeeper. Look, if there's a problem with the bill, I'll handle it."

"No, nothing like that, señorita." The nurse's voice grew gentle. "I'm sorry to tell you this, but the lady you ask about died about an hour ago."

Alex's breath caught in a hitch, as if someone had belted her in the stomach. Her eyes filled with hot tears and she gripped the desk frantically. "Oh, no! That's not possible! Are you sure? Check again! It just can't be! Not my Teresa! We haven't even found her daughter Jenni yet! God help me, not both of them!"

Immediately, several nurses converged to handle the *norteamericana* with blond hair and very blue eyes who was nearly hysterical. For a period of time, Alexis Julian was beyond reason. Drab green walls threatened to close in on her and a certain horrifying scene in which a green car ran out of control kept replaying in her mind.

Finally, Alex quieted. Even in the sultry heat

29

she trembled uncontrollably. "Would you call my friend?" she requested in a hushed voice. "Rosemary Garza. Ask her to come and take me home."

CHAPTER TWO

"Thanks for picking me up at the hospital, Rosemary. I'm not normally so hysterical."

"You weren't hysterical, just upset." Rosemary smiled reassuringly. "And after what you've been through today, Alex, you have every right to be. Isn't that right, Sam?"

Her husband nodded. "You're doing fine, Alex."

"Well, I certainly didn't feel like facing an empty house this evening." Alex was still shaken, even hours later, as she drank coffee in the home of her friends and colleagues, Rosemary and Sam Garza.

"That's what friends are for, Alex." Rosemary smiled sympathetically. "This has been a horrible day for you."

"So much has happened, I still can't believe it. Oh, my God, I forgot all about the party tonight!"

"Don't worry about it," Rosemary soothed gently. "After they called from the hospital, we figured no one would be in the partying mood tonight. Sam phoned everyone and canceled."

"Thanks, Sam." Alex sighed with relief. "You

were absolutely right. I'm in no condition to do anything tonight. I hope they understand."

"Of course they do. I explained, and they sent their condolences." Sam took another sip of coffee and studied Alex's drawn face. Although he was Mexican, Sam had fair skin and blue eyes that harked back to his Spanish ancestry.

Sam had been educated at the University of Arizona, then returned to his native Mexico to teach. His dynamic American wife, Rosemary, worked with Alex in the Early Childhood Department at Sonoran University in Hermosillo. During the two years Alex had been an exchange professor in the industrial city, she and the Garzas had become good friends. Now, in the face of tragedy, they pulled together.

"You'll find most of the university staff very compassionate," explained Rosemary, a brunette with dark, snappy eyes. "They'll look on your tragedy as one of their own. In fact, they might tend to smother you with sympathy and covered dishes, so it's probably just as well that you're here until you compose yourself and decide what to do next."

"I don't want their sympathy. If anything, I need their help." Alex pressed her lips together in an effort to control her emotions.

"Alex, please spend the night here." Rosemary smiled warmly and patted her friend's arm. "I know how difficult it must be to go back to your house alone, so don't do it until you're ready."

"Thanks, Rosemary, but I'll be all right. You two were so wonderfully calm in the face of a crisis, and I needed that. I'm afraid I fell apart at the hospital. It was so unexpected. I still can't believe Teresa's gone—" Alex's voice broke off in a sob.

"I've called the police twice this evening, Sam," she continued after she'd gotten a grip on herself, "and they still claim there are no leads on Jenni. Why haven't they found her? What have they been doing all this time?"

Sam took a deep breath. "Nothing. To be perfectly honest, they're probably doing nothing active right now, Alex."

"What?"

"Please try to understand, Alex. The police are extremely busy. And understaffed."

"You mean they probably won't do much more than the rudimentary questioning they've already done?"

He nodded. "I'm afraid so. I'm sure this case isn't high on their list of priorities."

"What do you mean? A child is missing! What could be more important than finding her?"

"It's important to us, but to them . . ." Sam shrugged. "Remember, they have violent crimes to deal with and—"

"Isn't this violent? A child abducted! I just can't believe it, Sam!" Alex rose and began pacing the floor.

"Alex," Sam said, trying to calm her. "You must have patience. There is also a chance—a chance, mind you—that they may not find her."

She wheeled around, her indigo eyes snapping at her friend. "No! I won't accept that, Sam!"

"Alex, be reasonable. This isn't the U.S. Things are done differently in Mexico. You can't stomp into the police station and demand your rights. You have none! You're on foreign soil!"

"My God, Sam, who cares what soil this is? A child has been taken! A child we all loved. No, I won't accept the possibility that she may never be found! I have to find her!"

"Alex, I know you don't want to hear these things, but you must be realistic."

Rosemary gave her husband a warning glance. "Please, Sam . . ."

They sat in silence for a while, then Sam apologetically said, "Alex, I didn't mean to upset you this evening. Surely you know we care about Jenni. But I don't want you to harbor any false hopes for finding her."

"Are you saying you don't think I'll ever find her?"

Sam took a deep breath. "No, I won't go that far. But realistically, it may be tough. A young Mexican woman was killed today. She had no family. No husband. Her illegitimate child is missing. The only person asking about that child is an American exchange professor. Face it, you don't have much clout, Alex."

"Dammit, Sam!" Alex exclaimed, close to tears. She knew, deep in her heart, that he was right. Perhaps there wasn't much chance of finding Jenni. But she wouldn't give up.

"Sam, hush!" Rosemary scowled. "Can't you see you're upsetting her?" She put an arm around Alex's shoulders. "Don't worry, honey.

We'll find her. I'll go with you to talk to the police again tomorrow, if you want."

"Maybe he's right, Rosemary," Alex admitted hollowly. "It's going to be damned tough. I need time to decide what to do next."

"Well, you don't have to decide tonight. You can take all the time you need right here. I insist that you spend the night with us. Come on. A good hot bath will work wonders. I know you're bushed. It's been an exhausting day. And look, you have scratches on your knees and elbows. We need to put some disinfectant on those."

Alex allowed Rosemary to guide her to the back bedroom and put antiseptic on her scraped elbows. The act made them both feel better, gave them something to be concerned about besides the crisis. Long after Sam and Rosemary went to bed, Alex lay wide-eyed and alert. The questions that had driven her all day long still plagued her.

Where is Jenni? How is she? Is she being taken care of? Is she lonely and crying? As long as there were no answers to those questions, Alex wouldn't give up the search.

Realizing that sleep was not imminent, she slipped out of bed. From a desk in the bedroom she took out a pen and paper and dashed off a missive to her friend Carol, relating the terrifying events of the day.

Nick Diamond checked his watch.
Two twenty-nine.
He set the chopper down and cut the lights.

35

They sat in the pitch dark for a minute or two, neither speaking.

Finally, Juancho broke the silence. "You okay, Capitán?"

"Yeah. Close call, Juancho. I don't like it."

"You think someone squealed?"

"Damned if I know. I just hope no one saw us escape. They came in too damn fast. I'll talk to the boss tomorrow. See if timing can be controlled. Otherwise, we're goners."

"Si, Capitán."

Nick sighed heavily and ran a large hand roughly over his angular face. His finger lingered on the scar that ran along his cheek. Another close call. A few more inches and . . . "I'm tired, Juancho. Tired of these late-night runs. Tired of the risks."

"My wife, she is tired of it, too, Capitán." Juancho chuckled nervously. "Every day she asks me if this is the last time."

"When we have a night like this, when somebody else screws up and my life is at stake, I wonder if it's worth the risk involved. Of course, for you it's a greater risk. What is it, three kids?"

Juancho nodded. "Twins and a little girl."

"Aw, hell. We're just tired tonight. Tomorrow it'll look different."

"It's already tomorrow." Juancho pointed to his watch.

"Yep," Nick growled. "Well, maybe I'm getting old."

"Maybe you need a woman waiting in your bed at night, Capitán. She would rub your back.

36

Keep you warm," he said as he moved to get out of the helicopter.

"Hell, a woman wouldn't solve anything. She'd only create more problems!"

Juancho chuckled in the darkness.

"What's up for tomorrow?" Nick asked.

"Nothing."

"Good. That's exactly what I want to do for the next three days. Nothing!"

The next morning, Alex and Rosemary sat on the small back patio eating breakfast amidst the bougainvillea and fragrant gardenia bushes.

"Sam's gone to play tennis. He has a couple of buddies he would love to beat." Rosemary smiled as she poured them more coffee.

"I hope you didn't stay home because of me."

"Not at all." Rosemary tucked her robe tighter before sitting. "Sometimes it's fun to be lazy. I wanted to stay and keep you company. Besides, he's beat me three Sundays in a row and I think it's time for him to work out with someone his own size and skill!"

Alex smiled and reached for another pastry. "I can't believe I'm eating like this."

"After yesterday, I'm sure you can afford a few extra calories. I'm sorry that Sam was so rough on you last night, Alex. He means well, it's just that he's so realistic!"

"I understand, Rosemary. Maybe I needed someone to plant my feet solidly on the ground."

"Leave it to Sam to do the planting." Rosemary rolled her eyes dramatically. "I don't think he understands how deeply you feel about Jenni, Alex."

"Do you remember the night she was born?" Alex mused softly.

"Oh, God, do I ever! We paced the living room of your house like a couple of prospective fathers. And when the midwife called for help, I knew I couldn't do it. I'm the one who faints when I prick my finger."

Alex laughed gently. "I'd never done anything like that before. It was an experience I'll never forget. . . ."

When Alex's voice trailed off, Rosemary picked up the memories. "The sound of that squeaky, little cry . . . what a feeling! It meant everything was all right."

"I love her, Rosemary. And I won't give up until I find her," Alex vowed in a shaky voice.

Rosemary hugged Alex quickly. "You *are* determined. And I admire you for it. I have every confidence that you'll find her. I just hope the University stays solvent long enough for you to do it."

"What do you mean?"

"You know the rumors about financial difficulties that have been floating around for months? Well, there was a private meeting Friday evening of several irate professors. There were complaints about budget cuts, lack of modern equipment, and salary freezes. They're going to present a petition to the president."

"Is it serious, Rosemary?"

"I'm afraid it's very serious. Of course, this university has been through upheavals before and weathered the storms. But lack of money is hard to argue."

"Has the administration announced budget cuts? And salary freezes?"

"No, the official budget hasn't been released publicly. Unofficially, though, the word is that no salaries will be increased and that some departments will be cut . . . departments like Early Childhood."

"Ours?" Alex lifted her brows. "I don't have tenure here to protect me."

"What better place to make cuts than the children's department? We aren't strongly influential in the country, like agriculture or business. We just teach women how to take care of their kids."

"But ours is one of the most important for the future. If the kids aren't educated and prepared for taking over responsibilities and problems, who's going to do it?"

"Take it easy, Alex. You don't have to convince me. I'm on your side, remember?"

"Sorry, Rosemary. If the budget for our department is cut, guess who'll be the first to go? Me! The exchange professor from Arizona State. And if I haven't found Jenni by then—"

"Now, Alex, don't jump to conclusions. Wait and see what happens."

"I have no alternative, do I? Wait and see what the University is going to do with my job. Wait and see if the police find Jenni. Just wait. . . ." In frustration, Alex paced to the edge of the bougainvillea-lined patio and back. "It's not easy to wait. I want action now!"

"Well, sounds like we're going to have action sooner than we planned. I think I hear my darling husband returning from the ravages of a morning of tennis. So much for our time alone, Alex." Rosemary went to greet her husband and Alex could hear her murmuring to him.

In a few minutes, Sam poked his head out the door. "Morning, Alex. Feeling better?" He stepped out on the patio. "The coffee smells great! Mind if I join you two? Alex, I'm sorry about last night. You've suffered a terrible tragedy, and I'm afraid I've been insensitive to your feelings."

"It's okay, Sam," Alex muttered. She was taken aback by his sudden apology. It was probably prompted by Rosemary. "Actually, you made me think about alternate ways of looking for Jenni."

Sam draped a towel around his neck and mopped his brow with one end. After pouring a cup of coffee, he sat opposite her. "You're serious, aren't you?"

"As serious as I've ever been about anything. She's like my own, Sam. I'm all she has, especially now that Teresa's . . ." Alex swallowed hard and didn't finish the statement. It hurt too much to say it.

Sam nibbled thoughtfully on an empanada, a small fruit pie. "There is someone who might be able to help you, Alex."

"Who?"

"Padre Ramón, the priest at Our Lady of Guadalupe."

"Padre Ramón? I know him. In fact, he'll be conducting Teresa's funeral mass tomorrow. How could he help?"

"He knows everyone, and probably knows more about what's going on in this city than anybody I can think of."

"I'm willing to try anything at this point."

"I'm just looking at this realistically. You're going to need all the help you can get in finding that baby."

Alex studied Sam's sincere eyes. "Okay. I'll go talk to this priest."

The old priest's rich chestnut hair was sprinkled with gray and slightly shaggy along his white collar. His eyes were steady and kind, his chin square, his back straight and proud. He was a man who, Alex decided, had probably been quite handsome in his youth.

"I'm glad to see you, Alexis. It gives me a chance to practice my English. Please, come in and sit down."

"Thank you for seeing me, Padre. I must talk to you. It's urgent."

"Certainly." His voice was kind. "This is a hard thing you must face. I understand you are Teresa's only family. Is it about her funeral?"

"No, I . . . I need your help with something else."

"How can I help you?" He folded his hands benevolently.

41

She sighed. "I'm having no luck in finding Jenni, Teresa's little girl. She was with us the day of the accident and disappeared right under our noses."

"Are the police looking for her?"

Alex shrugged and the discouragement showed in the sag of her shoulders. "They say they're looking. But nothing has come of it."

"And you think I can do something the police cannot?"

"Can you do something? Anything? Padre . . ." Alex lifted anxious blue eyes and began her appeal. "You know I'm the only family Teresa had. There is no one else to take care of her child. I'm her godmother, and I . . . I love her."

Padre Ramón nodded. "I can see that you do."

Alex spread her hands helplessly. "Then do something to help me. I have to find her!"

Turning away from Alex's stricken face, the priest studied a crack in the old stucco wall for a few terse minutes. "There is a man . . ."

"Yes?" Alex prodded him.

He shook his head. "I don't know if he can help you or if he will. But if there is anyone in this city who could—"

"Who is he?" Alex asked anxiously, leaning forward.

The priest began to jot something on a slip of paper. "You must promise—"

"Yes! Anything!"

"Promise not to tell him, or anyone, that I sent you to him."

She gave her word.

42

"His name is Nick Diamond, but he is known around here as *El Capitán*. He has a business of sorts in town. This is his address."

Alex leaned back reflectively. *"El Capitán?* I've heard of him. He's an American? A wheeler-dealer type?"

The priest shrugged silently.

Alex's eyes dropped to the slip of paper and she mumbled a response to her own ponderings. "Why else would an American have a business here in Mexico, but to make money?"

"Be prepared to pay, Alex."

"Pay for my own little girl?"

Father Ramón's eyes met hers steadily. "Whatever it takes to get her back."

Alex's back straightened as she drew up tightly. She was dealing with a different breed now. Someone who was devious enough to steal a child. "I'll do whatever is necessary. Thank you, Padre Ramón." Even as she said it, Alex wondered where she would get enough money.

CHAPTER THREE

Alex paused outside the shabby office door and took a deep, shaky breath. In the distance, she heard the plaintive wail of a siren and instinctively shuddered. It would be a long time before the reminders of the tragedy were gone from her mind. There was still the most visible reminder —her own empty house. She had yet to face those hollow rooms by herself.

The sultry April air was suffocatingly hot and heavy. Perspiration trickled beneath her hair and down her back. She should have pinned her hair up for comfort. It would have hidden the frizzy curls that always busheled her hair during the rainy season. But she didn't think of it. In fact, Alex hadn't thought of anything except Jenni for the last two days. And nights.

She gripped the doorknob. It rattled loosely and threatened to fall off in her hand. Across the thick patterned glass of the upper half of the door were painted the words: AIRCRAFT SERVICE —We Fly Anyone Anywhere. By American standards the place was seedy. Was this the office of the *norteamericano,* the one who could help anyone do anything? Or was he just down here in Mexico to make a buck? He advertised to fly anyone anywhere. Well, all she needed from him was help in finding Jenni.

Alex stiffened, wondering what she would do if he wasn't willing to help her. But she preferred not to think of that now. She was desperate.

Pushing the door open, she stepped inside. The interior of the office was hotter than outside, if it was possible. There wasn't a breeze stirring, no fan, nothing. Two men sat in straight-back wooden chairs, their feet propped up on desks and sombreros pulled over their faces.

A slow, unreasonable anger that she couldn't quell grew inside her. They seemed so uncaring in their nonchalance. A life was at stake here! The precious life of a child! Perhaps she should have called first so they would be expecting her. A quick glance at the two battered desks revealed there was no phone. It was just as well. A phone call wouldn't have the impact that she had planned for this meeting with *El Capitán*.

Alex glanced at the first figure. He was short and stocky and his feet barely reached the desk. His legs were thick and powerful looking, and his broad hands exuded strength. Head turned to one side, he snored loudly.

She turned disdainfully to the other man. He was tall, his body stretching easily from chair to desk. His legs were long and his scruffy boots with a hole in the sole caught her eye. Her gaze traveled up his length, past the noticeable male bulge where his legs connected to his torso. She

45

couldn't avoid the erotic sight in those loose-fitting pants of his. Tanned, long-fingered hands were folded across his flat stomach. Her indigo eyes flickered for a moment, pausing to admire the bold virility of his physique, then quickly moved on to the expansive chest and the ridiculous broad-brimmed sombrero that covered all of his face except his chin, which rested on his collarbone. He must be the American, she thought.

"Mr. Diamond?" she asked.

Neither man moved or answered.

"Mr. Diamond!" she said more loudly.

As she stood watching him, a strange sensation came over Alex, bathing her with fury, filling her with something akin to hatred for this man who ignored her, just as he ignored the impoverishment around him. How could he be so blind? And uncaring! That's the way it was with a man whose total interest was in making money! She had him pegged, all right.

She didn't know what made her do it as she stepped to the side of the desk, placed her hand on the man's shabby boots, and swept them off the edge of the desktop. With a loud noise, they clumped to the floor, and before she had time to utter another scornful "Mr. Diamond!" he was on his feet, legs widespread, hands reaching.

Behind her, Alex could feel the close presence of the other man, who was also on his feet and poised. They reminded her of two dark animals, ready to spring.

She stepped back, the rabbit in pursuit, suddenly frightened by the quick moves of these two ruffians. Sam's words rushed back. *Don't forget you're in a foreign country, and anything can happen. You have no rights!*

Alex gave the taller man an innocent gaze. "Sorry to interrupt your siesta, but I couldn't get your attention any other way."

"Well, you have it now," he responded angrily as he straightened his broad shoulders. No cause for alarm, Nick thought. Take it easy. Just a woman. And damn good-looking too.

"Are you Nick Diamond?" Suddenly she felt very foolish. Of course he was. The man standing before her was tall, arrogant, more masculine than handsome. A scar deepened the crease on one side of his face, but still, he was appealing.

He nodded, his hard, umber eyes assessing her in one glance. Ah yes, this was one very attractive tourist. And American, at that. Already they spoke the same language. A devastating smile broke beneath the dark bushy mustache, his straight white teeth clearly visible. "Good guess. I'm Nick. And this is my partner in flight, Juancho Rios."

She turned to shake hands with Juancho first. He was just a little taller than her own five feet four but seemed very short beside his tall American partner. Juancho's handshake was gentle yet he exuded a tremendous amount of strength from his great, broad body. His arms and chest were well developed. Alex guessed he probably weighed close to two hundred pounds and had the force of solid steel. But his face was round and friendly, and she couldn't help smiling at

47

him. His long mustache extended beyond the width of his face and was elaborately groomed. He reminded her of Pancho Villa, the renegade Mexican hero.

"Mr. Rios," she nodded. *"Mi gusto."*

"Juancho, please," he answered, speaking partially in Spanish. *"A sus ordenes, señorita. Mi gusta."*

When she turned back to the tall American, he gave her his best sales pitch along with his most winning smile. "Where can we take you, miss? Over the devastating volcano, *El Chichon?* To the Mayan temple of Palenque where lives of the most beautiful young virgins were sacrificed to the gods? How about the remote beauty of Copper Canyon, hidden from the world in the Sierra Madres? It's bigger than the Grand Canyon."

Alex stared at him, hating him and his jaunty attitude more and more by the minute. He was everything she despised in an American on foreign soil. Arrogant. Foolhardy. Caring for no one or nothing but his own stupid tourist service. And the money he could make doing God-knows-what! She shook her head. "I didn't come here for a tour. I need your help. I was told you could help me if anyone in Hermosillo could."

His dark, devil eyes grew sharp, but he folded his arms casually across his broad chest. "Who sent you?"

"It doesn't matter. I was instructed to come to *El Capitán,* and you would help."

He glanced quickly at his partner, then back to Alex. "I'll try. You aren't a tourist, then."

48

"Hardly. I'm a teacher at the University. Alexis Julian is my name."

Nick extended his large hand and quickly shortened her name. "Pleased to meet you, Alex. What can I do for you that seems so urgent?"

She took his hand, the warmth of it penetrating her own clammy palm. But she wouldn't be swayed by his raw masculine appeal—she had a job to do and she would do it, with or without this man's assistance. "You can help me find a missing child."

He shook his head. "Sorry. I'm not a private eye. That's a little out of my line. Tourism is my business. And flying."

"Who knows what your business is!" A cold, hard anger mushroomed inside her breast, threatening to choke her if she didn't let it explode. "A child is missing, stolen from beneath my nose right on the street, Mr. Diamond, and you sit here sleeping!"

"Now, wait a minute—"

Alex rubbed her temple nervously. "I-I'm sorry. I shouldn't take my frustration out on you," she amended, realizing irritation would not persuade him. "I will pay, Mr. Diamond. I will pay you to find her for me. Or pay you for her."

"Hey, you aren't suggesting that I know anything about this?" His abusive tone jolted her.

"No," she said quickly. "No, of course not." She really didn't want to offend this man, and didn't want his refusal either. "I thought you might know where I could find her."

49

He looked down his aquiline nose. "I don't know anything about your missing child. Or any other kids, for that matter."

His tone was dismissive, and Alex was disappointed. How could she convince him to help her if the prospect of money didn't work? Alex whipped out a newspaper clipping and flung it on the desk. She tapped the accompanying photo. "This woman's child has disappeared. She's the one I'm looking for."

"This is hardly my concern." He lifted the paper to look at it more closely. It was a poignant photo, the one that had made the front page of the newspaper the day after the car accident in the market. It showed a young Mexican woman lying lifeless in the foreground, and a blond woman kneeling beside her on the street. In the background was a chaotic scene of overturned wagons, fruit scattered everywhere, and vendors gathered in shock. Nick was unmoved. He had seen worse, much worse. Something familiar flashed back to him, and he murmured, "The wreck in the marketplace last Saturday. Oh, yes."

Alex nodded and proceeded eagerly. "The child's mother was k-killed that day and Jenni has disappeared."

He shook his head. "I'm sorry, but like I said—"

"Capitán—" Juancho began.

Alex interrupted frantically, "The young woman who was killed in that wreck was my housekeeper." Choking on the words, Alex swallowed convulsively before continuing. "And

50

now, her child is missing. I want . . . I *must* find her. But I need your help to do it, Mr. Diamond. Please say you'll help me find her!"

He shrugged. "What could I do that the police haven't already done?"

"You have the resources, Mr. Diamond. *Resources,*" she emphasized. "I don't know where to turn. You do. Even though I've lived here two years, I'm still the gringa. A foreigner. But you . . . just look at you. You're like one of them. You dress like them. You act like them. You've even earned a title of respect—*El Capitán.*"

Nick Diamond shrugged his broad shoulders. "You seem to have a misconception about me. I just run an aircraft tourist service."

Alex slipped the news clipping from his hands with a sinking feeling in her stomach. She should have known better than to expect anything from a man like him. "I had two misconceptions about you, Mr. Diamond. I was told that you were something of a hero. That you saved lives. That you had the resources to help me find my missing child. And I believe you do, but for some reason, you're refusing to help me.

"The other misconception was my own fault," she said. "I thought that somewhere in that American heart of yours was a shred of compassion. Someone who would care about lives torn apart, of people in need. But I was wrong about you. You're a hard-hearted bastard, down here to make a fast buck!" Alex wheeled around and made a fast exit before she could humiliate herself by blubbering all over the place.

As the rattling door slammed shut, Nick Diamond looked at Juancho. Their eyes met in an understanding flash.

"Damn good-looking woman!" Nick said as he moved across the room toward the door. "Check on her story, Juancho," he clipped, then added with a twinkle in his deep, dark eyes, "I've got to protect my reputation. Can't have her thinking I'm a hero, now, can I?"

"And the shred of compassion in your heart?"

Nick answered readily. "There's plenty of passion there, my man. Passion, not com-passion!"

Juancho chuckled. "This is the one, Capitán."

"Huh?"

"The blond American I told you was looking for a child after that wreck in the market."

Nick paused and narrowed his gaze. "Then she's telling the truth. Maybe the child *was* stolen, after all. It's possible we're on to something. Another commodity smuggled out of Mexico!"

"Si, Capitán."

Juancho watched Nick tear down the street after Alex. A smile twitched his lips beneath the wide, dark mustache. *El Capitán* was hard-nosed, all right. He had defied the melancholy blue eyes and quivering lips of the beautiful señorita. Even the sad story about the missing baby had failed to break through his steel facade. Then why was he following her? To investigate the possibility of another smuggling ring? Or because he wanted that blond woman called Alex to warm his bed?

Juancho shrugged and walked around to the back of the desk. He bent to open a wooden door near his feet, and with a low grunt, pulled out a hidden phone.

Alex's heels clicked on the sidewalk as she hurried away from Nick Diamond's shoddy office. She wished a cab would come by and whisk her away from this part of town. There were bad memories here. A clap of thunder rumbled overhead, warning her it would begin raining soon. She didn't care. Right now she just wanted to calm down and decide what to do next, now that *El Capitán* had turned her down.

What should she do? Go back to the police or to Father Ramón? Feeling panic growing within her, Alex feared she was on the border of hysteria. A drop of rain hit her arm, and she frantically stuffed the newspaper article deep inside her purse to protect it.

"You're going to get soaked, you know. It'll be pouring soon."

Alex looked up as Nick Diamond fell into step with her. She had been so deeply absorbed in her own thoughts, she hadn't even heard him coming behind her. He was impressively tall, she noticed, as they walked together. His shoulders were level with her ears, and that wide-brimmed sombrero he wore made him seem even taller.

She stared ahead and ignored his comment. Right now she didn't care if she got wet, or about this *El Capitán*, Nick Diamond. She only cared about Jenni and how to find her.

A crazy thought struck Alex. *Was Jenni getting*

wet this minute? She clamped her teeth together, determined not to cry in front of this
arrogant man.

"I'd like to know what happened that day in
the marketplace. How would you like to take
refuge in that cantina? We could have a cup of
coffee and talk," he offered quietly.

She continued walking ahead and raindrops
started to pelt her head and shoulders. Was he
making a pass? Or was he saying he'd help? "Are
you saying I was wrong about you?" she asked,
looking up at him.

"No, your assessment of me is about as accurate as any. I'm certainly no hero. And compassionate is not a word used to describe me."

"Then what do you want with me?"

"Well, we could have some coffee and—"

"It's a little hot for coffee."

"A fruit ice, then. We could talk about—"

Impatiently, she said, "Talk, Mr. Diamond?"
She grasped at a shred of hope that he was considering her plea. "I need help."

"Look, I . . ." He put his hands in his pockets
and hunched his broad shoulders against the increasing rain. At least he was protected somewhat by the sombrero. The rain was hitting her
unmercifully, and she didn't even flinch. "We
could talk about the kid. I'll see if there's anything I can do."

Alex stopped and faced him. Now he was talking turkey! Large raindrops bathed her face and
smeared her mascara at the corner of each eye.

"Would you listen to my story? Will you try to help me, Mr. Diamond?"

He gazed down at her, tempted to wipe the smudges from her big eyes. *Big, beautiful eyes,* he thought. "I'll try. No rash promises, though. We'll talk about the situation." Her mouth looked incredibly appealing, especially as it was moist from the rain. She opened it slightly in a slow, hesitant smile. Her hair hung in tawny wet strands to her shoulders and dripped on her blouse. Nick tried not to notice how the damp blouse clung to the rounded curves of her breasts. *Nice breasts.*

"Yes! All right! Thank you, Mr. Diamond!" Alex grabbed his hand and pumped it up and down jubilantly. "Thank you for trying to find *my* child."

He held onto her hand a little longer than necessary and they stood staring at each other in the rain for a moment. "If we're going to work together on this, call me Nick."

"Okay . . . Nick." Her eyes crinkled as she smiled through the rain, smearing her mascara even more. "Call me Alex."

Even in the rain, with her wet hair now plastered to her head, she looked beautiful. At that moment Nick would have done anything she asked him, but what he wanted to do was take her to bed. "Damned monsoons started early this year. You're soaked."

Alex felt a little breathless as she smiled up at him through the rain. "So are you. Sorry about dragging you out in this." The man was a symbol

55

of strength, a hope she could cling to. Maybe he wasn't completely corrupt, after all. He certainly had an aura of efficiency about him. He would take charge. "Let's get out of the rain so we can talk. You grab a table with an umbrella, and I'll get us the fruit ice."

In a few moments they were huddled cosily under a blue canvas umbrella. "Tell me what happened that day. The day of the wreck," Nick began, scooting closer to her side of the table.

Alex nibbled some of her fruit-flavored ice and took a deep breath. This would not be easy, but she knew it was necessary. She would probably have to tell her story a hundred times, but she was willing, if it brought her closer to getting Jenni back. "My housekeeper, Teresa, and I went to the market Saturday. I had planned a party for some friends from the University that night and wanted to get the freshest fruit. One of Teresa's friends was supposed to keep Jenni, but her mother got sick at the last minute. So, we took Jenni with us." She stopped suddenly and pressed her fingers against her lips.

"What's wrong?"

"It all seems so insignificant now. The reasons for going to the market, the party . . . everything. I'm sorry. I promised myself I wouldn't do this."

He kept his businesslike reserve and tried to remain detached. "Take your time." She used the napkin to dab at her eyes, missing some of the smudged mascara in the process. He wanted to grab that napkin and finish the job.

"Well," she continued when she was more composed, "a car came around the corner. It was green."

"What make? Did you notice?"

She considered for a moment. "Chevy, I think. But old."

"You're a good observer. Most people wouldn't remember."

"Are you testing me?"

"No," he laughed. "Just wondered how much you remembered in a time of stress. Go ahead with your story."

"The car crashed into everything in its path, including us. I . . . I lost sight of Jenni. Then there was Teresa, lying on the sidewalk, unconscious—"

"Were you knocked out too?"

"I don't remember. Maybe for a few seconds."

"When did you start looking for Jenni?"

She paused, again remembering. "Five minutes. Maybe a little longer. I asked one of the bystanders to get her. But she wasn't there."

"Have you talked to her friends? Maybe some member of Teresa's family has Jenni and intends to take care of her."

Alex shook her head sadly. "There is no family. Teresa was from Naranjo, where her mother was killed when the volcano erupted a few years ago. There was no one else. She had no husband. I don't even know the father of her child. I took care of her funeral. Teresa's local friends have been questioned by the police. No one has seen Jenni. She has completely disappeared."

He shook his head tightly. "I just can't buy that. She's somewhere. Someone has her."

"Do you . . . do you think she's safe?" Alex asked hesitantly, her vulnerable side revealing her real concern. The loving, nurturing part of her, the part that cared deeply for the well-being of this child, wanted reassurances.

Nick didn't fail to notice it. He smiled, sensing that she needed a positive answer, deciding to keep his doubts to himself for now. "Of course," he replied.

Alex sighed and squeezed her hands into fists. "I hope so. Oh, God, I hope so. We've got to find her! And soon!"

The urgency in her voice again told him of deeper feelings than one might normally have for a housekeeper's child. "You mentioned earlier that you had to find *your* child. Alex, is she your child?"

She smiled as tears began to fill up her large blue eyes. "No, she isn't mine. But I was there when Teresa gave birth, and feel very close to her. I'm Jenni's godmother. She has always lived with me. She was like my child, and I . . . I love her. I must find her."

Nick nodded curtly and looked away from Alex's tears. "Okay. We'll see what we can do. You understand, though, there isn't much to go on here."

Alex quickly flicked the tears away. Now wasn't the time to get sentimental, not when she was so close to acquiring the help she needed. She had to be tough. "I understand. Where should we start? Maybe with this." She slid an envelope beneath his tanned fingertips. "I don't know how much you normally charge for something like this, but I'll do the best I can. Here is a retainer fee, and I'll pay you more later."

"Huh?" Nick's eyes dropped to the table, then angrily sought hers. "I told you, Alex, I'm not a private eye. I don't normally do this sort of thing, therefore, there is no fee." He pushed the envelope back toward her.

"Then we'll negotiate as we go along. I want this to be a business deal, with money exchanged. I'm serious about wanting that child found." Her sharp eyes caught his, level and hard. "I'm hiring you, Nick."

"No money," he asserted. "I can't take money for this."

"Don't get maudlin on me, Mr. Diamond. I know you couldn't possibly give a damn about Jenni. If I didn't put up the money, you wouldn't be looking for her. I thought you said we had a deal. So far, it seems like you're humoring me. I want someone to work for me. Someone who will use every resource possible, including money, to find Jenni."

"The name's Nick, remember?" he said tersely. "We're still at the talking stage. Talk and time are cheap, and that's where we start."

"And, we'll never get any further than talk with your attitude. I'm sorry, Mr. Diamond." She reached for the envelope and began to rise. "I want action, not talk. We're running out of time."

His hand shot out and snapped the envelope

from her fingers. "Dammit, woman! You are impossible! Now, sit down."

"If you think you're going to talk to me like that, you're crazy!" She took another step in the rain.

"Alex!" His other hand grabbed her arm. "Do you want my help?"

Her eyes lifted to his, questioning their sincerity. For a second his eyes pinioned her. She read more than sincerity in them, something fiery and combustible. More like controlled animal lust, she told herself, but decided not to repel him further. She needed his help too much. "Yes."

"Then sit down."

Dropping her eyes from his riveting gaze, Alex sat down and said in a quiet tone, "Okay. We'll try again, Nick. Now, where should we start with the search?"

He pulled his chair a little closer to hers and grumbled, "Uh, we should start by questioning those closest to Teresa and your home, then branch out."

"But the police have already done that."

"Well, I'd like to conduct my own inquiry." Damn her, anyway! Who was this woman, pushing him into something he had no business doing, then telling him how to do it!

"Could we start now?" she asked eagerly. "The rain's almost over."

"First, do you have a photo of her? One I can keep?"

"Yes, right here." Alex fumbled in her purse and drew out a child's snapshot.

Nick looked at the photo of a very pretty Mexican child with large dark eyes and soft curls that framed a small face. She smiled jauntily at the camera.

"This picture was taken at school," Alex explained.

"Do you have others? A more somber shot?" Nick knew that if they found the child, she probably would not be smiling. However, he didn't want Alex to know that.

Alex turned a puzzled look at the snapshot in his hand. "I thought this was the best one. But I'll see. What's wrong with it?"

"Nothing. I'd just like to have another. You said this picture was taken at school?" Nick continued. "She doesn't look old enough for school."

"Jenni's not quite two. She's enrolled in a pre-school program for toddlers at the University. I took her to work with me three days a week and her mother picked her up after lunch."

"So she was exposed to a lot of people?"

"Yes, Jenni's very bright," Alex said proudly. "We feel she should be exposed to as much as possible. That's all part of the learning process."

"Sounds as though she almost had two mothers."

Alex nodded silently. "Almost."

"Can you tell me anything else about her? Anything unusual or interesting. Any scars or handicaps?"

Alex studied for a moment. "She's bilingual."

"Bilingual? She talks?" A frown deepened in Nick's forehead. Everything Alex had said so far

61

could work against their chances of ever finding this child. But he couldn't say that. Alex's blue eyes were already too full of pain. And he was fighting hard to stay objective.

"She has a good vocabulary for an eighteen-month-old child. Jenni's mother spoke Spanish, and I speak both Spanish and English, so it was only natural for Jenni to pick up words from both languages. I told you, she's very bright. Anything else you need to know?"

"No, that should just about do it for a start."

"Then let's go."

"First, I'd like for you to make me a list of everyone who knew Jenni. Especially those who might have a reason for wanting to take her . . . and keep her."

Alex looked shocked. "Who would want to do something so cruel and heartless?"

He drew the words out slowly. "Think about this from the opposite perspective, Alex. Who would desperately want a child? Someone, perhaps, who's lost a child recently; or someone who's lost another loved one and needs the unconditional affection a child can give; or maybe someone who lost a baby at birth." He wondered did he dare add "or someone who wants to make money"?

"But you're talking about almost everyone I know," Alex nearly wailed.

Nick leaned closer. "Desperate is the key word, Alex. Someone who's desperate. Who would want a child badly?"

She sighed. "Well, I don't know about that. I'll have to think."

"Go home and make me a list. Think about it. We can meet tomorrow and discuss—"

"Tomorrow? Why not today? Now! The rain's almost stopped!"

She was rushing him again. "Give me a chance to investigate this on my own," Nick said slowly. "I'd like to check out a few things and I'll be back in touch. Tomorrow, I promise."

There was distinct disappointment in her face, but Alex smiled faintly. "You know, you're sounding more and more like a private eye. Are you sure that's not your business?"

He shrugged and returned the grin. "I've just seen lots of *Magnum* reruns. I'll need your phone number."

Alex scribbled her number on a slip of paper then handed it to him. "Well, I'd better go make that list." Although Alex preferred to sit and talk with the enigmatic Nick Diamond, she stood up and tried to straighten her drenched and rumpled clothes.

"I'll call soon, Alex." He offered her his hand.

She took it and smiled warmly. "Thank you . . . Nick. I've changed my mind about you. You aren't the mercenary Yankee I originally thought you were." Her indigo eyes grew soft, and she looked at him frankly.

Nick laughed off her admiring gaze. "Don't fool yourself, Alex. I'm no hero."

She gazed at him stubbornly, her eyes defying his remarks. "Oh, yes you are, Nick Diamond.

You're the man of the hour. The only one who can help me."

Nick stood in the rain, watching her hail a cab. He was somewhat dumbfounded by her assertion. It was like a mandate he had to live up to.

As she got into the cab, he rubbed the scar on his cheek reflectively. Alex Julian was a damned attractive woman, good legs, nice body, beautiful eyes, just the kind of woman who might be sent to seduce him. He wondered if he was risking his hard-earned reputation by agreeing to meet her again. He'd have Juancho check her out. Knowing his wily Mexican partner, Nick figured Juancho would want to shadow her.

As the cab pulled away from the curb, Alex glimpsed the masculine and mysterious *El Capitán*. His damp peasant clothes clung to his triangular frame, emphasizing broad, prominent shoulders and narrow hips. After meeting him, she couldn't believe he was as shady a character as the rumors would have her believe. He was even appealing. Not handsome in the classical sense, but strong and powerful and rugged. He exuded a kind of raw masculinity she found impossible to ignore. Plus, he had *resources*.

Alex felt a distinct sense of exhilaration for the first time in days. She had accomplished what she set out to do. Nick Diamond was going to help her find Jenni!

But the exhilaration was short-lived, as other questions crowded her mind. Why did this man agree to help her? It certainly wasn't money he was after. He never even looked at the envelope he'd tucked inside his shirt. Was it the plight of Jenni, a poor homeless waif? Or because Alex was an American . . . a woman? Could Nick be trusted? According to rumor, she should beware.

Juancho tapped a pen on the notepad before him. "Her story checks out. At least, so far. The Mexican woman who was killed was her maid. And the woman had an illegitimate daughter about a year and a half ago."

Nick listened as he changed clothes in the adjoining bedroom of the upstairs flat. "What about her job? Any subversive activities?" He slid his long, muscular legs into a clean, dry pair of *calzones*.

"Works at the University in the Early Childhood Department as an exchange professor from Arizona State. Does a good job. Speaks fluent Spanish. Works well in the field." Juancho clicked off Alex's brief history in Mexico. "Her job's in jeopardy."

"Why?" Nick buttoned the clean *camisa* across the breadth of his chest.

"Tight budget at the University. Her department will probably be cut. Some teachers presented a petition to the president today. Threatened to strike."

Nick raised his dark eyebrows. "Is she a part of that?"

"No. She attended a funeral today."

"Can I trust her, Juancho?"

"If you can trust yourself, Capitán." Juancho

smiled intuitively as he leaned against the door frame, his powerful body filling the doorway. "Just don't look too deeply into the señorita's eyes."

Nick laughed roughly. "Don't worry, Juancho. I won't let this woman get to me. But I'm making no promises that I won't get to her. She could warm a bed nicely."

"Si, Capitán. You can take care of yourself." He chuckled deep in his huge chest. "Ready to go?"

"Yep." Nick moved toward the door. "Let's see if there's a baby for sale out there. This might be just what we've been looking for."

Juancho followed Nick. "You think this one might be involved in a baby ring?"

Nick nodded, his expression turning grim. "Selling Mexican babies is a big business. Let's hit the street and check with some of our contacts. Somebody, somewhere, knows about this kid."

CHAPTER FOUR

Nick called Alex the following afternoon. "Meet me in an hour," he said. "Our Lady of Guadalupe. Bring the newspaper clipping, along with your list of suspects."

"What suspects? They're friends! Why?"

"I'll explain later. Just be there."

Alex was on time. Nick Diamond was late. She sat alone in the church, nervously twisting a handkerchief. Maybe he wasn't even coming. Maybe he just wanted to get rid of her today by sending her to the church. Maybe he had no intention of finding Jenni. How did she know if he was trustworthy? She had been foolish to disregard the rumors. Maybe they were true.

She bent her head and looked at the row of empty wooden pews, then let her eyes travel to the rear of the church. Her gaze moved along the stations of the cross, where brightly colored murals decorated the walls. The biblical figures in the ancient pictorial, including the Christ, were dark-skinned Mexicans.

Two robed figures moved silently to prepare the altar for the next mass; an old woman knelt in prayer near the front. A constellation of candles flickered, projecting shadows on the somber murals.

Although her attitude was one of supplication, and her heart repeatedly cried out one particular prayer, Alex's mind raced in many directions.

Was she too trusting with this man she hardly knew? Yet she knew she had to trust someone. She had reached a dead-end in her search very quickly and knew she needed help. Both Sam and Padre Ramón knew it too. Did she think that just because Nick Diamond was an American, she could trust him? Or because he had been recommended by a priest? There had been qualifications, even then. What if the things they said about Nick were true?

He didn't look like someone working outside the law, but that's what she had heard. After one meeting, she decided he wasn't a man just out for money. What kind of man was he, though, this Nick Diamond? A local hero? Or a criminal in exile? Neither? Both? Someone to fear or revere? Well, now was not the time to doubt her decision to seek his help. He was already involved. Already hired!

Maybe it was the undeniable physical attraction between them that swayed her opinion of him. Perhaps his devastating smile made her think he would find her darling Jenni.

Alex's heart wrenched every time she thought of the little girl, alone and frightened now for three days. Nothing would deter her from finding Jenni. She wouldn't stop until the little girl was back where she belonged—in Alex's arms.

"Alex . . ."

She jumped at the sound of the low masculine voice and opened her eyes to the tall dark-haired figure of Nick Diamond. He wore a pale blue shirt tucked into tight jeans and looked devastatingly masculine. Maybe she should have prayed for restraint! "I . . . I thought you'd changed your mind about coming," she mumbled.

"I thought you were praying." He looked different without the Mexican sombrero to hide his dark hair and canny eyes. Now, thick sable curls capped his head, and daring golden-flecked eyes assessed her boldly.

She shivered involuntarily. Even seated next to her in church, he reminded her of a wild animal ready to spring. Alex could only hope he would apply that energy toward finding Jenni. "I was thinking . . . about what to do if you didn't show."

"Sorry I'm late. Something came up." He wouldn't tell her he had to have time to scout the place out and make sure she was alone. He couldn't trust anyone, especially strange women with beautiful blue eyes. *Seductive* blue eyes.

"I have a list of Teresa's friends for you, and another picture of Jenni." She fumbled in her purse. "Here's the newspaper clipping of the accident."

Nick watched her carefully, his well-trained eyes observing the knotted handkerchief she stuffed in the corner of her purse. He inhaled the

69

faint flower fragrance of her freshly washed hair, and noticed the way her casual blouse and skirt hugged her slender, very feminine body. His hand brushed hers when he took the items she offered, and he wanted to clasp it and pull her closer.

"Good. This is exactly what I need. Okay. Ready to talk to the priest?"

"P-priest? What are we doing, confessing before we get started?"

"No," he chuckled. "Gathering a little information."

"From Padre Ramón?"

"Yes, do you know him?"

Alex held back. "He conducted Teresa's services. But he, uh, can't help on Jenni's disappearance." What would Father Ramón say if she trailed in with the notorious Nick Diamond, especially after he had warned her not to tell anyone about this man?

"How do you know? Have you talked with him about it?"

"Why, yes, as a matter of fact, I have. He was no help."

Nick nudged her with his hand at her back. "He's the only one I know who can answer my questions."

Against her better judgment, Alex moved along the aisle with Nick. He was nothing if not determined. Strangely, though, his light touch on her back felt reassuring and she found his dark, dominant presence comforting.

70

Alex preceded Nick into the priest's office and fumbled with the introductions.

Padre Ramón glanced into the hall before quickly closing his office door. "Did anyone see you come in?"

"What's wrong, Father?" Nick laughed. "Don't want to soil your good name by entertaining the likes of me?"

"I do have a certain reputation to maintain, you know," Padre Ramón countered with a twinkle in his brown eyes. "What can I do for you?"

Alex had the distinct feeling the two men had met before. Maybe she was being conned, by both of them.

"We need some information." Nick spread the news photo on the desk. "Can you tell me the names of the people in the background here? They were all witnesses to this accident that claimed Teresa's life. Maybe they saw something that will give us a clue to the child's disappearance."

Padre Ramón spent the next half hour relaying individual names, relevant data about families and where they lived. Nick was right. The priest was probably the only one in town who could have given so much information about a group of apparent strangers.

When they left the office, Nick seemed satisfied. "Now I have a place to start. Perhaps these people saw more than you did, Alex. After all, you were personally involved and had to be distracted."

"Makes sense," she said, pausing outside the church.

"Come on. I'll drive you home." He motioned her toward a battered gray Volkswagen van.

Alex followed him but had other ideas. As she climbed into the passenger's seat, she commented drily, "Father Ramón knows you, doesn't he?"

Nick hopped easily into the driver's seat and revved the motor to life. "We've met."

"Knows you well."

"We've worked together a couple of times."

"I feel like an absolute fool. You probably know that he sent me to you for help."

"I'm not surprised."

"With instructions not to mention who sent me. What is he? Your referral agent? Do the two of you split fees?"

Nick's eyes cut sharply to her. "It's imperative that you not mention it to anyone, Alex. You haven't, have you?"

"Well, no, but—"

"Then, don't! Don't even say that you and I went to see him today. He shouldn't be associated with me."

"Might sully his reputation?"

"Something like that."

"Or break up your racket?"

His dark eyes flicked with a certain wickedness. "There is no racket, Alex. And we don't split fees."

"You know something, Nick?" Alex's indigo eyes flashed fire. "I don't even care about that. I

72

don't care what kind of racket you run or if the rumors about you are fact or fable. I only care about one thing. Can you find my child?"

"No guarantees, Alex. All I can do is try."

She stared at him steadily for a long moment. It wasn't even a question of trusting him. She had no alternative. "Then that's enough for me."

"You'll keep quiet?"

"I won't breath a word to a soul."

He nodded curtly. "Let's get you home."

She reached out and touched his arm. "This may sound presumptuous, but I'd like to go with you, Nick. To interview these people."

"That isn't necessary, Alex." He turned the next corner and drove directly to her small white stucco house.

"But I want to go." She frowned when she realized that he'd known exactly where he was going. "How did you know where I live?"

He grinned and cut the motor. "Juancho is very handy to have around. He's persnickety about details, especially regarding the company I keep. And, he and I *do* split fees. We also share the work load, like this interviewing."

"In other words, you don't want me interfering in your business."

"Actually, I'd like to talk to you about this list." He dug into his pocket for the list of names Alex had given him. "Do any of these people live around here?" He motioned to the pleasant tree-lined street.

"Yes. Most of them do."

"Nice neighborhood."

"Too nice for someone who wants to hide a baby," Alex said bitterly.

"You can never tell someone's innocence merely by looking at them," Nick warned. "Although I agree with you. These people probably had nothing whatsoever to do with Jenni's disappearance. Can we go inside and talk? I'd like to go down the list with you anyway."

"Sure." She led him into the house with no reservations. Regardless of his sullied reputation or what an association with him might do to hers, Alex's only concern was furthering the search for Jenni.

Nick followed her, knowing Juancho would be pulling at the curly end of his mustache when he saw them disappear into her house. But Nick needed to know more about this woman, and more about this child she sought. At least that's what he told himself.

Alex motioned toward the tile-floored living room. "Have a seat. I'll have the coffee ready in a minute."

Nick made no move to sit where she indicated but followed her into the kitchen. "Can I do anything to help?" His glance swept through the small, neat house as they walked down the hall.

Alex tried to ignore the tall man's domineering presence and went about her task in mock casualness. "No, thanks. I can handle it."

Nick leaned easily against the door frame. "Nice house."

"Nice house, nice neighborhood," Alex

mocked. "What is this? An analysis? Do you have to report my social status to Juancho?"

He shrugged off her testiness. "It was just an observation. Do you rent?"

Alex nodded, instantly regretting her sharpness. But this man set her on edge, and she wasn't sure what was going on with him or if she could trust him. Even Father Ramón looked suspicious to her now. She sighed and tried to take a more amiable approach. "The University provided it when I came here to work. It's only a few blocks from school or town, close enough to walk to either. They also helped me find Teresa." She halted and chewed her lip.

"You have a pretty good set-up here."

"Had," Alex amended. "Teresa was an excellent housekeeper and a good friend—" Her eyes clouded and she lost count of the number of dips of coffee she had already put in the basket.

"You said you were present at Jenni's birth," Nick probed. "How did that happen?"

"Not by choice, believe me." She smiled softly, remembering her near panic at the time. "Teresa was pregnant when I hired her, although no one knew it. When it became apparent, some of my friends advised me to fire her, said it was too much trouble to train a maid then have her leave when she had a baby."

"Why didn't you let her go?"

Alex shrugged and turned up the flame beneath the coffee pot. "I don't know. I liked Teresa from the start. She was a good worker. And she wanted to stay on after the baby was born.

75

She even talked about going back to the States with me. You see, she wasn't married and had no family. I became the family she didn't have."

"And she became yours?" he posed.

"Yes, I suppose. Working in a foreign country can be a pretty lonely business."

"You're all alone? No friends or, uh, anything?"

She smiled directly into his eyes. He was asking, rather awkwardly, about her personal life. "No one. I left everyone and everything in the States."

Nick watched her steadily without raising an eyebrow. "Had you ever lived in Mexico before?"

She shook her head and chuckled softly. "I was so naive, I didn't dream Teresa'd have the baby right here. In the States one normally goes to the hospital. That's what I assumed she'd do."

He smiled, understanding. "But she insisted on a midwife."

Alex nodded affectionately. "Jenni was born right in there." She motioned to the small room in the back of the house that Teresa and Jenni had shared. Abruptly, Alex changed the subject. "While the coffee's brewing, let's go down that list."

Nick read a couple of the names and Alex responded with whatever information she had.

"Dominga lives here in Hermosillo during the week. She works for an English professor at the University. She goes home to her village on weekends. Maria and her mother live about four blocks away. Her mother is always sick. Cecelia has a little boy and works across the street in the pink house. It's all she can do to feed herself and her son. I feel sure that none of these people have a desire for another child. They're all struggling." She hoped her explanation convinced him that Teresa's friends couldn't possibly have taken Jenni.

"What about Dominga, who goes away on weekends?" Nick asked stubbornly.

"She goes home to her village where she has six children of her own!"

Nick nodded silently.

The rich aroma of fresh-ground coffee beans filled the room, signaling the coffee's readiness. Alex turned to set out two cups for their coffee. "Cream and sugar?"

Before Nick could answer, her phone rang. Alex excused herself and went to the hall to answer it.

Nick listened to her half of the conversation while giving the place a closer inspection.

"Thanks, Rosemary . . . I'm okay. I made it through the night. It seems strange and lonely without them here, but . . ." She paused. "Yes, I'll be back at work tomorrow. No, I won't be able to make it tonight, but thanks for the invitation. Maybe tomorrow we can have coffee and talk? Fine. See you then." Alex cradled the phone. She had purposely saved this afternoon and evening in case Nick changed his mind and let her tag along to interview the witnesses.

When she returned to the kitchen, Nick was not in sight. Where could he be? She moved swiftly, following the shuffling sounds that came from an area where Nick Diamond had no business. Teresa's room!

She halted in the doorway with a slight gasp. There he stood in the middle of the room, his broad back to her as he examined the place where Teresa and Jenni had lived for the last two years, where Jenni had been born.

"What are you doing in here?" Alex demanded resentfully. She hadn't been inside the room since the accident. It felt a little strange to walk in, almost a sacrilege.

Nick turned around, a small brown teddy bear clutched guiltily in his hands. "Just looking. You say Jenni was born in here?"

With a clumsy lurch, Alex took the teddy bear from him. "You have no business in here! This was . . . is . . ." Her voice trailed away to a croak as she looked down at the frayed, well-loved teddy bear in her hands. The brown, lumpy object blurred. "Dear God, I didn't want this to happen. Get out of here! Just get out right now!"

"Alex . . ." His voice was a gentle urging, but she wanted none of it. "I was only—"

She turned away. He mustn't see her tears. Damn him, anyway! Just when she thought things were moving forward smoothly, he had pushed her to the edge of emotional disaster.

Nick's large hand reached out to her, a force of strength on her shoulder. "Alex, I need to know as much about them as possible." *And you*, he almost added. "You'll just have to trust me."

78

Alex tried to jerk away from his touch but he remained steadfast. He felt secure and strong, and oh, God, she needed that right now. She fought the tears and tried to gather her depleted emotional reserve.

All she had left of the little girl she loved was this stuffed teddy bear. And memories. The police had all but dismissed the case. Now she had nowhere else to turn. Nick was right. She had to trust him, whatever his reputation or racket. At this point it didn't matter if he were involved in illegal activities. She was desperate for his help.

"This is all I have left of her, Nick. And she's so little . . ."

For a wild moment Nick wanted to pull her into his arms and feel her feminine softness around him. "Alex . . ." he whispered.

She lifted her chin ever so slightly. It was just enough to crumble the wall of restraint he had been struggling all afternoon to build. His lips lowered to hers and claimed them with the strength of passion. Alex struggled to prevent the kiss but he held the back of her head with one large hand, cradling it firmly.

Nick had watched those lips the last two days as they railed and pouted, smiled and quivered, until he thought he would die if he didn't taste them just once. But the taste was a seduction, a feast of honeyed sweetness which tempted him beyond reason. His tongue twisted lazily against the sensitive inner edges of her mouth and Alex gasped at the brazen intrusion.

Her response was one of surprise—surprise

that she actually enjoyed the kiss, this intimacy with the man who jolted her senses so incredibly. Although she tried to push him away from her, she could feel her body growing limp against his.

Her lips allowed his entry and her breasts rose to be crushed against his chest. His hand pressed the small of her back, thrusting her body against his, and she felt his rigid maleness straining between them. Wildly, she wished there were no clothes separating them, just flesh against flesh. She could feel the heat of him and wanted to know the fire.

Alex moaned softly and tasted the minty warmth of his tongue. Oh, how she wanted to resist him, to shove him away, yet her body defied such action. Every feminine part of her betrayed what her mind knew was right. From the first moment she saw Nick Diamond, she'd felt attracted to him, regardless of his reputation.

Oh, dear God, she had lost all sense of decorum with the man hired to find Jenni. She had allowed this kiss, maybe even invited it, certainly relished it. As his lips moved sensually against hers, Alex vowed silently that this would be the last time she would allow this kind of shameless expression between them. The valley between her breasts tingled with a new sensation that spread like wildfire to the very tips of her nipples.

Alex's arms felt weak as she clung to Nick. An embarrassing warmth flooded her lower body, making her realize that she wanted this man, wanted him more than she had ever wanted any man, wanted him to make love to her.

But she couldn't let it happen!

Alex pushed weakly against his chest, and to her amazement, he raised his head.

"My God, Alex. I could take you now, you arouse me so."

"No, Nick," she muttered shakily. "Not . . . not now. It isn't right."

"Oh, yes, Alex. What I feel for you is just right. You feel it too."

"No. I don't."

"You're lying."

She stared at him. Nick was right. She'd never been so thoroughly aroused by any man, by any kiss. But she had to resist. For both of them. Alex shook her head. Abruptly, he thrust her away.

Alex hugged her arms and realized she still clutched the teddy bear. She would have to remember what it was like to be kissed by Nick Diamond, for this was the first, last, and only time it would happen.

"Alex, you must know I want you. From the minute we met, you could feel it. Standing in the rain that day, you were so damned sexy with that blouse clinging to you. Don't say you didn't want me to kiss you. To touch these." His hands cupped her breasts and his thumbs rubbed across her firm nipples. "See? You can't help but respond to me."

"No!" She took a step backward. "Nick, please. We have a job to do. A baby to find." She straightened her blouse.

"I haven't forgotten about Jenni. You'll just have to trust me."

"I have no other choice, do I?"

"Of course. You always have a choice."

"Then I suppose you're it, Nick Diamond."

He shifted away from her fresh-flowered fragrance. "Let's have that coffee, Alex. And finish the list."

She nodded, placing the teddy bear back in Jenni's crib, and allowed him to steer her out of the room. Suddenly, Alex had to exercise a great deal of restraint to keep from burying her face against Nick's strong shoulder and sobbing her heart out. But they had a job to do. Together, they would find Jenni. Alex had to believe it, just as she had to trust this man named Nick Diamond.

"I'd still like to go with you," she said as she poured the coffee.

"No. Not this time."

She gritted her teeth. Boy, he was stubborn! "What if you find her?"

"I won't. I'm just looking for information."

"Then why are you going through all this if you don't expect to find her? I want her home tonight!"

"We have to be patient. And follow through."

She shoved the cup of coffee toward him. "Patience is not one of my virtues. It isn't fair, Nick! It just isn't fair!"

Nick's large hands hovered around the coffee cup, as if harboring an inner rage. "No, Alex. It isn't. But give me time."

Alex looked into Nick's deep umber eyes and

saw an alarming viciousness. She knew that she would hate to be the object of his wrath.

Later, after Nick departed, Alex felt the strong urge to tell someone of her strange alliance with Nick. And yet, she didn't dare tell Rosemary. He had all but sworn her to secrecy and she didn't want to jeopardize his investigation. She reached for a pen and paper. Carol lived in Phoenix. It would be safe to confide in her.

April

Dear Carol,

I've met an American who has agreed to help me find Jenni. He runs a charter airplane service. It isn't much of a business—takes tourists to Mayan temples and over volcanoes. I can't decide if he's a hero or a heel. I'm told that he has contacts to do almost anything, and if he can help me find Jenni, that's all I ask.

It sounds crazy, Carol, but I have confidence in this man. I believe he'll find her. My spirits are higher tonight than any time since the accident.

Love,
Alex

CHAPTER FIVE

"How do you Americans say it . . . squeaky clean?" Juancho smiled grandly and handed Nick the folder with Alex Julian's name penciled lightly on the corner.

Nick nodded, his eyes gleaming amber in the lamp's yellow glow. He stuffed several papers into the folder. "So are all her friends. These people have no reasons to want another kid. Although most of them need money, I'd be damn surprised if they had any connections with the disappearance of this kid."

"You talked to all of them?"

"Yep. Most are females who work as house-keepers, like Teresa did. I also talked with the Garzas, who are both professors at the University and close friends with Alex Julian. Sam Garza was educated at the University of Arizona in Tucson and worked there for a few years before moving back here. Rosemary is his American wife. She was present at Alex's house the night the child was born, so that part of the story is confirmed." He tapped the closed folder with the back of his large hand and pursed his lips. "Like you said,

Juancho, squeaky clean means no leads. How about you? Any luck with that list of witnesses?"

Juancho pressed his massive body into an overstuffed chair and scanned the sheet of paper listing names and addresses. The weak light from the lamp added golden highlights to his thick, dark hair and elaborate mustache. "Without Padre Ramón's input, we would never have found all these people. I've seen most of the vendors and about half the other witnesses. So far, no information on this little Jenni or on knowledge of a baby ring."

"Or they're just not talking," Nick said tersely.

"That's possible." Juancho shrugged and tugged at the curly tip of his mustache.

"Did you talk to the man who runs the blended fruit stand? The one who spoke to Alex that afternoon?"

"Jorge Alvarez is streetwise. Now, he may be holding back information, but so far, nada."

"You left your number, in case he changes his mind?"

"Of course." He pulled out the two snapshots of the large-eyed Mexican child. "What do you think, Capitán? Any chance of finding her?"

Nick ambled to the darkened window and looked out over the sparse lights of the city at night. "Don't know, Juancho. She might be out there right now, or she might be . . . hell, anywhere!"

Juancho's brown eyes softened as he gazed at the photos. "*Dios mio!* She's beautiful!"

"Don't get soft on me, Juancho," Nick

85

growled. "You know how this search might end *if* we find her."

"Si, Capitán. I know."

Nick paced back and forth, stopping to ponder the light-studded view again. His tall, broad-shouldered form practically blocked the entire window. "I just have a feeling this one's connected to a ring. A ring that sells babies. They happened to make the mistake of getting involved with an American woman who won't let it drop. As much as we've heard about the baby-selling businesses from Mexico into the States, this is the closest we've come to touching one. We have to pursue it."

Juancho watched the man stalking before him and saw the slow-building, seething anger behind his umber eyes. Nick Diamond was a cool character, and as calm as he now appeared on the surface, Juancho had never seen him so agitated.

"Si, Capitán. What next?"

"You finish interviewing the witnesses. I'll check with Alex again and see if she has any new leads. There's always the possibility of a ransom. Then we'll reevaluate the situation. What do we have going tomorrow?"

"Nada."

"Good. Then we can work on those witnesses."

"But the next day, a tour of Mayan pyramids."

"Legitimate?"

"Si. A family from Kansas. Including the grandfather, who's seventy-eight. Then, a Thursday night pick-up—"

"Not another bunch of coffins loaded with aliens!"

"No, Capitán." Juancho chuckled. "This time, it's citrus. Grapefruit, oranges, lemons, and limes. Heading for Santa Barbara."

"Fruit!" Nick heaved a sigh. "It's hard for me to get excited about a load of goddamn fruit when we're on the trail of this baby! And I feel we're so close too! This'll have to be overnight. It'll delay us another day!"

"Thousands of dollars for uninspected citrus, Capitán."

"I know, and that's why we're here. Never underestimate the power of the tiny fruit fly if it threatens the U.S. economy. Hell, in the early eighties the fruit fly was the governor of California's downfall, so they say. Yeah, I know it's important. But this other thing has me distracted.

Juancho watched Nick pace the floor with a glimmer in his dark eyes. *I wonder, Capitán,* he mused, *if it's the tragic situation of the missing baby, or the woman with the deep blue eyes that has you distracted?* "Is that all tonight, Capitán?" he asked.

"Yeah, Juancho. It's getting late. You'd better head on home. And . . ." He paused and caught Juancho's eyes. "Give my love to Yvez and the little ones. Tell her how important your work is."

"Si, Capitán. She understands. *Hasta mañana.*"

Juancho slipped out quietly. Nick continued to study the midnight view but his thoughts were on a certain woman with blond hair, indigo eyes, and lips as soft as silk.

"Your friend questioned me yesterday, Alex."

"What are you talking about, Rosemary?"

"The man with the scar on his cheek and the broad shoulders and wonderful mustache. The big one who breathes sex appeal! The American." Rosemary smiled knowingly and stirred her coffee. "Why didn't you tell me you had hired a private eye to find Jenni?"

"I haven't. I mean, he isn't. He's . . . well, he's just someone who has agreed to help find her." It sounded lame, and Alex ducked her head and sipped her coffee. She had no idea that Nick would interview everyone on that list, especially her friends from the University. But if he was thorough in his investigation, it made sense.

"Just *someone* you hired?" Rosemary scoffed with a grin. "Sure, Alex."

"Now, look. I told you I was serious about finding Jenni. And the police reached a dead-end the first day. So I was forced to take matters into my own hands."

"And you did an excellent job of it too!" Rosemary leaned forward with her elbows on the table. "Tell me about him, Alex. How did you ever find him?"

"I . . . I can't tell you. That is . . . please don't ask me because I don't know very much about him.

"Now, tell me what's going on at the University. After being gone several days, I can tell something's brewing. I heard rumblings today but no one is willing to explain things to the *professora gringa.*"

Rosemary was clearly disappointed that Alex wouldn't give her more information on the intriguing American, but obliged her friend with shoptalk. "I told you things were not smooth at work."

"But they can't cut the Early Childhood program! It's too important! We've just gotten it off the ground. What will happen to those programs out in the field?" Alarm clouded Alex's eyes as she thought of the two remote villages that depended on the University's assistance in running their child-development programs.

"I don't know what will happen. I don't even know if it's entirely true. As I said, it's a rumor. And you know how scuttlebutt flies among the staff just before budget time."

Alex had been so preoccupied during the last few days, she had forgotten everything connected to the University: the grumbling faculty, the talk of a strike, her tenuous position as an exchange professor. Her thoughts had been riveted to the accident and finding Jenni. This new turn of events could affect everything, including her search for her godchild.

"If they're cutting human services, who's the favored department?" Alex caught a glimmer in Rosemary's eyes. "Agriculture?"

Rosemary pushed a wisp of brunette hair behind her ear. "Believe me, it has not made for the most pleasant home life. Realistically, though, I know how desperately that department needs to be upgraded. Why, two years ago, Sam presented a proposal to the department head. It's taken that long for action, Alex. Now it looks like they're going to supply the money he needs for more modern equipment and trained staff. They've got to catch up with the twentieth century in agriculture. All of that takes money, lots of it, and the University has only so much to spend."

"Sounds like you've been properly brainwashed. I understand about budgets, Rosemary. I'm just thinking about how all of this effects me." Alex sighed. "I'll be the first to go."

"Well, I'll be soon after you. I don't have that much tenure either. And I, too, am a *norteamericana.*" Rosemary motioned to the waiter for more coffee.

"How can they do this? People, not plants or equipment, are involved in our programs. They're important to the future of Mexico. People—*children*—are the hope of the future! Not some damn machines!"

Rosemary shook her head. "I can't agree with you more, Alex. But some things are out of our control."

"Can't we do something?"

"The department heads are meeting with the president and board of regents at the end of this week. We'll know more after that."

Alex paused as the waiter refilled their cups. "Then final decisions haven't been made?"

"No. That'll be done in a few weeks, when the

90

proposed budget is presented and discussed. Department heads will be consulted and counterproposals submitted."

Alex lifted her chin. "Counterproposals?"

Rosemary seemed to have the same idea that flashed in Alex's mind. "Yes, objections can be submitted. They may not carry much influence, but it's a chance to state your department's needs and how the new budget will affect it."

"A chance is better than nothing!" Alex said eagerly. "Why don't we work on a counterproposal, Rosemary?"

"Well . . ."

"Come on." Alex nodded enthusiastically. "Our jobs are at stake here, not to mention the programs out in the field. The kids need them! We've got nothing to lose. This is our only chance, our fighting chance to present something to the board, something that shows our belief in the worthiness of our program."

Rosemary nodded, her enthusiasm not equal to Alex's, but she was agreeable to the idea. "We probably should do something."

"Okay, it's settled. Each of us should make a rough plan and meet again tomorrow to discuss it. We'll combine our ideas and write a counterproposal."

When they parted, Alex wore a smile of determination on her lips. Rosemary's expression wasn't quite so resolute.

Later that afternoon Alex's determination had dwindled somewhat, replaced by a look of urgency when she barged into Nick's ramshackle office. "We have to find her, and fast, Nick. If my job is eliminated, I'll be forced to return to the States. And I refuse to leave without—"

Alex stopped when she saw the shapely dark-haired woman sitting on Nick's desk. "Oh, I didn't know you were busy, Nick."

He motioned nonchalantly to the attractive woman on his right. "We were just discussing a tour. Alex Julian, meet Lia. . . ."

Alex nodded curtly.

Lia slid off her perch and stood enticingly close to Nick, who was still seated at the desk. His eyes, Alex noticed, were focused on Lia's curvaceous bosom. "I'm so excited because Nick's taking me to the Mayan temple of Palenque!"

"The one where virgins were sacrificed?" Alex asked sarcastically.

"Oh! I hadn't heard about that."

"Well, you won't have to worry," Alex said. "That happened hundreds of years ago, and I'm sure Nick is a very capable pilot. Well, nice to meet you Lia. I have to go."

Alex pivoted and left the office. Nick lunged into the hallway after her. "Wait. I thought you came by for a reason."

"It's nothing. I can see you're busy."

"You were saying you're on the verge of losing your job."

"I was saying that time's running out for me to find Jenni. Do you have any information on her?"

He shook his head.

"Then what the hell are you doing here?" She

caught her tongue, knowing full well: that woman kept him occupied!

"Do you have any brilliant ideas?" he countered, releasing the frustration he felt at the lack of leads on the case.

"Yes, as a matter of fact, I do. I'm going somewhere I hope I don't find her. But I have to go."

"Where?"

"The hospital."

"The hospital?" His voice gentled. "She's not there, Alex."

"How do you know? Have you been there?"

"No, but—"

"What if Jenni was injured that day and carried off to the hospital by someone else and has never been identified? Or is lying up there unconscious! I asked about her the day of the accident and they hadn't seen her, but maybe she's been brought in since then—" Alex stopped with an emotional hitch in her voice.

"Well, it's possible, of course," Nick replied. "But not probable. The police would have been notified. And they would have called you."

"Don't tell me what the police would do. They've given up on it. They don't care if I find her. Not really." She gave him an accusing look.

"I have more important things to do this afternoon than to go off on wild goose chases looking for this kid," he said.

"Nobody asked you to go."

"But that's why you stopped by here."

"I came by to see if you had any leads." She motioned impatiently. "Please go back inside and plan your Mayan temple tour. Just let me know if you discover anything important while you're sitting around on your ass. Or possibly you'll get a brilliant idea while flying over Palenque." Alex wheeled about and strode down the hall, not realizing until that very moment how absurdly jealous she was of Lia. And dammit, she had no right to be!

"Wait a minute!" Nick called out to her. "I want to go. You might just find her. Then I'd be out of a job!"

Alex halted. "Don't feel obliged to follow me around."

"I don't *feel* anything!"

The door to his office had opened during this exchange, and now a tremulous voice broke into the verbal jabbing: "But Nicky, what about our trip?"

"Another time, Lia," Nick said.

Alex turned large indigo eyes on him, then let her gaze flutter over a pouting Lia. "Don't let me interfere with your business . . . *Nicky.*"

His eyes flickered angrily. "I will decide what is and is not interference. Now, let's go." It was a command, and his expression told her she'd better not push him further. "You don't mind, do you, Lia? This is very important business."

"I'll bet!" She sashayed past them, her three-inch heels clicking on the tile floor.

"I'll be in touch, Lia."

"Don't bother!" she flung back.

"This is probably just a waste of time," Nick fumed.

94

"Well, we certainly don't want you to waste your precious time. So why are you going with me?"

"Damned if I know," he said, but he was thinking more of spending time with Alex than of finding the child. And being with her wasn't wasting time. He flipped the cardboard sign so the other side was visible through the cracked glass door. *Cerrado.* Closed. "I'll drive you over there."

Alex considered him for a moment. "Nick, are you taking this job seriously?"

"Of course." He grinned devilishly as he locked the door. "I feel like an honest-to-God detective doing this. Why, Juancho is out questioning witnesses today. Don't I remind you of Magnum, P.I., or Mike Hammer?"

Alex rolled her eyes upward as they left the building.

"Actually, this new detective stuff has given my career an added dimension. I may include it on my door, under where it says Aircraft Service. Something like Private Investigation—We Find Anyone, Anywhere." He opened the rusty gray door of his VW van.

"Don't be in such a hurry to add that line. So far, I'm afraid I couldn't give you a recommendation."

"Why? Don't you think I've conducted our business professionally enough? If you're thinking of that one little indiscretion at your house, I can assure you it won't happen again. I intend to exercise the highest degree of restraint whenever I'm around you in the future. Anyway, you asked for that one."

She paused at the open door to the van. "What? I did not!"

"Well, I don't mean in so many words. But that look. Those eyes! Why, I just couldn't resist." He flashed her a smile then left her to mount the step-up into the van by herself while he hurried around to the driver's side.

Alex decided Nick was teasing about his reasons for the kiss, and wasn't about to argue whether she had invited it. Not only did she want his kiss that day, but a broad shoulder to cry on. "Nick, I couldn't recommend you as a detective because you haven't come up with one tiny clue. You don't have one lead or suggestion for finding my child. Why, even this trip to the hospital was my idea."

"And I'm not so sure it's a good one either." He jerked the van into gear and concentrated on the traffic.

"What if she's there?"

"Then it'll be a good idea."

"You're impossible, Nick Diamond! I'm beginning to think I'd get more help from the police!"

"Please, don't compare me with them!"

"But you've both come up with the same thing. Nada!"

"The police aren't willing to do this with you." He pulled to a stop in the hospital's parking lot.

"No, they aren't, Nick. And I appreciate your coming." She grew quiet as they approached the large, looming building. Her face told of the stress she felt, and the fear.

They took the elevator up to the children's floor and approached the nurse at the front desk. "I'm looking for a little girl," Alex said in Spanish. "A year and a half old. I think she was injured in an accident a few days ago."

"Her name, señorita?"

"Jenni. Well, I'm not sure." Alex groped for the right explanation. "She . . . she's my friend's child and could have been registered under another name."

The nurse looked at Alex strangely for a moment, then checked her roster. "We have two little girls of that age. Neither one is named Jenni."

"Could I . . . could we see them? Just to make sure?"

The nurse inclined her head in a reluctant nod. "If you'll follow me."

They stepped into a large room lined with beds filled with dark-eyed children of all sizes. Alex gave a slight, tiny gasp.

Nick was right behind her, his words warm against her ear. "Are you sure you're up to this, Alex?"

"I couldn't leave now, Nick. I have to know." She walked stiffly behind the nurse.

They stopped beside a small, white crib. Alex moved to the side and peered into the face of a child playing with a doll. Both her legs were confined in hard white casts from toes to hips. The little girl gazed up into Alex's anxious face and immediately broke into loud sobs.

Alex backed away and gave the nurse an apologetic look.

"It isn't you. She is expecting her mother soon and cries when anyone else comes toward her," the nurse explained.

"I take it that's not her," Nick said softly, as they continued their somber journey.

"Pobrecita," Alex murmured, obviously shaken.

As they moved on, Nick took her hand. The nurse led them to another crib with white metal bars. Nick squeezed Alex's hand as she stepped closer.

The child lay inert, sleeping peacefully beneath a clear plastic oxygen tent. A young woman sat beside the bed, lovingly caressing the tiny brown hand that lay limp on the sheet.

"Pneumonia," the nurse said. "Is this your friend's child, señorita?"

Alex held Nick's hand tightly and shook her head. "No, gracias. This isn't the one, either." She shrank back, suddenly feeling weak, depressed, and saddened by the unhappy little faces she had just seen. They reminded her of Jenni. Alex shuddered and leaned against Nick. He braced her with his strength, putting his arm around her, and ushered her out of the hospital.

"Oh, God, Nick," she breathed when they were outside. "They should be out here, running and playing in the sunshine."

"I thought you said you could handle this," Nick growled.

"I lied. You were right, Nick. It was devastating. And I still didn't find my Jenni."

The sky rumbled above and the air felt still and hot.

"Alex, if you don't loosen your grip on my hand, I'm afraid I'll be maimed for life."

"Oh, Nick. I'm sorry." She immediately let go of his hand. "I . . . I want to thank you for coming here with me, Nick. You knew how awful it would be, but you came anyway. Why?"

"There was a chance she'd be here. There's always a chance."

With a gentleness seemingly uncharacteristic for a man so tough and rugged, Nick helped Alex into the beat-up van. It was a small haven, away from the sadness and disappointment she'd just seen. Perhaps, Alex considered quietly, being with Nick Diamond was the haven she needed. He climbed into the driver's seat and drove away from the hospital. Alex stared blankly out the window, lost in thought. When he stopped, they were in a part of town unfamiliar to her. They sat for a moment, listening to the rumble of thunder. She looked at him questioningly.

"El Jardin makes a great margarita. Care to join me, Alex?"

"Is this a professional courtesy?"

"I consider it my duty, señorita."

"In the line of duty, then." She nodded and smiled.

Just as they started down the street, large

drops of rain began to fall. Instinctively, Nick's arm went around Alex's shoulders and they hustled into the garden restaurant. They sat under a canopy in the garden and watched rain splatter over the brick floor of the uncovered portion.

"Dos margaritas, por favor," Nick told the waiter, then turned his dark eyes on Alex. "You okay now?"

"Better." She smiled, her face fresh from the quick shower. Again, her mascara was a bit smudged at the corners of her intensely blue eyes. "Thanks for being there, Nick. And, for this. Even the rain helps. Helps me forget her for a few minutes. I can't help thinking about her all the time. I wonder if she's getting wet."

"Promise me something, Alex. That you won't go off hunting for Jenni again by yourself. That you'll call me first. What if you had gone by yourself today? I wish you'd leave this investigating to me."

The waiter brought their drinks along with a bowl of crunchy corn chips and a very spicy salsa.

"After all," he continued. "That's what you hired me for. To find her."

Alex slid her finger and thumb along the narrow stem of her glass. "Yes, I suppose it is. Is the advice a part of your investigative service?"

Nick stiffened. Damn! She was getting to him. He was only a man, drinking in the beauty of a woman with sad blue eyes. "Strictly business, Alex. Here's to finding Jenni."

Alex tipped the salt-rimmed glass to his and sipped her margarita. Nick was only doing a job.

Accompanying her to the hospital, the drinks, maybe even the kiss were professional courtesies. And she'd better not forget it.

Nick's large hand lifted a damp strand of hair from her forehead and smoothed it back. "The rain was later than usual today. Waiting on us. We seem to attract it." He gazed at her, feeling the powerful attraction between them, a charge so magnetic it was difficult to resist. "This is the second time we've had to seek refuge in a downpour."

Third time's the charm. Alex felt herself sinking, swirling, drowning in the safe haven of Nick's dark eyes. "The monsoon season is strange. You can never rely on the weather, although it's supposed to rain every afternoon. . . . What's wrong? What are you staring at?"

"Do you mind if I fix your mascara? It's smeared on your cheeks."

She laughed, grateful for something to do, and dug into her purse for a tissue. "Be my guest. I suppose I should use waterproof mascara, especially if I continue to run around in the rain."

"Do you? Plan to continue running around in the rain?" Carefully, Nick wiped at the corners of her eyes, then let his fingers caress each cheekbone and trail down one cheek. He continued to stroke her silky, soft skin. He'd like to stroke her all over like that, he mused. "There, now. I've needed to do that since we . . . since the other rain."

"Needed?" Alex murmured, somewhat staggered at the surge of warmth she felt when he was so near, his arm brushing her shoulder, his fingertips driving her crazy.

"Uh, wanted. Yes, wanted to touch you."

"Is this part of the service to clients too?" Suddenly she was dry-mouthed and hot.

"Only to you, Alex. I told you before, I've never known a woman like you, not one who takes my breath away. You're very beautiful, you know, Alex. . . ." He whispered her name again, the way he did that day in Teresa's room. "Especially in the rain."

Suddenly she wanted the solace of his cool, reassuring kiss again, wanted desperately to believe him. Then she remembered Lia, perched so alluringly on his desk, and she knew he was lying. "Did you get it all off? The mascara?"

He surveyed her eyes, touching her cheeks lightly in a mock examination. "Clean. And smooth. Very smooth."

"Would you like to order now, señor?" The waiter stood beside their table.

"They make a very good *pesole*. Care to try it?" Nick asked.

Alex shook her head. "I don't think I could choke down a bite."

"Another margarita, then?"

"Dos margaritas más," Nick answered for both of them, dismissing the waiter then turning to Alex. He had to be honest with her, to warn her of the risks little Jenni faced and their chances of getting her back. "Alex—" He stopped abruptly. Her eyes revealed the confidence she held in his ability to find the lost child, and he couldn't de-

stroy that trust. Not now. She put too much faith in him, he thought. It wasn't a good sign. Not good at all.

As they sipped the fresh margaritas, Alex figured it was a good time to find out something about this man. "How long have you been here, Nick?"

"A year."

"Only a year? What brought you here?"

"My business went down the tubes."

She nibbled on a tortilla chip. "That's a strange reason. Not everyone flees to Mexico when their business in the States fails." Why did she use the word *flee?* she asked herself. It sounded like something a criminal would do.

He shrugged. "A friend of a friend offered me something here."

"So you just left everything and moved to Hermosillo, Mexico?"

"Yep."

"From where? Where was your business?"

"Nevada."

"Vegas?"

"Yep."

"And what was your business?"

"The same thing. Helicopter tours."

"Tours? What did you do? Fly people over the desert? What's to see out there but cactus and sand?"

"Mostly we'd fly over the Grand Canyon. But that was the trouble—not enough business."

Several hours and another margarita later, they decided to leave El Jardin. Alex felt as though she were floating through paths of flowers, buoyed by the sweet fragrance of a thousand gardenias. The tequilla had a tranquilizing effect on her. And, it was very nice, indeed. Nick's hand nudged her back and she leaned willfully against it, enjoying the full pleasure of his nearness.

Alex stifled a giggle as she considered that Nick might be involved in more serious trouble than she ever imagined; like gambling, or the Mafia in Vegas. It would be easy to get in trouble with the law in Vegas. Or, worse yet, the underworld. And the perfect solution could be to escape to Mexico for a few years until things quieted down. Oh, who had she gotten herself mixed up with? Who *was* this *El Capitán?*

It wasn't funny . . . then why did she want to laugh?

Before she knew it, they were standing at her door in the darkness. The rain left the air smelling fresh and her attraction to Nick was stronger than ever. She could hear his heavy sigh and felt the power of his maleness, his rugged dominance over everything he touched, including her. "Would you like to come in, Nick? It's early. I could fix us some coffee. . . ." She needed coffee to clear her head.

Nick hesitated before answering. If he went in her house, he would stay. He would spend the night in Alex's bed and in her arms. There'd be no stopping him. He knew it as surely as he knew his name. His response came in definitive spurts. "I'm supposed to meet Juancho on business. And he has a family. He needs to go home soon."

"Could we . . . could we meet tomorrow and discuss the investigation? I want to know what the witnesses had to say."

"No, I have a tour to the pyramids. It'll take all day."

Alex thought of the voluptuous Lia and wondered if the tour included her. Or some other woman. "Then what about tomorrow night when you get back? I could fix you a bite to eat."

"Not tomorrow night either. I'll be out of town."

"Oh." Her heart fell. Obviously he had other plans, quite likely with a woman. She couldn't expect him not to.

"Business. Overnight."

"It's okay, Nick. What you're doing isn't any of my concern. Just don't forget about finding Jenni."

"I won't forget. She's foremost on my mind. It's just that I have these other things to do that are very important. Look, Alex, don't ask questions. Don't press me about things I can't tell you."

Alex inhaled sharply. She *was* pressing. And he was resisting. "Sure, I have no right." She pressed her fingers to her lips. "Nick? Nick, are we going to find her?"

"I won't lie to you, Alex. I won't make promises I can't keep."

She could feel the emotional frustration swelling within her, threatening to explode. "Tell me *yes!* Please, tell me a lie!"

"The truth is—"

"Damn the truth, Nick!"

"Alex, take it easy!" He gripped her shoulders forcefully. "One promise, Alex. I'll stick with you. I'll be here beside you, no matter what happens."

Her hands rested naturally on his chest and she drew a deep breath. This was what she wanted. To touch him, to absorb his strength, to lean on him. She swayed toward him, relying on Nick to keep her upright. "Thank you, Nick." Slowly, quite logically, her hands climbed up to his chin. "I'm glad you're here. I need someone calm, someone strong. I trust you'll find her if anyone can. . . ." She moved closer and placed a gentle kiss of appreciation on his lips.

"Alex . . . oh, God, Alex . . ." Nick breathed her name raggedly before he abandoned all resistance and covered her lips savagely with his. He hauled her against him and molded her entire length to his body. His strong arms slid around her back, engulfing her in his power, barely giving her space to gasp for air. He wanted her, wanted to make love to her until she forgot her fears and her fruitless search for this baby. He wanted to hear her cry his name.

Alex gave herself up to him, unable to avoid the passion that surged through her at his touch. She allowed the kiss to deepen and drank eagerly of his intoxicating lips. Mindlessly, she swirled in the splendor of his arms.

Nick held her tightly, crushing her breasts to his chest, pressing his hard thighs against her unsteady legs. His lips forced hers open and his tongue dipped into the savory crevasse of her mouth. She moaned softly and met his strength with a teasing probe of her own.

Alex was filled with desire for this man who whipped her into a frenzy with only one look, only one kiss. If he wanted to, she would take him inside, to her bedroom. If he resisted, she would persuade him with every female wile she knew.

With an audible gasp, she caught herself. What was she thinking? All those margaritas must have worn down her inhibitions. Here she was, ready and willing to fall into bed with a man who might be a criminal!

Alex forced their lips apart. "No, Nick—"

"Alex . . ." His voice was ragged and low. "Let's go inside."

"No! Not now. I'm sorry, Nick."

His eyes burned with dark desire. "You're giving me double messages, Alex. Don't tease me. You'll be sorry."

"No, Nick. Only one message. Find Jenni. Nothing else."

"You're hot next to me, Alex. And I'm on fire for you. Feel it."

"Please, Nick, we mustn't."

He shoved her away from him. "I don't think you know what you want, Alex. You're a grown woman. When are you going to act like it?"

She placed a steadying hand on the door as he angrily strode away.

He was right. Again. She had lured him on, had taunted him, had given him an enticing message. Then, she'd naively denied their sexual attraction. It was the margaritas, she decided sullenly.

They left her muddle-headed. She almost ruined the working relationship she had with this man she'd hired to find Jenni.

Quite obviously, he only wanted to get in her bed. If she allowed that to happen now, would he then be satisfied and turn his back on Jenni? No! She couldn't let that happen.

Alex went inside as Nick's van screeched away from the curb.

CHAPTER SIX

"What do you mean, you can't sign your name? You worked on this proposal too. You deserve credit—"

"Credit is exactly what I have to avoid!"

"But, why?"

"Sam says—"

"Sam? What do *you* think, Rosemary?"

"Would you please hold it down, Alex? And let me explain."

Alex clamped her jaws together and rose to pour them more coffee. "Okay. Explain."

Rosemary shifted in the chair and folded one leg beneath her. "Alex, remember we aren't in the States, and I'm not married to a liberated American man. There are cultural differences, and at times like these, they appear. Otherwise, Sam is a wonderful man, and I love him. How would it look if Sam Garza's wife objected to how the University's money is apportioned, especially if Sam's department is getting most of the money? Now, Alex, think about it realistically."

"I thought we decided together that the Early Childhood program here is of utmost importance. That doesn't mean we're against agriculture."

Rosemary spread her hands expressively. "That's the way it would be interpreted. At least, Sam doesn't want to take that chance."

"Nor do you." Alex leaned back, resigned to Rosemary's abdication from the project.

"That's right. I just can't sign the counterproposal, Alex. I hope you will try to understand it from my viewpoint."

"Well, how's it going to look when the *professora gringa* presents this proposal to the University president?"

Rosemary laughed delightedly. "Like a typical American woman!"

"Thanks a lot, Rosemary, for leaving me holding the bag!"

"Alex, you know I'd do anything I could to help you keep your job. But this is something I just can't do."

"Okay. So you can't." Alex tossed her hands up in frustration and began to pace the floor. "Do you know what losing this job will do to the search for Jenni? Oh, hell, I didn't mean that the way it sounded. I don't want to lay a guilt trip on you, Rosemary. This isn't your responsibility. It's mine. It's just that I'm so worried about her, I really don't have time to be bothered with this problem at the University. And yet, it's vital to me."

"Alex, you can stay on here. You could live with us, if necessary."

"Oh, Rosemary, thanks. But it isn't just funds

110

for my basic existence. It's . . . it's paying for the search. All of this costs money, you know!"

"You mean, the big guy with the dark eyes?"

"Well, he's not doing this for nothing."

"How's the search coming along? Is your private detective earning his fee? Has he found anything substantial?"

"No," Alex muttered, perching nervously on the edge of her chair. "Nick isn't exactly a private investigator, Rosemary."

"What is he, then?"

Alex blinked, wondering silently how many times she had asked herself that very question. "I don't know, exactly. He's . . . he and his partner have been interviewing all the witnesses to the accident. They haven't finished that yet. Then . . . I don't know what next. They're out of town for a few days."

"On the case? Do they think Jenni's been taken out of town?"

"No. This is their other job. They take people on helicopter tours."

"Helicopter tours?" Rosemary screwed up her face. "How the hell can they make a living at that?"

"I don't ask." Alex looked away and didn't catch the astonished expression on Rosemary's face.

"Well, do they do other things, like this private investigation stuff?"

"I don't think so. Actually, Rosemary, I don't know."

"Alex, are you mixed up with some kind of weird scheme?"

Alex studied the billowing clouds out the window for a full minute. "I don't know what I'm mixed up with, Rosemary. I only know that Nick said he'd try to find Jenni. And that's what I'm banking on."

"I just hope you aren't making a mistake, Alex. If you know what I mean. . . ."

"So do I." Alex ran an impatient hand through her hair. "What the hell, Rosemary? As a last resort, I was sent to *El Capitán* for help. When he agreed to investigate the situation, I didn't ask for his resumé and a list of credentials!"

"El Capitán?"

"Oh, it's just a name some people around here have tagged on him." Alex shrugged without meeting Rosemary's eyes.

"Oh, God, Alex. It's sounding worse all the time."

"Please, Rosemary. Don't make any quick deductions. Don't tell me your fears or opinions on my dealings with Nick Diamond. I have enough of my own. And I won't give you my opinion of Sam telling you what to do at the University!"

Rosemary gave her a slight smile. "Okay, Alex. I just hope—"

"So do I, Rosemary," Alex finished wistfully, knowing instinctively what her friend was about to say. "I can tell you one thing for sure. I'm going to submit our counterproposal to the University president, with or without your signature.

We've worked too hard to let it go down the tubes. And my job along with it!"

"I'll help you type it," Rosemary offered with a wicked smile. "Sam certainly can't tell me what to type! Or what to do for my friends."

When Rosemary left, the neatly typed proposal was stacked on the table. What a friend! She really wanted to help, but like Alex, was hampered by circumstances beyond her control.

With a crash of thunder, the afternoon rain started. Alex studied the pattern of rain on the flowering hibiscus in her backyard. She was reminded of the times she and Nick had encountered a sudden downpour and the way he looked with a rain-drenched shirt clinging to his shoulders. Shoulders broad enough to provide strength and a refuge for someone who needed help; someone like her, who needed a strong man to lean on. Oh, how she wished he was here right now.

Reluctantly, Alex admitted there was an overwhelming attraction between them, something neither could deny. Apparently it was also something neither could resist. She remembered their breathless moments together and the hot, surging sensations she felt when he whispered her name. That was a dangerous sign.

She hugged her arms in frustration, thinking of Rosemary's unspoken fears, for she had them too. They were amplified now that she had felt the magnetism of Nick Diamond's kiss and knew of the passion he aroused in her. She was well aware of the strength of passion she aroused in Nick too.

113

Where was he right now? Was he really taking somebody on a tour of the pyramids? And what about tonight? The more she learned about him, the more doubt was cast. Where could he be going overnight? Was he meeting a woman, as Alex originally suspected? Perhaps Lia, with the voluptuous body. Or was he off on a smuggling mission?

Alex knew she shouldn't care if he was involved in smuggling or other illegal activities. He wasn't the man for her, not a hard criminal-type like Nick Diamond. Yet for some crazy reason, thinking he was a criminal was preferable to knowing that Nick lay in another woman's arms!

What difference did it make? she asked herself. She was only a client to him, regardless of the passion of his kisses. Obviously, he was only interested in getting into bed with her. Why else was he helping her with this search for Jenni? Well, she'd have to make sure that his interest in her remained keen but unsatisfied. Nothing must interfere with the search.

Dear Carol,

Well, I did it! I'm out on a limb by myself since Rosemary refused to sign that proposal. The official protest of budget cuts to the Early Childhood Dept. is lying on the University president's desk at this very moment. It may be one of the dumbest things I've ever done, or the wisest, but it was my only alternative. I figured I may as well go down fighting, stubborn American that I am!

We should hear something in a week or so.

Of course, I'm not ready to leave Mexico. Certainly not without Jenni.

So far, no leads. Nick is pursuing the investigation slowly. Too slowly for me, but he's running this show.

You mentioned Jack in your last letter. No, I do not want to see him! Please don't give him my address.

Can you help me find a job in Phoenix? I may need it sooner than I expected.

Love,
Alex

Nick had only been gone two days, but the way Alex felt, it could have been two years. She thought of him constantly and paced the floor and worried. Although she went through the motions of going to work, her mind was often occupied by Nick Diamond. Her reassuring hope of finding Jenni. When he wasn't around, she had none of that assurance. She felt completely alone in her fruitless search.

What if Nick didn't return? What if she was left once again with no one to help her find Jenni? What if she never saw Nick again? Alex tried to stay busy, tried not to think about the what ifs. She was ashamed to admit her obsession with this ruffian, Nick Diamond.

It was after dark when she heard the knock. Cautiously, Alex approached the door. *"Quien es?"*

"It's Nick, Alex. Nick Diamond," a weary voice rumbled.

Feverishly, Alex flung open the door. "Nick!"

115

Deep in her heart she felt tremendously relieved to see him, though she tried to hide her feelings.

"Alex, we have to talk." Nick teetered on her doorstep looking so big and rugged and . . . awful!

"Oh, God, Nick, what's wrong?"

"Does that offer of coffee still hold?" His eyes looked darker than usual, and tired. Gone was the spark she had seen there the last time they were together. Now she saw only fatigue, and that he needed her.

"Of course! Come in!" Instinctively, she reached for his wrist and pulled him toward her into the hall. Then, realizing what she was doing, she released his hand abruptly. "What in the world have you been doing?"

Nick sighed, his eyes drinking in Alex's refreshing beauty. "You wouldn't believe it. Actually, I'm just very tired. I didn't sleep very much in the past two days."

She closed the door behind him. "I thought you . . . might not return, Nick."

"What gave you that idea?"

She shrugged. "I didn't know where you were or when you'd be back."

"You don't have to know those things, Alex. Only that I'll be back." He loomed, rather than stood, in the hallway.

"How do I know that for sure? I don't know anything about you."

"You know that you can trust me, Alex," he said quietly. "That's enough."

She shook her head and her blond hair rustled

around her face. "It isn't enough for me. I want to know more, Nick."

"I thought we made a deal. You don't ask questions, and I'll help you find Jenni."

She nodded and looked down. "We did. But you haven't exactly held up your end of the bargain either. We're no closer to finding her."

"Oh yes we are. Investigations take time. We've only been working on this a week. And we're further along than we were at the beginning."

A week? Only a week? It seemed like a year! "Yes, I guess we are. Sorry, Nick. I'm just so anxious to find her. And these last two days have been long." *Without you!* she wanted to add. She gulped and left her feelings unsaid.

"That coffee? I need it, Alex."

"Oh, yes. And I'll fix you a sandwich. You must be hungry too." She turned away from him and started for the kitchen.

Nick followed her. "The reason I'm so grimy is that I just flew back into town tonight. Didn't take time for a shower or anything before coming over here. I'm dead tired, but something has developed and I figured you'd want to know."

The coffee pot clattered to the stove and Alex wheeled around. "You found her?"

"No! Now, take it easy, Alex. Just listen." He heaved himself into the chair and rested one muscular arm on the table. Even in his near-exhausted state, Nick looked so powerful and sexy that Alex wanted to run to him and soothe his tired body.

117

"Father Ramón got a tip that an orphaned child might be found at Guaymas, a small fishing village on the coast. Now, there is nothing definite about this at all. An anonymous tip. There was no specific information. The child could be ten or two, boy or girl. It might not be a valid tip at all. It might be the first of many wild goose chases. Like the hospital. I thought you'd like to go and see."

"Of course I'll go! It might be her!" Alex felt a flush of excitement. "This might be it!"

Nick shrugged, dousing her enthusiasm with his nonchalance. "At this point, we can't discount it. But chances are one in a million that we'd find her there. And so soon."

"Soon? My God, she's been gone a week!"

"Alex! Get ahold of yourself!" He had a mind to shake some sense into her but instead motioned impatiently at the coffee pot. "The coffee? I really need it." Nick looked at her askance, his usually sharp eyes bleary and dull. Just when he wanted to take her in his arms, he was demanding that she fix him a stupid cup of coffee. He must be losing his mind.

"How can you be so casual about this? So uncaring?"

"I'm not uncaring, Alex. Just tired. And if I'm going to sit here and stay awake long enough to talk to you, you'd better give me a little caffeine."

"All right, I'll fix the coffee. You talk." Alex forced herself back to the abandoned task. "Tell me everything. When did Father Ramón get this call? Who made it? Why don't you trace the caller? When are we going to Guaymas?"

"The only question I can answer is the last one. Tomorrow morning."

"Tomorrow? Why not tonight?" Alex demanded, her emotions playing havoc with soaring highs and plummeting lows in a matter of minutes. "What if she's there now?"

"If she's there tonight, Alex, she'll be there tomorrow. Anyway, I'm in no shape to fly anywhere tonight. I have to get some sleep."

"The claim on your door says you fly anyone anywhere," Alex accused, slapping packages of ham and cheese on the counter. "If you can fly tourists to the pyramids, why can't you fly me to Guaymas now? You fly that . . . that Lia anywhere she wants to go. I've hired you too!"

He ignored her jealous outburst. "I want you to meet Juancho and me at the airport tomorrow around ten. There's a little yellow building off to the right side where we keep the chopper. Juancho and I have to go over the mechanics and gas it up. Then we'll check out this rumor. And remember, Alex, that's all it is, a rumor."

Alex spread mustard on the bread and dug out lettuce and pickles while the coffee perked wildly. Why was he doing this to her? Building her hopes up only to kick them down. The rich aroma of strong coffee filled the room, and she placed a plate of sandwiches and a steaming cup of coffee before Nick. "If that doesn't keep you awake for at least thirty minutes, nothing will."

119

"Thanks. I'm starved." He dove into the first sandwich without another word.

Alex fixed herself a cup of coffee and sat opposite him. "You don't think she's there, do you?"

"I don't know. I told you the odds. But it's possible that they would try to get her out of town. Away from Hermosillo."

"They?"

"Whoever has her."

"And you think someone has her? That she's been stolen?"

"Definitely. I think . . ." He paused and looked into Alex's frightened eyes. "I think she's safe. But they probably don't want to ransom her. We would have heard something by now. They want her."

Alex froze. "F-for what?"

Nick took a deep breath. Damn, he shouldn't be telling her this. He was just so tired, he couldn't think straight. He jerked to full awareness when she gripped his arm fiercely. Her fingernails pricked his skin and he felt the sting all the way to his soul.

"Tell me! What do you think, Nick? Why do they want her?"

Nick's eyes hardened and he wrenched his arm from Alex's frantic grasp. His angular face grew taut and he rose to pace across the floor. Running a large hand through his dark hair, he turned back to Alex. "Maybe . . . maybe to sell her."

CHAPTER SEVEN

Alex felt as though someone had stabbed her in the stomach. She stared horrified at Nick. "Sell? Sell Jenni?" Her voice was shrill as her emotions pitched and rolled with another of those roller coaster surges. "Oh, my God, *no!* Surely not! It just can't be!"

"Oh, hell! I didn't intend to tell you my suspicions so soon, Alex, but I guess it's time you knew—"

"When were you going to tell me? After she was sold . . . when it was too late?"

Nick gripped her arms and shook her roughly. "I didn't intend to tell you because I didn't want a hysterical woman on my hands! For God's sake, calm down!"

"How did you expect me to react when you told me something so . . . so outrageous!" Her eyes were like blue flames, dancing with panic.

"Alex, the only way we're going to see this thing through and get Jenni back is by calmly calculating the actions of the enemy. We will get nowhere by losing control!"

"Calculating the enemy? You sound like we're fighting a war!"

He released her. "Well, in a way, I feel as if we are. It's a hard business, taking a child like this. It's cruel and barbaric. We have to be the same if we're going to win."

"I don't think it's possible for me."

"Then leave that part up to me. Just don't get hysterical on me."

"Are we? Going to win this . . . this 'battle', as you say?"

"It's going to be tough. I don't know yet."

Alex took a shaky breath, verging on tears yet not able to fully release her emotions. "It's easy for you to be hard and unfeeling because you aren't emotionally involved with Jenni. You just think of her as a thing, a name of something, not a little girl who might be afraid and hungry and crying for her mama!"

Nick's eyes flickered with something close to a savage viciousness. "I'm more involved than you think. But one of us has to be calm about it!"

Alex turned her back on Nick and hugged her arms in distress, trying to block out the inner pain she felt. "I'm sorry, Nick. It's hard to be calm when I've just learned someone might be s-selling Jenni."

"What that means, Alex," Nick's voice became gentle and another side of him surfaced, "is that she's being well cared for, that she's warm and dry and being fed and . . . whatever is necessary to keep her in good condition."

Alex turned around slowly and lifted her eyes

to meet his. The savage expression was gone, replaced by a tenderness that surprised her. "Do you really think so, Nick?"

He nodded. "Yes, I do."

"And cuddled?"

He gestured impotently. "If that's necessary."

"It is. For a little child. For Jenni. She's accustomed to lots of attention. And love."

"Then, I suppose . . . oh, hell, Alex. I don't know. I don't know much more about this situation than you do."

She narrowed her eyes accusingly. "Yes you do, Nick. And you're only telling me what you have to, when you have to. I feel like I'm the last to know anything that's happening."

"It's better this way, Alex." His hands hung limply by his side, itching to touch her, to feel her softness. He flexed them once, trying to eliminate the urge to embrace her, to claim her as his own, to protect her from the pain she now felt. Maybe she needed the comforting. Maybe he was the one to give it. He lifted his hands, then let them drop. Oh, hell, that was crazy. There was only one way he wanted to hold her: the way he'd hold her if they were making love.

"I'd better leave, now," he said a little too quickly. "Thanks for the sandwich and coffee. If you want to go to Guaymas, meet us around ten tomorrow."

"I'll be there." She swallowed hard, wishing he'd pull her into his arms. Wildly, she wanted his touch, his hot, hungry kiss. Her eyes grew

123

misty. "It'll be difficult to sleep tonight, thinking about her . . . about Jenni."

Nick's eyes flickered sharply. "Yeah. Difficult to sleep. See you tomorrow." He hesitated, then turned and bolted from the room.

As Nick jerked the gray rattletrap van into gear, he knew how close he'd come to losing that degree of restraint he tried to force on himself whenever he was around Alex. Tonight he needed to be lost in her softness, and she needed his strength. It was an intangible feeling, but something he knew. She wanted him, and how he wanted her! Wanted her with more driving desire than any woman he'd wanted in a long time. But now was not the time, he thought. And this was not the woman. Alex was too vulnerable; she'd been hurt too much already. And he was no good for her.

Nick squinted in the bright sunlight and wielded a huge wrench over the rotor head. After rechecking the rotor blades, he jumped down from the helicopter. "The newspaper photographer! Hell, Juancho, I don't know why we didn't think of him first! As an eyewitness, he was probably the most observant person there that day."

Juancho nodded in agreement. "I bet he has more photos than the one in the paper. They always take more than they need."

"Oh, hell, yeah. You've got to get to him soon. Today!"

"And forget about Guaymas? What about the tip from Padre Ramón?"

124

"We'll check it out. Alex and I. It's senseless for you to make this trip. Might be a waste of time for us too. But I'd never rest easy if we didn't see it through, and Alex would be a basket case."

Juancho climbed on the helicopter and leaned over the turbine engine, watching its action with calculating eyes. "But what about the change in plan and tonight's pick-up at Guaymas?"

"I'll take care of it. No big deal."

"You sure you can handle this haul by yourself?"

"What's to handle? It's just birds! Anyway, I'll have Alex along to help."

Juancho rolled his eyes comically. "That's what bothers me, Capitán."

"Not to worry, Juancho. I won't expose our game. She doesn't know a thing."

"But how do you expect her not to question these extra passengers?"

"We have a deal," Nick answered simply.

"Ah, si. I should have known." Juancho slid off the helicopter and bent to adjust the main under-carriage wheels, hiding a smug smile. "I won't ask what kind of deal."

"Good." Nick shrugged amicably. "Then I won't tell you. Besides, it's more important for you to talk to this photographer as soon as possible. I'll take care of Alex and the birds, you take care of this photographer while we're gone."

"Then you don't expect to find Jenni in Guaymas?"

Nick sighed and leaned against the helicopter's tail. "I just have a feeling we're heading up an empty street. It was a poor tip, and Father Ramón even said there were strange circumstances about it. But . . ." Nick shrugged and left the rest unsaid. "Our cargo is getting stranger and stranger, Juancho. Whoever thought we'd be going for goddamn birds?"

Juancho stood and reached inside the helicopter's back cabin. "Exotic birds are important, Capitán. Thousands of dollars are exchanged in their safe transport. Avoiding the thirty-day quarantine period and excess costs of feeding and testing them is the key to big profits." He waggled a brown paper bag. "This is for the birds. Not too much, now, or you'll kill them. But, used discriminately, it'll quiet them down."

Nick smiled wickedly. "Is there any for the pilot?"

"No, Capitán. You have to keep a clear head."

"Hell, Juancho. It's a cinch."

Juancho stuffed the paper bag in the rear cabin and slammed the sliding door. "Okay, you have plenty of rags to hide the birds in the back."

"No cages?"

"Won't need them. Except for the boas. And they're already crated."

"Boas? Goddamn! You didn't tell me about them!"

Juancho smiled, making his mustache waggle at the ends. "It's a cinch, Capitán. You can handle it. I'm confident. There is much money hanging on this deal!"

"Birds!" Nick fussed. "I'd rather haul crates of

oranges! At least they're quiet! Now how the hell am I going to explain boas to Alex?"

"How are you going to explain birds, Capitán?" Juancho taunted.

"Damned if I know." Nick looked up at the sound of an approaching car. "That must be Alex's taxi. Now you get to that photographer as soon as possible, Juancho. We'll be back tonight, birds and boas in transport. I'll bring Alex here, drop her off, and pick you up. Then we can take them on to the border drop."

"There will be a message confirming it, Capitán. Same place."

"I'll call you just before we take off." Nick nodded curtly and turned to watch Alex as she paid the taxi driver. He felt an unbidden swell of masculine admiration as he observed her approach, her shoulder bag banging jauntily against a slightly swaying hip as she walked. She looked devastating in a white peasant blouse and a full colorful skirt. On closer inspection, he could tell she hadn't slept much. Well, hell, neither had he.

"*Hola*, Juancho," she smiled in greeting. "Nick . . . ready to go?" Expectation buoyed her flagging spirits. Nick could tell she was anxious to get started.

"*Buenos días, señorita*," Juancho returned happily.

Nick tossed the wrench into a nearby metal case of tools and wiped his hands on a damp rag. "Alex, there's been a slight change of plans. Juancho isn't going with us. He has work to do here. So it's just the two of us."

127

"Fine," she murmured nonchalantly. "Are we ready to go?"

"You anxious? You look like you didn't sleep much last night."

She cast him a weary glance. "What did you expect, after the news you dropped on me? Who could sleep?"

His dark eyes looked at her with tenderness. "Neither could I. Come on." He reached for the door.

She paused beside the door, fumbling in her purse. "I know I owe you some money. How much for this trip?"

Nick stared at her for a moment. "Nothing. You don't owe anything, Alex."

"Oh yes I do. This trip wasn't a part of the original bargain. I realize that. I expect to pay extra for trips."

"It's included," he muttered gruffly and took her arm to assist her into the helicopter.

Stubbornly, she resisted. "But, Nick, I realize that gas for this thing is expensive and—"

"No! I tell you, I had to make this trip anyway. It's business." He practically shoved her aboard the helicopter.

"Business? What kind of business?"

"I'll explain . . . later." Nick slammed the door and gave Juancho a weary glance. Dealing simple answers to this woman might not be so easy after all.

Juancho gave him the thumbs-up sign and backed away as the overhead rotor blades started rotating. He had watched the exchange between

Nick and Alex, observing their unspoken communication with an uncanny understanding. Their eyes said everything. He piled the tools into the back of the gray van and watched the chopper as it whirled noisily over Hermosillo, heading for the west coast. *Ah, Capitán, she is very pretty. Big, beautiful eyes. A little sad. And you are caught, whether you know it or not!*

The seaside village of Guaymas nestled like a multicolored pearl against the clear blue Bay of California. They set down at the miniature airport between jagged mountains and the bay. If it weren't for their emotion-charged mission, the place could be beautifully romantic. Alex almost wished . . . then she quickly dismissed such thoughts. Nothing must interfere with that mission. Jenni must be found! Maybe it would be today!

"This is the man we are to meet," Nick said, helping her out of the helicopter. He showed her a slip of paper. "Name's José. He'll meet us at a local cantina, El Corral."

Alex looked curiously at the common name as they walked to the airport office. "Is that all you have? How will we know him?"

Nick grinned, his dark mustache contrasting with his white teeth. "Not to worry. The plan is that he'll find us, my sweet." He opened the airport door. "You did bring your passport, didn't you? The immigration officer here takes his job pretty seriously. Plus, I need to make arrangements for the helicopter. It'll only take a few minutes."

"What plan?" She preceded him inside the small red-tile-roofed building. "And what did you call me?" Alex arched an eyebrow at him. "My sweet" just wasn't like Nick Diamond. What was he up to, anyway?

"I'll explain later," he said mysteriously. "But first let's take care of this business."

She had to wait for the explanation until they were tucked into a local cab, careening through the streets of Guaymas. Alex could feel the excitement swelling in her breast. They were getting closer! "Okay, enlighten me!" she demanded. "What plan?"

Nick leaned closer to her ear and the faint masculine scent of him accosted her senses, making concentration difficult. "José is looking for a blond American woman. Very pretty. And her . . . American husband. He's tall, dark, and a little rough around the edges. Has an old scar right here." He ran a finger down his own cheek, then switched to touch her soft skin.

"What? Did I hear *husband?*"

"Remember now," he whispered, tucking a finger against her lips. "Not a word of Spanish. You're a *tourista* through and through. And here." Nick dug into his pants pocket. "You'd better wear this. Looks more authentic."

Before Alex knew what he was doing, Nick had slipped a gold band onto her ring finger. "Nick? He actually thinks—"

"Yes, my sweet. He thinks we're an American couple looking for a child to adopt. Or buy."

Alex stiffened against the cab seat. "A child to buy?" she rasped.

"Shhh." Nick motioned to the cab driver. "Yes, my sweet darling."

"Oh, God, Nick! I can't believe it!" Alex struggled to keep her voice low. "I can't go through with this charade!"

"Of course you can. You'll do anything for a baby. Well, almost anything." He smiled reassuringly at her as the driver pulled to a screeching halt in front of El Corral. Nick paid the cabbie and ushered Alex out of the cab, keeping an arm protectively around her.

"Nick, I'm so nervous. I don't think I'll be any good at this." Her feet felt as though they were planted in the concrete sidewalk; her knees felt like lead.

He took her hand and lifted her fingers to his lips for a tender kiss. "You can pretend anything for an hour, Alex. Come on, my sweet, smile. We're a very loving couple. Our story is quite tragic. We lost a child in infancy and were unable to have another. Money is no object when it comes to mending our broken hearts. What we want most in the entire world is a little girl to replace our precious Jenni." His arm braced her back and propelled her toward the cantina.

Alex took a shaky breath. "I . . . I can't believe I'm doing this."

Nick hovered close, granting her a wink and a reassuring squeeze. "Just remember, you're playing a role. You'll do fine, Alex. Whatever you do, don't mention Father Ramón. An anonymous contact directed us here. That's very close to the truth anyway. Said we could find a kid. For the right amount. And we're a wealthy couple, so don't be concerned about the money. I'll handle that part. You just keep quiet about it. Come on, now, my sweet. If someone is watching, you don't want them to see us arguing."

"Give me a minute to compose myself, Nick. I'm just so damn nervous." She gave him a skittish smile. "Don't loving couples argue?"

"Yes, but not about getting babies. These people want this kid." His arm embraced her tense back, drawing her close to his firm chest. "We make a perfect couple, Alex. A man and woman always make a good foil. That's why I wanted you along instead of Juancho." Before she could resist further, they were inside the darkened bar. Nick sat so he could have a view of the door.

The place was small and the bartender was also the waiter. He ambled over to their corner table. *"Bebida, señor?"*

"My wife and I would like a good margarita," Nick announced boldly. "One of those slushy kind."

The waiter's brown eyes assessed Nick quietly before he shuffled away. Alex observed the man beside her in amazement. He was playing his role to perfection! He was the paragon of a wealthy, arrogant American. Thank goodness she only had to remain quiet through this whole ordeal. She could at least do that. *You can pretend anything for an hour,* Nick had said. If it involved getting Jenni back, yes, she could!

Alex tried to hide her shaking hands and concentrated on breathing smoothly. She barely had time to take a sip of her slushy margarita and to adjust to her newly acquired marital status before a swarthy man, slight of build, stopped beside their table.

"Mr. and Mrs. Smith? From Detroit?" he asked in a heavy accent.

"Yep, that's us," Nick responded quickly, glancing from side to side before extending his hand to the man. "You José?"

"Si." He pulled out a chair and joined them.

"Bring this man a drink," Nick called to the bartender.

Alex marveled at the change in Nick. She had never seen him like this and had to admit he portrayed a slightly nervous, arrogant gringo to the hilt. She tried to take another sip, but found that her throat was constricted and refused to allow anything to go down. She pretended to drink and quietly watched the action.

Nick leaned across the table and muttered in a low voice, "I want you to know, señor, that money is no object in this transaction."

José's heavy-lidded eyes narrowed as he calculated this American couple before him. "Si, señor. I understand. We have everything you need. Papers for emigration. And the baby is in good health. Happy too."

"Good, good. That's important." Nick nodded and took another substantial drink of the margarita. "The, ah, the kid, José. It *is* a girl, isn't it? We're looking for a girl. Our little Jenni." His voice softened at the end, and Alex had to admire his apparent tenderness, contrasting with his obnoxious arrogance.

José smiled readily, an evil gaping-toothed grin. "Si, señor. *La niña* is very beautiful!" His dark gaze settled on Alex and she quelled a shudder.

"Good," she managed hoarsely with a weak smile.

"My wife is a little nervous about this," Nick said in an apologetic tone, patting Alex's arm, then letting his large hand slide down to cover hers. With an affectionate squeeze, he tucked her hand to his lap, and Alex's heart skipped a beat. It was damned hard to concentrate and play an unfamiliar role when her hand was resting on Nick's thigh. *You can pretend anything for an hour* she kept reminding herself.

José dabbed some salt on the web of his thumb, licked it off, then turned his glass of tequila straight up and emptied it in one gulp. "You like to see her? Let's go, Mrs. Smith!"

The three trooped out of the cantina, and José drove them to their destination in a vehicle that made Nick's rattletrap van look like a Rolls. They halted before a hovel of a house with ancient, brown, crumbling adobe brick walls and a thatched roof. Dark-eyed, skinny-legged children gathered at the corner of the neighboring houses and stared at the gringos.

Alex's heart was working overtime. She had never been so nervous, scared, and excited—all at once—in her entire life. She clung to Nick as if he were truly her husband. She glanced up at his face for signs of stress but found none. Just tight-jawed determination. He could pull this off, if anyone could. *El Capitán* could handle it. She hooked her hands more securely around his arm.

They stepped inside the house and stood uncomfortably on the hard-packed earth floor. Alex felt Nick's arm slip securely around her back, giving support. Children scattered to the rear of the house and a burly dark-haired man rose to greet them.

The formalities were simple and handled by José. "Mr. and Mrs. Smith. This is Ricardo."

"Please to meet you, Ricardo." Nick shook hands with the man who could speak no English.

In an unsteady voice, Ricardo began to explain the child's circumstances in Spanish. José interpreted the story and Nick and Alex listened politely, as if they couldn't understand what the man was saying.

"Ricardo say," José began in halting English, "this is not his baby. The sister of his wife is only sixteen. She has no husband and left the baby here. But Ricardo, he has too many children of his own to feed. He want you to know he would never do this if it was his own child. And he know you take good care of this baby."

"Certainly. Oh, yes. Of course, we'll take good care of her. Like our own." Nick nodded curtly, in complete agreement with everything that was being said.

Alex felt as though a movie was playing before her and she was somehow standing apart from it.

Even Nick wasn't himself. She didn't know whether to believe Ricardo's story or not. If it were true, then this child definitely was not Jenni. Ricardo left the room. From the rear of the house muffled sobs could be heard—a woman's cry.

Oh God! It's her baby! Alex felt dizzy and clung desperately to Nick.

Ricardo reappeared with a small child clinging to his neck. She turned her tawny pixie face away from the strangers and buried it against his shoulder. Alex could see the man go rigid as the child frantically clutched the one person she trusted. Yet he was about to betray her! Instinctively, Alex reached out to pet the child's sturdy back. Yes, she was tiny, but well-fed. And barely over a year old. She definitely was not Jenni.

Nick watched Alex's reaction until she whispered, "It isn't her." Large tears rose unbidden in her eyes and she bit her lip, trying to control the raging sobs that threatened.

"José," Nick began haltingly. "This child, she just isn't right for us. You see, we were looking for one who was a little older."

"What's wrong, señor? This is fine baby!" José's voice was angry. "Why are you backing out of the deal?"

"Nothing is wrong with her. She's a fine baby. Like you said, very beautiful. I'm sorry, José. But, my wife . . ." He stepped back and motioned to Alex. Obviously, her role was that of the strange wife who couldn't be pleased. She was the reason they were refusing to buy the child.

Alex lifted her face in agony to the circle of men and shook her head, unable to speak. Tears streamed silently down her cheeks. She was playing the role to perfection. Only deep inside, Alex knew the tears were for real.

Nick stuffed a twenty into Ricardo's hand, the one holding the baby, and said to José, "Tell him to buy his children some milk and bread. Explain about my wife, that we're very sad this didn't work out. And here. You take this for your trouble." He gave José another bill and pushed Alex toward the door.

They left amid a noisy commotion. The men were angry. The child began to whimper, and in the distance, a woman's cries of joy could be heard. Alex's legs, her whole body, were numb. She wanted to scream, to sob hysterically, but she kept a stoic face. They were leaving without her precious Jenni.

CHAPTER EIGHT

"I could easily hate you, Nick Diamond, for putting me through that. Only, I know you aren't responsible for what happened."

"Thanks a lot. You probably won't believe this, but I hated what we went through too. I wish I could say it won't happen again, but I can't guarantee it. It might happen again and again . . . until we catch the bastards." Nick stuffed his hands in his pockets as he walked down the street. "Until we find her."

Alex hurried after him, simply because there was no other alternative. "Where are we going? Do you plan to walk back to the airport?"

"No. There's a restaurant a few blocks away. I thought we'd—"

"I don't want to eat. I want to go home!"

"Can't."

"Can't? Why not?"

"Have to wait. At this restaurant. I have more business."

"Well, I'm tired and emotionally drained, and I'm ready to leave this place. . . . What business?"

He ignored her question and continued walking. Alex struggled to keep up with Nick's long-legged strides.

"Why don't we just take a cab?"

"I need to walk. Need to think. It isn't far."

Nick seemed preoccupied with other thoughts, and when they reached the restaurant, he took a sidewalk table without a word. Alex gratefully slumped into a chair opposite him and didn't protest when he ordered, *"Dos cervezas, por favor."*

Finally, he spoke to her: "I know you're disappointed, Alex. So am I. I'm sorry."

"I'm afraid I set myself up for this pain. My expectations were too high." She sipped dejectedly at the beer the waiter brought. "I actually thought we'd find her."

"I tried to warn you. At least you aren't hysterical."

Her indigo eyes narrowed. "It's because I'm keeping a tight lid on my emotions. What I'd really like to do is scream at the top of my lungs about the cruelty and injustice of everything that's happened recently."

He took a long swig of beer. "I doubt that. You aren't the emotional type, Alex. I think you've been pretty steady through it all."

She leaned forward on the table. "You're forcing me into being the emotional type by exposing me to such heart-wringing situations. That baby . . ." She shook her head helplessly.

He touched her hand in a soft gesture, a gentle caress, then rested his large hand over hers. "I

139

think you've done very well, Alex. You played your wifely role to perfection and held yourself together at that house. I realize it was tough, especially knowing this child wasn't Jenni."

She snatched her hand away from his. "Don't placate me, Nick Diamond!"

"What do you want from me, if not understanding?"

"I want you to find Jenni!" Her voice rose.

"It isn't the simplest request you could make," he growled. "You never know what will come of this. José may come back with another offer."

"*Another* child?" She pitched forward and rested her forehead in her hand. "Oh, God, Nick! How could he?"

"Maybe another one. Or he may find Jenni."

Alex turned her face away and took a deep breath. "José was repulsive. Only interested in money."

"Yes, Alex. That's what we're dealing with here. People whose only interest is making money. They're cold, hard-hearted bastards. When are you going to get that through your stubborn head?"

She cast angry eyes at him but said nothing. Alex wanted to hate Nick but she couldn't. She wanted to cry, but tears wouldn't come. She wanted to go home, wanted to do anything but sit here and drink beer with him. Yet Nick had other plans, other concerns. She'd never felt so torn apart.

The waiter returned and Nick asked, "Do you like turtle soup? They fix the best I've eaten."

"I'm not hungry."

"You need food. We haven't eaten all day." He gave the order anyway and the waiter left.

"Here. I won't be needing this." Alex reached across the table and placed the gold band on the table before him.

Nick's eyes dropped to the ring, then lifted to hers. "We may have to use it again, you know."

"I hope not. I hated every minute of it."

"It wasn't that bad, was it?"

"Only the 'my sweet' part . . . and in the restaurant, when you were such an obnoxious bastard . . . and at the house, when they brought out the baby."

"I thought I made an understanding husband. And you were a very convincing wife." Nick smiled for the first time in hours.

Alex softened, ever so slightly, and smiled too. "It just shows that in a pinch, I, too, can act . . . my sweet."

"The act's over now." He matched her sarcasm then glanced around warily. It was a motion he would repeat many times while they sat there.

The waiter brought their soup, and they ate in silence. In spite of her protests, Alex found she was starved. She couldn't help wondering if the act was truly finished. Would they have to go through this again in the search for Jenni? Was this whole thing an act for Nick? Even his kisses?

They topped off the meal with coffee and flan. Nick took his time and chatted aimlessly about local customs and history. They had more coffee and he relayed stories about the biggest, longest, and meanest fish caught in Guaymas. They'd been there about two hours when Alex realized he was dallying.

Finally, before she could confront him, she understood the reason for the delay. Or part of the reason.

"Are you *El Capitán?*" A boy of about twelve stood by their table.

"Si." Nick nodded.

The boy handed Nick a slip of paper and was gone in a flash. Nick slid the paper inside his shirt, quickly paid the bill, and ushered Alex away. They took a cab immediately. Digging out the paper, he scanned it then ripped it apart and stuffed it into two different pockets.

"Delayed," he muttered. "Damn!" He gave directions to the cab driver then turned to Alex. "Plans have changed."

"What plans? I thought—"

"My plans. We'll have to spend the night here."

"What? Why?"

His eyes were hard and dark. He glanced behind the cab as if checking to see if they were being followed. "No questions, remember?"

A sudden chill went through Alex, and she wondered what in hell she'd gotten herself into. Who was this man beside her? And what was he doing? In all the time she'd spent with Nick, she still couldn't answer the questions she had about him. She still didn't know him.

It was a modest hotel by American standards. Alex walked into the cool, clean-smelling room and pushed on the near corner of the bed. It seemed adequate enough. She peered around curiously. The shower was small, but completely tiled; the walls were white-stucco and decorated with framed charcoal drawings of Mexican women in the marketplace.

At the end of the room a window overlooked a lush courtyard. People milled about, bringing food and arranging decorations. Musicians gathered on a small stage, tuning their instruments. Obviously, they were getting ready for a party. Alex turned away. The thought of gaiety repulsed her.

She could hear Nick in the room next door and leaned her body against their adjoining wall as if to absorb more of his sounds. What was it about the man that drew her to him? Here she was, spending the night in a strange place because of his so-called plans. And she had no idea what his plans were. Or how she fit into them.

She heard his door click and realized Nick was leaving the room. Maybe he was coming in here to see her. She waited and listened breathlessly, suddenly aware that that was exactly what she wanted him to do. The sound of his footsteps, however, receded down the hall, and she felt a small, sad pang. Alex took a deep breath and tried to shake her mounting melancholy mood. Maybe a shower would help. She pulled the blouse over her head, slipped out of the skirt and then her underwear. Standing barefoot on the cold, Mexican-tiled floor, she looked down at her gently rounded breasts and wondered if Nick liked a woman with a larger bosom. She pressed a palm to her flat stomach and the feminine curve between her hip bones. She wondered what it would be like to have Nick touch her there, and to feel him inside her. Shaking the thoughts away, she adjusted the water and stepped inside. With gratitude for the warm wetness, she turned her dusty face up to the refreshing spray.

Nick made a phone call to Juancho, explaining the delay, then chatted amiably with the hotel manager. There would be a wedding soon, and hotel guests were invited to participate in the celebration. Feeling dusty and mentally fatigued, Nick made his way back down the hall. A brisk shower was what he needed. Then he would tell Alex about the wedding celebration. Maybe it would cheer her to attend.

She was angry with him. He could feel it. Hell, maybe she had a right to be. All he'd done was build her hopes up, only to dash them today in that house with the earthen floors.

Nick stood beside the door to his room and paused. He heard something. The sound came from Alex's room, the mournful sound of someone crying. He hesitated. Should he let her alone? But he couldn't leave her like this.

He knocked softly. "Alex?" He pressed on the latch and the door opened. She hadn't even bothered to lock her door! Nick entered swiftly, prompted by the sight of her sobbing.

She sat against the wall that separated her

room from his, a towel wrapped around her slender body, her hair dripping wet from a recent shower. She hadn't even taken time to dry off and beads of water glistened on her bare shoulders and arms. She gazed, sobbing, at a charcoal drawing of a little girl, a dark-eyed Mexican child with unruly curls.

"Oh, God, Alex." Nick knelt beside her and turned her away from the framed picture. "There, there," he murmured clumsily, not knowing what else to say.

With his arms around Alex, Nick helped her stand up and gathered her protectively to his chest. He pressed her tightly to him and held her there until the two seemed as one, sharing the same passions, the same feelings. Without the encumbrance of words, his body told her of his caring.

Alex let Nick hold her, willingly relinquishing her limp body to his encompassing embrace. Like a child, she buried her face against his shoulder and cried until she felt a release of frustrations and grief that had built up over the last week and reached a dramatic peak today in the little Mexican house.

Nick's shoulder was sturdy and sheltering, just as she'd imagined it would be. When Alex's sobbing abated, she could hear the steady beat of his heart, strong and reassuring. She savored the sound and stood very still, listening, not allowing any other thoughts to crowd her mind. Nick was with her now and he would make things right. *El Capitán* could take care of everything.

His hand caressed her wet hair then slid to the bare skin of her neck, pressing her head to his chest. She was still wet from the shower and he ran his other hand down her slick back. Oh, how he wanted to touch her all over like that! To dry her with his hands!

"It's been a week," she said, turning her face to the side. She wiped some of the tears away. "And, when I saw that . . . that drawing on the wall . . . I remembered Jenni and . . ."

"It's been a hard week for you, Alex."

"Nick . . . I'm sorry."

"Don't be."

"I . . . didn't intend to lose control. To get hysterical on you."

"You aren't, Alex. Anyway, you deserve a good cry after all you've been through. I've been too rough on you."

"Why didn't you leave me alone just now?"

"I couldn't. . . ."

"Nick . . . what will happen to her?"

"To Jenni?"

"No. To the little one we saw today."

He sighed heavily. "I don't know."

"Do you think they'll find another buyer for her?" Alex's voice quivered when she spoke.

"We can't rectify every injustice we encounter, Alex. We have to concentrate on our own. Jenni is our main concern."

Struggling with his reasoning, Alex finally nodded against his chest. "You're probably right. I've got to get tough. I just hate leaving that little kid in that situation." She began to wiggle and Nick loosened his hold. "I think you're pretty generous, letting me cry all over your shirt like this." She reached up and stroked futilely at the wet spots on his shirt, at the same time petting the hard chest behind those spots.

"It gave me an excuse to hold you."

"An excuse?" She lifted her head. "Nick, the act's over, remember?"

"Act?" he repeated roughly. "Can't you tell when I'm being honest? Surely you've known . . . felt . . . that I wanted to do this." He kissed the back of her neck and her slick, bare shoulder. She was still wet and tasted sweet and fresh. He wanted to relish every moist, feminine inch of her!

She tried to ignore the rush of warmth that filled her when his lips caressed her like that. "I'm all right now."

"Maybe crying was what you needed."

"Sometimes a woman just needs to be held. Does this go along with the job, Nick?"

"You know better, Alex." He kissed her mouth, then slid his lips down a moist trail along the sensitive column of her neck. He tried not to notice that the towel was loose around her breasts. But his male instincts knew it had slipped to reveal the rose-hewed areolas encircling her nipples. Through the thin towel, he could tell they were tight and alert. Unable to resist the delicious sight, he dipped his face to the rounded tops of her breasts. His tongue lapped away the honeyed moisture gathered between them, then laved each tip.

147

"Alex . . . oh, God, Alex . . ." His voice was throaty and he could feel the swell of desire as he pressed his lips to her silky skin. His large hand cupped one half-clad breast and squeezed its cushiony softness. Oh, how he was tempted to rip the towel from her and take her right there on the cold, tiled floor! And, from the looks of her, he would encounter no resistance.

Alex leaned her head back against the wall and arched her breasts against his tantalizing kisses, content to enjoy the pleasure of her own mounting desire. His mustache brushed languidly across her sensitive flesh, awakening fresh sensations as her entire body grew tight and aching for his fulfillment. Ahhh, Nick's cool kisses were soothing, yet they lit a fire in her that threatened to consume them both.

He knew how to kiss her properly, knew exactly how to make her want him. And, oh, God, did she! She wanted him to kiss her all over like this.

But she couldn't let that happen! She didn't know him . . . couldn't trust him. This was all a part of the act. She and Nick had other things to accomplish and nothing should interfere.

She opened her eyes and drew a shaky breath. She was excited by the erotic sight of him hovering over her, kissing her, a man obviously wracked by passion. It was thrilling to know that Nick's desire was for her. It was what she had wanted all along. But she had to resist.

"Nick we can't lose control here." She squirmed to an upright position.

148

He lifted his head and looked at her for a moment, his dark eyes wildly passionate. He wanted her, oh, yes, he wanted her. But not like this. She wanted him too. But he could see the reluctance in her eyes, the apprehension, the distrust. Where was the restraint he'd promised himself from the beginning? Only one week with Alex and he was on the verge of toppling her into bed. "Alex, you're beautiful," he muttered as a way of explanation.

"Beautiful?" She smiled faintly. "Even with my hair wet?"

"Especially like this . . . and sexy." His dark eyes swept over her, taking in the bare, lengthy legs and the downy juncture that was scarcely covered by the towel. "Come here to me." With amazing ease and strength, he lifted her in his arms. The towel became a rumpled strip across her middle and he took full advantage of the moment to move heated kisses over the swell of her exposed breasts.

Alex struggled, but he pinioned her against his chest. She could do nothing stronger than push futilely at him and kick the air. When he raised his head, Nick's dark eyes flickered with the passion she'd seen before. Only this time, she was completely vulnerable to him.

"Nick, don't force this!"

"You want it, too, dammit!"

"No, I don't!"

"There's a phrase for a woman like you, Alex. I'm damned tired of your teasing."

"Me? Why, you're the one who entered my

149

room! I didn't invite you in here! You came of your own accord."

He glared at her. She was right. "Alex—" The name tore from his lips in ragged agony. Oh, yes, he could take her right now. He could force himself on her. But was this what he wanted from her? No, he wanted her willing and eager for him. To cry out his name in ecstasy. "Goddammit, Alex!"

The savage animal in him wanted to fling her from him, and his arms trembled with the beastly urges that threatened to possess him. Instead, he released her legs and let them dangle along his. One arm still held her securely to his chest, crushing her tender breasts. His eyes never left hers as he gradually released the pressure, letting her slither erotically down the tautened length of him. The seductive act forced her body over every inch of his muscular chest, his flat, hard belly, the aroused heat of his rigid manhood, the unyielding power of his legs.

When her toes finally reached the floor, she was weak-kneed and whipped into an inner frenzy. Her emotions were raw and jumbled, her desire soaring as never before. At that moment she thought she would be crazy to send Nick away. With hot, shaky fingers, she wrapped the towel around her steamy body. She looked up at him, her defiant face glowing with a rosy flush.

They stood gazing at each other for a long, somewhat turbulent minute. Both were thinking the same thing, and both knew it wouldn't happen. Not now. Nick's expression was filled with dark desire. And anger.

"Tell me you don't want me!"

"That was crude." Alex clasped the towel to her breasts. There was precious little between them. "I'm all right now. No more hysterics, so you may leave. This is no way to calculate the enemy, is it?"

"W-what?"

"It's what you said earlier. We can't calculate the enemy by losing control."

"I thought for a minute you considered me the enemy."

Her blue eyes softened. "No, Nick. I can't believe you're the enemy. As little as I know about you, I think you're on my side."

He stood rigidly, a man in turmoil. Strange emotions tore at his insides, threatening to explode. He knew only one thing. He wanted this woman with a desire so strong he wasn't sure if he could control it. It was something he'd never felt before and couldn't understand. "Believe it, Alex. I care about you. And about finding Jenni."

She took a deep breath and smiled. She had to go on trust with him, for he gave her nothing else. "You'd better leave, Nick." Even though she trusted him without really knowing why, she didn't trust herself. He was too virile and appealing. And she was essentially undressed.

"I'm going to take a shower." He shifted away then turned back to catch her eyes. "A *cold* shower. You get some rest. After that, maybe we could go out for dinner."

"Okay."

He reached the door then turned around again. "The hotel owner's daughter is getting married tonight. We've been invited to the wedding celebration. It'll be quite an extravaganza. Dancing. Fireworks. It might help you . . . forget."

Alex sat weakly on the corner of the bed. "I'd like that, Nick."

If body language could speak, Nick's jerky motions as he bolted through the door roared of his anger and frustration with this woman. And with himself.

It was a different Nick who knocked on Alex's door later. He looked the same—broad shoulders, tight jeans, dark, devil's eyes. But in those eyes she saw a tenderness in place of the usual hardness.

"Have you ever been to a Mexican wedding, Alex?"

"No."

"Lots of food and drink. And festivity."

She smoothed a wrinkle from the skirt she'd worn all day. "I hope I'm dressed appropriately for such an occasion."

After a brief once-over, Nick reached up and slid the scooped neckline of her embroidered peasant blouse off each shoulder. His hands stroked her bare forearms, then moved to tantalize her shoulders. "There, that's better." His eyes detected the small amount of cleavage now visible and nodded with masculine approval. "Much better."

Alex's skin sizzled beneath his warm fingertips. She realized it was quite apparent that she hadn't worn a bra tonight. Did Nick consider it a come-on? She wondered if the compelling passions between them were too strong to restrain. The expression on Nick's shadowed face told her there would be no resistance on his part. The feelings in her heart told Alex she could no longer deny this warm yearning she felt for Nick. "You don't think it's too . . . much?"

"You're perfect. Ready to go?" He pressed his hand to the small of her back, sweeping her away. "I know you think I planned this, but believe me, if I'd known we would be spending the night, things would have been different from the start."

"Oh? How?"

"Well, we could have brought along a change of clothes. And I would have reserved a room with hot water. *One* room."

"I thought you wanted a cold shower, Nick."

"I lied."

"My shower has hot water. You're welcome to use it."

"Only if we can share it."

"Well, I don't know about that." She laughed nervously. He was certainly honest about his intentions.

"Consider the shower, Alex. It could be rather . . . pleasurable." He moved closer and brushed her temple with his cool lips. "This celebration

153

tonight is just for us, Alex." He tipped her face up to his and covered her lips with his before she could protest or move away. "Just for us. . . ."

When they merged, the reaction was immediate and intense. Nick's lips covered hers, demanding, drinking, craving her as his body did. His tongue teased her lips until she opened to receive him, tentatively welcoming his invasion. His palm encased one thinly-clad breast, applying pressure to the aroused tip.

The message was obvious. He wanted more. Overcome with reckless abandon, Alex wanted to give him more. Nick's desire for her was fierce and strong, a rugged longing that threatened to overwhelm them both.

She moaned softly. "Nick, the fiesta."

Finally, he moved. "To hell with the party."

Alex felt slightly intoxicated from his kiss. "Yes. I'm starved. All I've had today was one tiny bowl of turtle soup."

"I'm starved for you, Alex. Do you know how alluring you are in that blouse?"

"I was afraid it was too much."

"You are too much," he said with a sigh of resignation. "I need you." He lifted her hand and gently sucked her finger, allowing his tongue to lave the length of it. For a wild moment Alex wanted to feel that tongue all over her, to know the excitement only Nick could give her. She was tempted to tell him so, but music blared in the courtyard and they became aware of the merrymakers.

"Later is for us," he whispered and steered her downstairs.

A huge table in the courtyard was piled high with food. As the music blared around them, Nick laughingly fed Alex tangy barbequed beef *fajitas* wrapped in soft flour tortillas and *pan dulce,* a kind of sweet bread.

Nick held Alex close when they danced to the Mexican *ranchera* music, then joined in the usual wedding festivities of the Dollar Dance by pinning money on the bride's veil and dancing with her.

Later, when the strolling mariachi band played old Mexican favorites, he and Alex sang the Spanish words to the rousing *"El Rancho Grande"* and the sensitive *"Cuatros Vidas."*

While the crowd was toasting the wedding couple, Alex and Nick tipped little shots of tequila, Mexican style.

"To finding Jenni." She smiled hopefully.

"To Jenni," he promised. *To us,* he vowed silently.

He whirled her onto the dance floor and murmured in her ear, *"Te quiero, te quiero, mi amor."*

Alex blushed and ducked her head to avoid looking into his sparkling dark eyes.

"You do know what that means, Alex. I want you. *Te quiero."*

"Nick, don't—" She tried to turn away from his grasp but he held her close, forcing their legs to move in tempo with the music. She gave him no answer, no more response. She couldn't be sure what she would do. Her mind said *no* but her will

155

was weak when Nick Diamond's arms surrounded her.

At the end of the evening's celebrations, they watched a spectacular fireworks display with the delight of two small children. Flashes of sparkling stars filled the black night. Brilliantly colored pinwheels made from exploding firecrackers rolled across the sky and a gigantic castle lit up the entire courtyard.

When they had eaten all they could and drunk all they dared, Nick and Alex left the celebration, his arm securely tucked around her. In the hallway Nick unlocked her door. "Does the offer for the warm shower still hold?"

"Sure," she agreed apprehensively, swinging the door open and stepping inside.

Nick moved with her. His hands slipped beneath the weight of her hair to the heated part of her neck. "Alex, I want more than a shower. *Te quiero.*" The door closed behind him.

As his lips closed over hers, Alex realized with a mixture of excitement and fear that Nick was hers for the night. Her resistance melted like hot wax as the kiss deepened and her lips parted with a hungry moan. Nick traced the sensitive inner circle of her lips with the tip of his tongue before plunging it into her mouth.

His whispers of pleasure muffled her gasps of objection and obliterated all but a delirious craving that swelled within her. His kisses danced over her face from her parted mouth to her flushed cheeks to the heat of her heaving bosom. Large hands reached inside the elasticized neckline of her blouse to lift her throbbing breasts to his eager lips.

Alex arched her back, thrusting her breasts outward to receive Nick's caresses. He pressed the soft, warm globes to his face, teasing the nipples to hardness, before his tongue encircled the sensitive pink tips.

"Oh—Nick!" Alex moaned.

"Alex, oh, my Alex. I want to know you all over. To see you."

With his help, she pulled feverishly at her clothes. Alex could hardly wait for Nick to discard his shirt and jeans. His caressing fingertips set her on fire. Then he bent to lick each breast with his tongue and blaze a moist trail to the most feminine part of her. He knelt before her, his tongue paying tribute to her beauty and arousing her inner frenzy to the shattering point.

Theirs was a leisurely loving kindling a fierce desire. The two had waited all evening, all week, all their lives, actually, for this moment. And the forbidden passion was released in a lusty and vigorous fashion.

Alex stood before him, nude and trembling. With a slight shaking of his hand, Nick's fingers glazed every feminine niche, sending whorls of flames whipping through her. First one tentative hand then both caressed and traced her slender feminine form. He brushed over the soft mounds of her breasts with his mustache then his hands traveled around her waist and to the charming swell of her hips. His darkly passionate eyes devoured her, sweeping her length with masculine approval.

"You're beautiful, Alex. So perfect. I've wanted you from the first moment I saw you. Touch me," he begged hoarsely.

She complied, trailing one hand from his chest all the way down to his thigh, as he had done to her.

His reaction was dramatic. With a sharp intake of breath, he pressed her hips to his, purposely forcing her to feel the strength of his arousal against her belly.

"See what you do to me? I want you, Alex . . . now!"

With no holding back, Alex arched against his hardness, pressing her breasts to his chest and her belly to his. He kissed her fiercely, his tongue penetrating her mouth with merciless passion. In another frenzied moment they were on the bed, Nick plunging into her with the same fierceness he'd exhibited in his kisses.

With a matching fervor, Alex eagerly accepted him. Her desire for this man was stronger than any she had ever known. Indeed, he elicited every emotion in her—anger, grief, happiness, excitement, and now a desire so desperate she couldn't get enough of him.

"Alex . . . I can't wait . . . can't hold back!"

"Don't wait, Nick."

His kiss muffled out further sound and she moved with him in the ancient ritual of men and women since time began. Higher and higher she rode to the precipice, the craggy edge of obscurity that threatens complete oblivion. Then she was past the threshold of caring, entering a suspension of time which she wanted to last forever. Only sensation mattered. Only she and Nick. Together they belonged, and together they swirled to the top.

With a frantic exclamation of joy, she reached the peak. . . . "Nick! Oh, God, Nick!"

He drove to his climax, plunging deeper and harder into her receptive body, unable to hold back.

When thought and time returned, Alex floated in a daze of heavenly gravity, only aware of the pleasure she felt with Nick. It was more than she ever dreamed possible.

Nick's voice was low, breaking into her euphoria. "Alex? You all right?"

"Hmmm." She didn't move, couldn't bear the thought.

"That," he sighed, "was barbaric. Too rough. Too fast."

"Pays me back . . . for yelling at you and crying on your shirt and hating you and . . . wanting you."

"All that?"

She ran a hand lightly across his buttocks. "I think all that made me want you more. And it's never been better."

"It'll be better next time." He sealed the promise with another kiss.

Later, their lovemaking was slower, more exacting, an unselfish sharing of feelings. And, as he'd promised, it was better. He admired her

159

body and touched her everywhere. She returned the favor with taunting hands and loving kisses.

"You are so soft here, and here. I love to touch you. Alex, you're beautiful."

"Not too small?"

"Just right!" His lips closed over each pert nipple and teased them to perfect erection.

"You, too, Nick. I love to feel these muscles." Her hand rode along his back. "You are so strong." She continued to explore until he directed her to the throbbing male protrusion that thrust against her hand.

"Now, Alex—"

"Yes, Nick." She smiled.

He was loving and gentle until passion overtook him. She was tempting and alluring, until she could wait no longer. Then she curved a leg over him and settled herself on him with an assertiveness she had withheld until now.

"I've got you, Nick Diamond," she teased as she moved sensuously up and down. "And you'll never be free!"

"Ahh, is that a promise?" he groaned with some effort. "We may stay here . . . forever. Oh, Alex—"

She had the satisfaction of bringing him to the brink, of knowing she had a sensual power over Nick, of feeling him inside her. Then the crest of her passion spilled over and she moved hypnotically until she fell in exhausted fulfillment against him.

CHAPTER NINE

Morning came too quickly for Nick. With sultry eyes he watched Alex sleeping peacefully against him. Her blond curls spilled over his arm like silk strands. Long gold-tipped eyelashes edged her fair cheekbones. Her heart-shaped lips, slightly swollen from his vigorous kisses during the night, were curved into a faint smile. He wanted to kiss them again but refrained.

What happened to the restraint he had pledged to himself the first time he saw her? He had been taken with her, even then. A man needed a woman, he rationalized. And this woman was *here* and willing. Even as he considered it, he knew that wasn't the reason. Alex exerted some kind of power over him. And it wasn't just her sexual attraction. He was tied in knots by her anguish and wanted to relieve her pain, wanted to help her forget.

The sheet crumpled around her waist, revealing her breasts, creamy white and inviting. He couldn't resist their silent supplication and with one finger traced circles around the pink tip until the nipple became firm. Then he brought the other to matching perfection. Still, she slept.

Unfair! he thought guiltily. *Irresistible!* the devil part of him insisted.

His dark hand was lazy in its intent, finally resting on top of one soft mound. The taut pink tip puckered firmly between his thumb and forefinger.

Alex moaned softly and shivered beneath his touch. "If you're trying to get my attention, you're succeeding," she mumbled without opening her eyes.

"Your full attention is needed for what I have in mind." He took one of her pink nipples in his mouth and sucked on it.

Inexorably, she arched in response to his actions. "And what is that?"

"Wake up, Alex," he rasped, throwing a heavy leg over hers. "Nothing worse than a sleeping, unresponsive female."

"Or an overly aggressive man."

"You didn't say that last night." His knee came up to separate her legs.

"In the light of day, things look different." Her eyes betrayed her with their sparks of passion. "Relationships have a different meaning."

"Does ours have to have a meaning? Can't it just be for . . ." he paused to kiss her lips, "fun?"

She turned on her side and pressed her body against his. "Sure." She kissed him squarely on the mouth just for the pure pleasure of it. "Tell me, Nick. How do I fit into this little scheme of yours? Was it all just a device to get me to spend the night? And into your bed? Just for fun?"

"You misunderstand my intentions, *mi vida*. The scheme, as you put it, didn't originally include you at all. Then I found how perfectly we fit together. This is where we belong, Alex." He moved over her and molded his length to hers. "Just like this!"

"Nick, I'm serious." She was pleasurably caught in the vise of his strong legs.

"I'm serious too." He cradled her head between his hands and kissed her deeply. "You've pushed me too far, Alex. I can't go back. Can't think. Mornings are a good time for making love," he murmured between kisses.

"Love? Are we making love, Nick?" she asked coyly.

"Yeah." He grinned devilishly as his hips moved sensuously. "Love lasts longer in the mornings."

"Oh, Nick . . ." she moaned softly as he thrust into her, filling her with his strength.

"Alex . . ."

In a silent fury they rose to passion's ecstasy. The peaks seemed to be even higher than those they'd reached the night before, and Alex settled into a feathery never-never-land encompassed by Nick's arms. "I love you . . ." she whispered and drifted off to sleep.

The sun was high when they woke the second time. Alex nuzzled his chest, resting her head on the dark mat of curly hair. What a pleasure to awake in Nick's secure arms, to know he was

163

close, to make exquisite love with him. *Was it love?* Her heart told her yes. But her mind was still whirling with questions. "Nick . . . you awake?"

"No," he mumbled, half awake. "This is too perfect. I don't want to disturb what we have."

"It's been wonderful."

"Umm-hmm." He caressed the arm she'd flung over him and pressed her palm to his heart.

"Nick, why won't you tell me something about you? I feel . . . I feel almost as if I've gone to bed with a stranger."

"What do you want to know?" His response was so eager, she felt encouraged. And excited. Now she would get answers to all those questions that plagued her!

"I want to know everything about you. Where are you from? Do you have a family? Brothers? Sisters? How old are you? How long have you been in Mexico? Why are you here?"

His answers came readily and required no thinking. "I'm from Oregon. My parents still live there, on the family farm. My only brother lives on the adjoining property. I'm thirty-five. I've been in Mexico about a year . . . and I'm trying to find a little girl for a beautiful American woman!"

"But Nick, what are you *doing* in Mexico?"

"Running a helicopter tour service."

"Besides that."

"That's it."

"No!" she insisted. "I know something else's going on! Tell me!"

164

He paused for the first time since her questions started. "I can't tell you."

"Why not? Is it illegal?"

He took a deep breath. "Now isn't the time to go into this. You'll just have to trust me, Alex."

She tightened inside. "It's hard when I have no basis for trust."

His hand rested on her bare shoulder. "I haven't deceived you yet, Alex, have I? Or given you reason to doubt me?"

"No, I guess not. But, I'm not satisfied with that. I want to know more. What did you do before you came to Mexico?"

"Ran helicopter tours over the Grand Canyon."

"Is that all?" She held her breath. Somehow she couldn't imagine Nick Diamond satisfied with merely taking tourists here and there.

"No." He shifted in frustration. "But don't ask. I can't tell you. Believe me, it's for your own safety, Alex."

She pondered the enigmatic answer for a while, then asked softly, "Were you ever married?"

"Years ago. Then I went to Nam. Came back a changed man. But you couldn't do . . . what I did there and not be changed. My wife didn't like what I had become. In fact, neither did I. But she didn't have time for me to get my head straight, and I had no choice . . . so we called it quits."

"Any kids?"

"No."

"Was it tough for you?"

165

"After what I went through in the war, nothing was tough."

She touched him softly. "What was it like there?"

"Makes all of Mexico look like the Ritz." He chuckled. "I was a chickenhawk. That's a pilot. I flew a chopper into the thick of battle every day. It was hell on wings, Alex, and that's why I enjoy what we have here. Every day is a pure pleasure, especially with you. You're soft and warm and . . . clean. How about sharing that warm shower with me?"

"Clean?" she shrieked with a laugh.

"Oh, God, Alex. You would never believe—" He shifted to a sitting position and swung his feet over the side of the bed.

Alex pulled on his shoulder. "Nick? I . . . I feel better . . . about you. About us."

"Me too." His deep, grateful kiss said more than any words could at that moment.

Later they found a lovely place for brunch and spent part of the afternoon walking on the beach, talking. Alex told him why she came to Mexico in the first place; how she applied to become an exchange professor after her love affair with Jack Kingsley fell apart. And how she fell in love with the country of Mexico, the culture, the people, and especially little Jenni. It was a reminder of her disappointment.

Nick draped his arm over her shoulder, and eventually they walked back to town. They ended up at the same little sidewalk café. Nick took the same seat at precisely the same table.

"Shall we splurge on turtle soup again? We may not be back this way for a while."

She leaned across the table eagerly. "Does that mean we're going home?"

He smiled. "Maybe."

She rolled her eyes. "Wonderful answer."

He shrugged. "It's the best I can do."

"Okay. Turtle soup. Why not?"

The mood was definitely lighter as they ate the soup then enjoyed rich, strong Mexican coffee. Then more coffee and more waiting. Finally the boy appeared with a message. Nick left money on the table and didn't read the scribbled note the boy had delivered until they were inside a cab. He gave her an easy grin. "It's on!"

"Great! Let's go home!" Alex didn't even know what the hell he was talking about but she smiled eagerly.

"Not yet. After dark."

"Wait! *What's* on? Why after dark?"

"Can't tell you. But trust me. We leave tonight."

She groaned and slumped against the cab seat.

He moved to whisper in her ear. "Gives us time for . . . you know . . ."

They lifted off at dusk. Alex's spirits were high even though the trip hadn't produced her darling Jenni. She had gained something else, a new and exciting relationship with Nick—and she prayed it wouldn't interfere with the search for Jenni, causing Nick to lose interest in her plight because he'd succeeded in getting her into his bed. Oh, God, that sounded so crude, reducing the beauty they'd shared to a base sexual satisfaction. It wasn't like that between them at all. Nick wasn't that kind of man. At least, she hoped not.

Before the lights of Guaymas were fully behind them, Nick was setting the helicopter down again.

"Where are we? Why are we going down out here in the middle of nowhere?"

"Now, listen, Alex," Nick began patiently, "don't say a word. And ignore whatever you hear. Sit here until I tell you to move. Then you can help me load."

"Load what?"

"The, uh, cargo."

Her eyes peered sharply into the darkness below. "Cargo?"

"No questions, please, Alex. Just—" They bounced to a halt on the ground.

"I know," she interrupted with a groan. "Just be quiet and do what I tell you."

"You've got it," he breathed low then hopped out into the darkness.

Alex could hear Nick conversing in Spanish. Others were there but she couldn't tell how many. Or who they were. She strained to pick up the exchange. *Ignore whatever you hear,* she recalled. Damn! It was hard to quell her curiosity!

Soon Nick slid open the door to the rear cabin of the helicopter. "Want to help?"

"Sure, if it'll speed up the trip." She slid to the ground. "What is that awful racket?"

Nick cast a glance toward their simple cargo.

168

There were only a few crates but the noise coming from that direction was astounding. He pointed to three quiet boxes stacked on top of each other. "Let's get them first."

Alex eagerly bent to lift one end of the oblong box. "What's in here? Lead?"

"This must be the boa."

"Boa?" she squealed and dropped her end of the crate.

"Damn, Alex! Now look what you've done! One side is completely loose!" He lunged against it as the arm-sized monster inside slithered against the gaping slats.

Alex's fear quickly reached the panicky stage and she wailed, "Oh, my God, Nick! It's going to escape!"

"Not as long as I'm holding this box together! And since I'm occupied, you'll have to get me the hammer. In the chopper, Alex. Go!"

"W-where?"

"It's in a tool box, just inside the sliding door. Next to the paper bag with the whiskey. You might even take a swig if you're feeling too jittery. Bring it over here too. Along with the canteen of water."

"Oh, no, you don't! I want you to keep a clear head and get us out of here!"

"Get the hammer," he intoned impatiently. "The whiskey isn't for me. It's for them." He nodded his head toward the squawking crates.

"Chickens?" she asked incredulously.

"Exotic tropical birds," he expelled angrily. "Will you please get me that hammer before I have this thing draped around my neck? And bring extra nails too!"

Alex hurried to the helicopter and returned with the requested items, including the paper bag of whiskey. Handing him the hammer, she held the nails out to him in a shaky, sweaty palm. "How did I get mixed up with a deal like this? What's going to happen next, Nick Diamond? First we pretend that we're married and looking to buy a child. Then we have to spend the night unexpectedly. Now you're hauling boas, for God's sake! And chickens or birds or whatever is squawking over there! Not once did you ask if I minded. Nor did you tell me what you were doing or why or even when. You just made the announcement and expected me to trail along like a little puppy! I came over here for a reason and it sure as hell had nothing to do with birds! Or with boas!"

He took the last nail from her hand and tapped it into the crate. "There. That should do it."

"Should? What if it doesn't hold that . . . that slimy creature in? What if—"

"He isn't slimy. Here. Touch."

She jumped away like a frightened toad. "Are you completely out of your mind? I wouldn't touch that thing if my life depended on it!"

Nick folded his arms and stared into her face. "Are you finished with your tirade? I don't think I can stand listening to you and those damn birds at the same time!"

"Dammit, Nick! I'm tired of this crazy stuff! And scared! And I want to get out of here!"

"So do I. But this won't cut it! I have work to do. Now, if you aren't going to help, go sit in the chopper. I'll do this by myself! I'm not leaving without the cargo."

She wheeled about, her first instinct hurling her back to the safety of the helicopter.

"But if you want to speed this process up a bit, you could help."

She turned back around with a deep sigh. "Okay. What do you want me to do?"

"First, shut up. Then, help me carry these crates."

Alex gritted her teeth together and lifted one end of the crate. They hauled the three quiet boxes to the helicopter and she tried not to look inside. She could tell that all of them contained some kind of reptile. She shuddered as Nick threw old rags loosely over them, hiding them from view.

"Now, the challenge." He motioned to her. "Where's the whiskey?" Nick poured a few drops of the intoxicating liquid into a half-rusted tuna can, then added some water from the canteen. "Okay, you little blabbermouths! This'll make you mellow and quiet! Bottoms up!" He opened one end of the crate and slid the can inside for the birds to drink.

One particularly aggressive parrot with a brilliant red head and lime-green body slithered past his hand. "This one's getting away! Catch him, Alex!"

Without even thinking, Alex lunged for the bird. She clamped her hands around the wiggling feathered body. Just as she smiled in satisfaction at Nick, the bird brandished his only available weapon, his beak.

"Ow! Damn!"

With a desperate fluttering of wings, the bird escaped into the blackness.

"Hell, Alex, you let him get away!"

"He bit me, Nick!"

Nick looked at her in exasperation. "There goes money on the wing."

"Looks like a little Mexican parrot to me," she jibed. "A *free* Mexican parrot!" Alex grasped his arm. "Please, Nick. Let them all go! I don't know what you're doing or why you're doing it, but it doesn't look good. It just isn't right to keep them penned up like this, and give them whiskey, for God's sake—" She drew a frantic breath. "Oh, Nick, let them all go free!"

He gazed at her stricken face. Maybe it was a mistake, after all, to bring her along. She was so honest and sympathetic. Her sense of justice was so straight down the middle, she was idealistic. She knew nothing about the harshness of the real world. Could he trust her to keep her mouth shut about this?

"I can't let them go, Alex. I have to do it. More rests on this than these few crates of birds. Now, if you can't help me, get back in the chopper. I'll do it alone. But I'll do it." His dark eyes looked hard with determination and the rest of him blended in with the darkness around them.

He was suddenly a frightening sight. Alex wondered if she knew him at all. Was this man with the evil eyes the same one who made love so gently? She shuddered and looked away. She had no alternative. Begrudgingly, she helped him.

Those birds that seemed too listless were taken out of the crate and laid out individually. All were then hidden with canvas and the rags Juancho had included. Finally they were ready to lift off, loaded with an impressive variety of exotic birds. Large groggy scarlet macaws, elegant snow-white cockatoos, small gray cockatiels with bright orange cheeks, and common red-headed and green-bodied Mexican parrots kept company with the boas. The cargo was now quiet.

As they flew back under cover of darkness, Alex's head whirled with confusion. Just when she thought she knew Nick Diamond and could trust him, he popped up with another crazy scheme that seemed damn close to being illegal. *Smuggling!* That was the rumor in Hermosillo about him. At this moment, she was damned if she didn't believe it! What else could she think? Why else would he be transporting all those exotic birds? And boas, of all things! She knew there were quotas on bringing animals into the States and she supposed it held equally for birds. There were quarantine periods because of diseases and inoculations and tariffs.

But why would Nick do such a thing as smuggle birds? For the money? After all, he had said of the escaping parrot, *There goes money on the wing.* Why, he was as bad as that awful José who found a baby for them to buy!

She gazed sideways at Nick. His angular face

was half-shadowed, his dark eyes steady and looking straight ahead, his chin set. Could he be involved in illegal activities? He'd told her no, but was he telling her the truth? Even though some of her questions had been answered during this intimate weekend with Nick, a hundred more had surfaced.

Juancho met them at the airport and had a cab waiting for Alex. He conferred briefly with Nick while she scrambled out of the helicopter.

"Alex." Nick reached her side before she could climb in the cab. "Alex, I know this is hard, but you'll just have to trust me. Can I . . . depend on you to—"

Her indigo eyes flashed in the muted airport lights. "To keep my mouth shut about all this? Of course! Because if I blow the whistle on your schemes, Nick, I ruin my chances of finding Jenni, don't I? It's a strange sort of blackmail."

"Is that what you think? About last night?"

She looked down, feeling crushed. "I . . . I don't know what to think, yet. I just know I can't deal with your cynicism. I don't understand it."

"No more than I can reason with your idealism."

"Not idealism," she countered with an upraised chin. "Sense of fairness. It isn't fair, what we saw yesterday with that baby. Even tonight . . ." she gestured futilely.

"That's idealistic nonsense!"

"How can you say that? You're an American too! Fairness and justice are what our country is based on!"

"Justice? Fairness?" he scoffed. "You forget I served in Nam! Tell me what was fair about that? What were you doing while I was watching my buddies die?" He turned away from her sharply. He hadn't intended to explode about all that pain.

"Nick . . . Nick?" She took his hand and brought it to her cheek. "I . . . I'm sorry."

He took a deep breath. "I shouldn't have said that. You had nothing to do with my life."

"But I do now. Or you have something to do with mine. I haven't decided yet if our involvement was one of my more foolish acts." She reached for the cab door but Nick's hand closed over hers.

"Alex . . ." He paused as she looked up at him. "I hope you decide it wasn't."

"For a while I thought it was wonderful."

"It was." He bent and kissed her quickly. "Come to the office tomorrow after work. There's been a new development."

She was suddenly alert. "About Jenni? What?"

He shook his head. "Tomorrow. You get some rest tonight." He opened the door and gave instructions to the driver.

When Alex arrived home, her phone was ringing. *"Hola?"*

"Alex, where on earth have you been? I've been trying to reach you for two days!"

"Nothing serious, I hope," Alex muttered vaguely, slipping out of her shoes. Her thoughts were filled with Nick Diamond.

"Depends on how you look at it, Alex."

"Rosemary—not the budget!"

"It's public. And final. All exchange teachers have been cut. Oh, Alex, I'm sorry!"

CHAPTER TEN

"My God, Nick, you look awful!"

"You don't look so great yourself." He drew her into the office. "Didn't you get any sleep last night?"

Alex smiled and shook her head. "Not much. Did you get your cargo delivered properly?"

"Yep. Only lost one little cockateil. Too much whiskey, I guess. You have to be careful about that. Or maybe it was sick before the trip. Anyway, we just got back a few hours ago."

"Just got back?" Alex raised her eyebrows in query. "From where—" She halted mid-sentence and gave him a cunning glance. "I know, I know. Don't ask."

"You catch on fast." Nick motioned toward his desk, where Juancho hovered intently. "I wanted you to come down this afternoon because we have a lead, Alex. Photos of the man we think took Jenni. And of Jenni too. We want you to make a positive identification of her."

Alex's heart pumped wildly and she rushed to Juancho's side. The desk was strewn with photos, various shots of the accident.

"These are from the newspaper photographer," Juancho explained. "He took all these at the scene."

"But where is Jenni?" Alex frantically scanned through the photos, her shaky fingers sorting them apart quickly. She tried not to look at the images of Teresa lying on the sidewalk and herself bending over the inert form.

Juancho's large brown hand lifted a particular photo and handed it to her. "Your eyes must be, uh, how do you say, looking into the pictures."

"Discerning," Nick offered from behind Alex.

"Si. Look carefully. See the child in the background? Near the right side."

Alex squinted her eyes to improve her discerning ability. "Yes, I see that child. It . . . it could be Jenni."

"What about this one?" It was a blow-up of the same child.

"Oh, yes," Alex breathed excitedly. "Yes, this is her all right!"

"You sure, now?"

"Yes! She had on a pink dress with ruffles on the front. And see her curly hair? Yes, yes!" Alex swallowed hard. She was torn by tender emotion at seeing Jenni and a growing euphoria for finding her. "But you said a man took her. Where is—"

"He's in this one." Juancho handed her another photo. "You can see a man's arm around the child. We believe he's in the process of abducting her."

Alex seized the photo and stuck it close to her

nose then held it at arm's length. "But, Juancho, you can only see part of him! And a *small* part, at that!"

"What did you expect? A mug shot?" Nick clipped, irritated by her lack of enthusiasm for their discovery.

"How can anyone identify him from this?" She threw it back down on the desk. Her balloon of hope was rapidly deflating.

Juancho gave her a patient smile beneath his elaborate mustache. "Ah, but these photos tell us much. Here you see a leg, an arm, and half a face."

"So, what can you tell from that?"

"Well, his limbs are rather thin. So, we know he's not as chubby as me." Juancho chuckled. "He's brown-skinned and has dark hair, so he's probably Mexican."

"Oh, that's just great!" Alex folded her arms and flopped disgustedly into Nick's chair. "There are only about a million men around here who look like that! No, only half a mil who are skinny! All we have to do is match them up with half a face! Shouldn't we start questioning them now? We might find a suspect by the time Jenni's twenty!"

"Dammit, Alex!" Nick turned his back and stuffed his hands impotently into his pockets. He stared angrily out the dirty cracked glass of the door. Sure, he could understand her frustrations, but he knew the potential of this lead too.

"Señorita," Juancho said gently. "It's better than nothing."

"Yes," she admitted bitterly. "Better than what we found in Guaymas."

"It gives us a start. We know now that Jenni definitely was taken, whereas before, we were only guessing. And we have a vague idea what her abductor looks like."

"And probably," Nick said, turning around and approaching the desk again, "probably, Jenni's tied into a baby ring. From the beginning, she was taken for this purpose. Trouble is, the adoptions take place in the United States."

"How do we know it hasn't already happened?" Alex asked, alarmed. Her large eyes searched his face for the truth.

Nick shrugged his broad shoulders. "We don't. We can only hope."

"Hope? That's not enough!" Alex stood hastily. "We need to get busy. Find out who this bastard is and—"

"What do you suggest? Start with the men on the street?" Nick's eyes flashed angrily.

"No." Juancho began to stack the photos and pondered the problem as he spoke. "We start with whoever might be able to help us identify half a face."

"The police?" Alex questioned with a frown.

"No!" Nick snapped his fingers as an idea struck. "There is only one who might. Just might. Becaue he knows so many people and faces in this town."

"Padre Ramón?" Juancho smiled determinedly and nodded.

"You bet! He's our closest link. And if he can't

identify this face, maybe he can direct us to someone who can!"

"I'm going with you, Nick!" Alex circled the desk.

"No, you aren't," he said firmly. "You go home and get some rest. You may need it later."

"But I want—"

"No, Alex. I don't expect Father Ramón to look at this photo and name the guy right away. This'll take time."

"But we don't have much time! Meanwhile, what happens to Jenni? She may be—"

"Wherever she is, señorita, she's being cared for," Juancho inserted gently. "I'm sure of it."

Alex's eyes grew large and sad. "That's what I want to believe, and it's what both of you keep telling me."

"It's as close to the truth as we can get at this time," Nick agreed. "You know I'll be honest with you, Alex. Now, there's nothing more for you to do here. Go home and get some rest." He led her to the door.

"Rest . . . and a new job," she muttered.

He nodded, tight-lipped. "Oh, yes. Your position at the university isn't being renewed, is it?"

"How did you know?"

Nick aimed a thumb over his shoulder. "Juancho keeps me informed."

"But I just found out last night! How could he know?"

Nick raised his hands defensively. "He has his sources. I don't ask how."

"And I shouldn't ask either," she murmured sardonically.

"You've got it."

"You will let me know if anything else develops?"

"Of course." He kissed her lightly. "You'll be the first to know."

"At least in time to play whatever new role you have for me?" She smiled weakly and closed the rickety door behind her.

May

Dear Carol,

I'm trying to be positive about everything, and as the British say, keep a stiff upper lip. But nothing seems to be going right! I lost the fight for my job. I refuse to even think about it right now. But I know one thing. I'm not leaving here until I know something about Jenni. Rosemary offered me her spare room. I may consider it.

One bright ray. At least Nick seems to think so. They have a photo of the man who took Jenni. But it isn't a good likeness; more of a profile. They're hoping Father Ramón can identify him.

Every day I feel like I'm on the edge of a new discovery! And yet Jenni remains out of our reach. Looks like I'll be heading for Phoenix before the end of summer.

Love,
Alex

She folded the letter and stuffed it into an envelope. She had purposely left out information on the trip to Guaymas with Nick. Her involvement with him was still too new, too puzzling to reveal. And there were all those questions still unanswered. For all Alex knew, she had fallen in love with someone on the lam from the American police.

Just as she stepped out of the shower, she heard a knock at her door. Thinking it was Nick with news from Father Ramón, she threw on a robe and dashed to the door. Not in her wildest dream did she think her guest would be Jack Kingsley, her former lover.

Alex stood mutely, staring at him.

Then reminders flashed through her mind. Carol mentioned him in a letter—was it just last week? She had said Jack would be in Hermosillo on business in May and wanted her address. But Jack was the last person she wanted to see right now. She never thought of him anymore when she was lonely, never missed him. When she'd left Phoenix, she never wanted to see him again. Yet here he was, smiling and handsome, arms eagerly opened to greet her.

"Jack! What are you doing here?"

"Surely you could come up with something more enthusiastic and heartwarming, like 'what a wonderful surprise to see you,' or 'I've missed you like hell,' or—"

"Jack, please. I thought it was over between us."

"That was a long time ago, Alex." He stood on the threshold with hands still outstretched. "Hey, am I invited in? After all, I did come five hundred miles to see you."

"Sure, come on in." She led the way into the living room.

"Hey, this is a nice place, Alex," Jack said, assessing the room as he followed her.

She shrugged. "It'll do. The University supplied it, furnished." There seemed to be no way out of this. Jack was already here and she supposed they could talk. But that was *all.*

"How do you like working south of the border?"

"Loved it, while it lasted. I lost my job yesterday." Alex smiled wistfully, thinking she should be more upset. Maybe she was still numb.

"How the hell did that happen?"

"Budget cuts due to the economy. Exchange profs were the first to go."

"That's a shame, Alex, especially since you like it so much here. Can't really understand why, though," he said sitting down on a loveseat in the living room. "But I must admit, I'll be glad to see you heading back to Phoenix."

"Not right away," she hedged, lowering herself into a chair opposite him. "Maybe by fall."

"I'm sure you can get your old job back at ASU. Or, you just say the word, and I'll get you a job doing something *really* interesting."

"Really interesting? As if teaching isn't?"

"Well, it isn't dynamic and high-powered."

"I like it," she said simply. She gazed at his handsome chiseled features and sun-bleached blond hair and honestly tried to determine why she had been so attracted to him at one time. He was still quite handsome, especially with that distinguished gray above his ears. Now, though, she felt no physical attraction to him at all, just comfortable familiarity, as she might feel toward a brother. "Working for the governor, now?" she asked.

"Yeah." He nodded proudly. "No more of this academic stuff for me. Now, it's strictly big time. Powerful position."

"Sounds like a good job for you, Jack. Is that why you're here in Hermosillo? Something important?"

"Nothing so important as seeing you again, Alex. And, I must admit, you're as beautiful as ever." His gray eyes softened appreciably.

Alex smiled a faint thank-you. "But you made the trip for other reasons."

"Delegation from the governor," he affirmed. There was a touch of pride in his voice. "We meet tomorrow to discuss contracts with the new Ford plant here, and to see about the viability of a couple of high-tech plants moving in from Arizona. They need industry desperately down here, and it will help our economy too."

She nodded, warming to his clipped, important manner. Conversation was easy. After all, she and Jack had spent a year sharing each other's lives. They did it very well. Jack told her how he'd lucked into this job as governor's advisor and how much he liked it. She could readily see that. And Alex related how she and Rosemary had worked on the proposal in a last-ditch effort to save her job. She even showed him the letter she'd received from the president of the University, thanking her for her excellent field work and urging her to consider teaching there again, when they were more solvent.

Jack's hand sought hers. "Let me take you out to eat tonight, Alex."

"Jack, I'm really very tired," she declined, pulling her hand away gently. "I just don't feel like going out tonight."

"Hey, how about if I go out for Chinese food? Remember how we used to love *mu shu* pork? I even have some Pinot Noir in the car. Good old California wine, Alex? Come on, babe. For old time's sake."

She smiled with a weak-willed submission. *Mu shu* pork did sound good, and a little California wine. "There's a Chinese section about four blocks away."

"Atta girl! I'll be right back!"

Alex watched Jack go and realized that he was good company. He knew all the right questions to ask and seemed genuinely interested in her endeavors. Plus, he understood her world, having worked in a university setting for a number of years in Phoenix. She hoped dinner and interesting conversation were all he expected tonight. While he was gone, she donned a clean blouse and jeans, but felt familiar enough to meet him at the door still barefoot.

By the time they'd finished the meal and polished off a couple of glasses of the specialty wine, she told him about Jenni. Jack listened patiently to her story and kissed away the two sparkling tears that edged unbidden to her eyes.

186

"Alex, I can't believe you've let yourself get so involved with a situation like this."

"I couldn't help it, Jack. I was just here and—"

"Then let it drop." He nudged her chin upward and kissed her unresponsive lips. "Alex, let me take you back to Phoenix when I go tomorrow. I'll take care of you—"

She backed away, startled. "You mean, let her go? Not try to find her? Let Jenni be sold?"

"Well," he motioned helplessly, "or whatever. This isn't your business. She isn't your child. What would you do with her if you found her?"

Without hesitation Alex answered, "I'd adopt her." She stopped and listened to herself. Alex had never even considered what she would do. But there was no doubt in her mind that she wanted Jenni as her own child. Maybe that was a little drastic.

"Adopt? Do you know how complicated an international adoption is?" Jack stared at her in disbelief.

"I don't care about that. I only care about Jenni. You obviously don't understand, Jack."

"Hardly! I thought I knew you, Alex, but you've changed. In a drastic way too."

"No, I haven't, Jack. You just didn't know me well enough. I was the one who wanted marriage, remember? You wanted a mistress."

"Not really, Alex. It's just that it wasn't the right time for marriage for me." He placed his hands on her shoulders and pulled her to him. "Look at us tonight, Alex. Two lonely people, free to love. . . ." His lips covered hers before she could protest. He kissed her with growing passion, his tongue lightly nudging her lips to part.

But her response was wooden, and he stopped. "I can tell I've offended you about this missing kid. Look, Alex, let me make it up to you. Let me show you a good time."

She turned away from him but felt his hands on her shoulders. "No, Jack. It isn't what you said about Jenni. It's just not the same between us. Can't you tell?"

"I can make it good again, Alex. If you just give me a chance." He pulled her sensuously against him and she could feel his arousal against her buttocks.

At that moment she wanted nothing more than to get away from Jack Kingsley. He represented a past she wanted to forget and a future in which she had no interest. "No, Jack. There is nothing I want to revive. Please leave."

"Dammit, Alex. If you only tried, if you could forget your hang-ups for one night, you might enjoy life a little. You're so straight, so honest, you can't enjoy one night with an old lover."

She looked curiously at him. Honest? Straight? Jack would be shocked if he knew she had helped Nick smuggle exotic birds across the border and had made wild and wonderful love with him after they had tried to buy a baby! The worst of it was, she'd do it all again if it were for Jenni or the man she loved!

Alex never wanted to make love with Jack again. Her feelings for Nick would get in the way.

"No, Jack. It's us. Whatever was between us is gone. I'm sorry."

"I won't forget your turning me away, Alex."

Jack walked out of the house, slamming the door behind him.

Alex cleaned up their dinner mess of boxes and wine glasses. Even with all that wine, she didn't feel relaxed, and after pacing for an hour like a caged tiger, decided to take action.

The cab stopped in front of Nick's office. Through the broken-glassed window she could see him bent over his desk, just as she imagined. When she rattled the door on entering, he looked up, startled. Then, with recognition, he smiled warmly.

"Alex!"

"I thought I might find you here."

"Just going over these photos again to see if we missed something." He laid aside a magnifying glass and closed the folder.

"Then you're still looking for Jenni? I mean, you aren't too busy or anything?"

"Of course not." He motioned to the desk but looked at her curiously. "We have this new information and—why do you ask?"

She shrugged and released a silent sigh of relief. Maybe she hadn't lost him, after all. Not yet, anyway. "Oh, nothing. Was Padre Ramón able to identify anyone in those pictures?"

Nick shook his head tightly. "Not immediately. I left two of the photos with him. He's going to work on it. I figured it would take time."

She nodded and began to pace. "I see."

"Alex, you all right?"

"Yeah. Sure."

He stood, rather uncomfortably. "Look, Alex. We're rushing this thing as much as possible. I told you it wouldn't be easy. But she's—"

"I know, Nick. I understand. It isn't about Jenni."

"What, then?"

"So much has been happening lately, I can't seem to keep track of it. On top of everything else, I lost my job. And tonight, Jack . . . Jack Kingsley came over. He, uh, flew in for business. He thinks I'm crazy to try and find Jenni." She stopped pacing and clasped her hands together nervously. "Am I?"

"You didn't have any trouble with this Jack, did you?"

"No." She glanced up and smiled weakly. "But he wasn't happy when I told him to leave."

Nick's big body moved quickly from the desk to Alex. Even without their touching, she received the impact of his energy, not in a torrent or rush, but a gentle outpouring cascading through her until she wanted to force him to her. This was why she came tonight—for the vitality only Nick could give her.

His powerful hands rested on her shoulders and the warmth radiated directly from his body to hers. The magnetism between them was intangible but real, urging her toward him.

For someone who functioned on the cutting edge of life, who spoke of calculating the enemy and demanded so much of her, his words were surprisingly encouraging and gentle. "You aren't crazy to want Jenni, Alex. We're going to find her, just be patient. I know this job thing has knocked you back somewhat, but we'll work something out."

She smiled shakily. "Thanks, Nick. Your confidence is contagious. I needed to hear that, especially tonight." Her hands sought the natural refuge of his chest. She could feel the pulsing vigor beneath the muscled wall and spread her fingers to encompass as much of him as possible.

"Why did you really come here tonight, Alex?"

"To check on the progress of the search for Jenni. To make sure you were still on the project." Alex broke down with a little laugh. "To hear you say this whole thing isn't crazy . . . oh, I don't know, Nick."

"I think I know," he murmured low and pulled her to him, slowly, ever so slowly. His eventual kiss was cool and tantalizing, not demanding as before, but beckoning, promising, sensual.

Alex swayed against him, then tried to pull back, but he held her securely. "Nick, I—"

"I think I know how you feel, Alex. Now that I've held you all night, I want you again. And again. It's damn hard to let you go."

She pressed her forehead to his chin. "I've never felt this way before. So mixed up." How could she tell him she needed him?

"I wish I could tell you that everything will be all right, Alex."

"Now, that's being too idealistic, Nick Diamond," she teased with a smile.

Nick took a deep breath, inhaling her alluring fragrance. "Being with you is the only idealism I want, Alex." He kissed her hair and slid his arms around her, pressing her close. His invincibility penetrated her being and Alex clung to his solid strength.

"I want to be with you, Nick."

"Tonight? All night?" Nick's voice reverberated with sensuality. "Don't tempt me, Alex. We aren't playing games anymore."

She nodded, admitting her true feelings to him and herself at the same time.

Nick locked the office and turned out the light. He tucked the files he'd been studying under one arm and looped the other around Alex. Without another word they mounted the back stairs together. Nick opened the apartment door and motioned her inside. "It isn't very fancy, but it's handy." He moved with familiarity in the room's darkness while her eyes adjusted. Alex heard him toss the files on a table before he returned to fold her in his arms.

"Alex, oh, my Alex . . ."

As she buried her face against his chest and joyously breathed his rich, masculine scent, her world became complete. Tonight, she would enter the secure fortress of Nick's dominion.

Nuzzling, urging her face upward, Nick's lips left a moist trail across her cheeks until they merged exultantly with her eager lips. Tasting and teasing, he kissed her until she thought she would cry out for wanting him. But, he was in no hurry. Nick's lips seduced her slowly and gently but ever so surely.

Alex matched his forays with her own darting tongue, nipping at his lips, meeting his licking flames with her passionate sparks of vitality. She bit at his lower lip with her white teeth and he moaned and thrust instinctively against her loins. The reflexive action revealed his arousal, and she took feminine pleasure in the sensation.

When the squall they created swelled to a raging hurricane, Nick trembled with the potency of his desire. Gone were the gentle, stimulating kisses as his tongue plunged the inner reaches of her sweet mouth with a pulsating rhythm. She moved erotically against him, her hips matching the rhythmic motions.

Alex opened wider to receive his male thrusting, allowing the female part of her to gratify his hunger. As his hands traveled over her curves, outlining each contour, Alex knew shamelessly that soon she would be the one receiving gratification to her craving need.

"Nick, I'm weak," she gasped breathlessly.

"I don't think I can ever get enough of you, Alex. You're driving me crazy. I've never been like this." He shifted and began to undress her.

"I need you, Nick. And, I trust you . . . so much." She waited, quivering nude, while he peeled away his clothes.

"Alex, I'm burning to touch you . . . everywhere."

As she stood before him, throbbing with the brushfire building within her, Nick explored every part of her body. Thick, swirling fingertips searched out and stroked each of her erogenous zones until she was moaning with pleasure. His lips followed, drawing her desire to the surface of every inch of her skin as he suckled her breasts and nipped the tender tips. Then his mouth plunged downward to her navel, and beyond to the fringe of her feminine crest.

Alex gasped as his fingers slipped inside to the moist softness awaiting him.

"Oh, God, Alex—"

"Nick," she murmured unevenly. "Don't stop. Don't ever let me go." Her hand closed over his extravagant arousal and his great body trembled with anticipation and agony.

Even as he lowered her to the bed, Nick wondered if he would hurt her worse by holding on or letting go now.

But it was too late to contemplate. With a compelling urge beyond his control, Nick immersed himself in Alex's softness, plundering relentlessly with each frenzied thrust. In the distant darkness, he heard her cry out in ecstasy.

"Nick! Nick!"

CHAPTER ELEVEN

"I've never done this sort of thing before."

"Never? Well, it's about time you did! Let your hair down, Alex."

"It's down, in case you didn't notice. And a ratty mess too."

"I like it like this."

"You should. It's your fault, Nick."

"I love to run my fingers through your hair. It's like silk. Yellow silk that smells like fresh flowers." He placed several kisses along her hairline, ending with soft, sensuous nibbles along the top edge of her ear.

"For someone so big, you certainly know how to be gentle." She shifted to plant indulgent kisses in the dark, curly mass of hair flourishing along his chest, pausing to taste the two hard, budding nipples. Her blond curls brushed across his bare skin, and she heard his breathing accelerate. With a satisfied smile, she laid her head on his chest.

"With you, *mi vida,* it comes naturally." He caressed her head then buried his large, bronze hand in her silken tangles. "Ahh, if you keep that up, Alex, you'll be forced to call in sick. But it'll be late this afternoon before I let you out of bed! You can claim you were dizzy every time you raised your head. That'll be close to the truth."

"Sounds enticing. You tempt me wickedly, Nick. But I do have to go to work today, and I intend to."

"Maybe you'll change your mind when I tell you what I'm going to do to you if you stay. No more gentle giant! First, I'll grab you like this . . . and kiss you like this. . . ."

"Wicked man! Nick! Nick!" she giggled and squirmed as his kisses tickled her unmercifully. "Using your brute strength against me is taking unfair advantage, you . . . you beast!" she panted when he finally stopped.

"But you use weapons that are just as unfair," he countered. "Like your hair, which I love to touch. And leaving those exposed." His eyes traveled to her bare breasts.

She quickly grabbed the sheet and scooted up to sit against the headboard. "I don't want to tempt you unnecessarily because I really do need to go soon. I only have a few more days of work left, anyway. There are some projects I need to finish. And I'd like to make one last check on the two pre-schools in the field. I hope they can make it on their own without University supervision."

"You are so damn righteous! Everything must be according to Hoyle, tied up in a bundle and finished. I'll bet you repeat the Golden Rule every morning!" He propped himself up on his elbows and his head swerved slowly from side to side. "My golden . . . golden girl who plays by the rules." Dark, unruly curly hair edged his forehead and a slow grin broke beneath his mustache.

"I am *not* righteous!" she denied indignantly. "Why, just look at me. I almost bought a baby in Guaymas a few days ago! I helped smuggle exotic birds across the border without a word to anyone! I'm sinfully infatuated with a rogue of a man I met in a foreign country, even to the point of knocking on his door in the middle of the night! Worse yet, he may possibly be hiding from the law. That means me too! And, all this without a question, or at least without a question answered! Now, does that sound like a righteous woman to you?" Her blue eyes danced spiritedly.

"Sounds like Bonnie and Clyde to me!" he hooted and grabbed playfully for her.

Rolling her over him, he kissed her nose and murmured with a hint of seriousness, "Señorita, when this is all over, we need to have a long talk."

"I know." She smiled sadly. "You aren't the infatuated type. It's all right, Nick. What we have is enough for me. I'm a big girl. I know the risks."

He sighed heavily and pushed her away. "It's not that, Alex. It's just, sometimes things get out of control."

"I understand, Nick." She scooted back to her seat against the headboard. "When . . . when will it be over?"

He swung his legs over the edge of the bed and

rested his elbows on his knees. "Probably when we find Jenni."

"Am I foolish to keep chasing her? And hoping?"

"It would be a sin to stop at this point, Alex."

"Now who's being righteous?"

He turned to face her with a guilty grin. "Damn persistent, at least." He grew serious then and his dark eyes flickered with something close to viciousness. "I won't stop until those bastards are caught. All the way up the ladder too. Not just the fool who snatched Jenni off the street, but everyone who's connected along the way."

"I guess I never considered the others," Alex admitted thoughtfully. "I just keep thinking of the guy in the photo with half a face. And how much I hate him."

"He's just a link, but an important one. He's probably already passed Jenni on to another link and is back on the street again. We figure he doesn't know anyone has a photo of him or can connect him in any way, so as soon as he gets rid of her, he may feel free enough to walk the streets again. That's what we're banking on— that he'll feel safe enough to let himself be exposed. And caught!"

She angled her head in admiration. "You and Juancho really have this thing figured out, don't you?"

He shrugged bare, broad shoulders. "Only figuring the angles. If this doesn't work, we'll try something else. You can see by what happened in

Guaymas, there are various ways these baby rings work. Sometimes direct. Sometimes down a chain. We intend to track the chain all the way to the end, even when it leads into the States."

"When? Then, you think it will lead into the States?"

"Eventually."

"Is that your cold, calculating mind at work, thinking like the enemy?"

"Whatever's cold can quickly be warmed up, if you'll just slide your hot little body over here by mine." He grabbed for her again but she rolled like a playful kitten off the bed, leaving the sheet behind.

"I have to get this hot little body in gear and head for work, Nick. Do you have a shower in this place?"

"Sure. A *warm* shower. A kitchen. And a bed. All the comforts of home."

She stood buck naked by the window. "It's a little small, but not too bad. Why you even have a lovely view of the city."

"Lovely?" he scoffed. "It's prettier at night. You can't see all the shacks."

"But in the daylight you can see the mountains. One of my field projects is a pre-school near there, in a small village. I hope they can keep it going after—"

"Alex, stay with me."

"What?"

His hands framed her bare shoulders. "Stay here with me. Until we find her and you decide what to do."

"Thanks for the invitation, Nick, but my rent is paid until the end of the month."

"That's only a couple of weeks away."

"I know, but I expect to find her by then." She turned abruptly and began picking up her clothes, discarded so carelessly on the floor. "Now where is this wonderful shower with the warm water?"

He watched her for a moment. She was hiding a lot, and denying even more. What would happen to *them* when, if, they found Jenni? "In there. I'll start the coffee while you test the water."

She gave him a teasing grin. "You can even cook too? My, my, what amazing skills go with a calculating mind."

He laughed. "Wait'll you taste my fabulous omelet!"

"And I make great toast," she claimed as she stepped into the shower. With an afterthought, she poked her head back out. "Do you have a toaster?"

It was a wonderfully leisurely morning, and they purposely ignored the time limit imposed on their relationship. As they lingered over a second cup of coffee, someone knocked on the door. Nick commented on rising, "Must be Juancho. No one else visits."

"Are you trying to convince me that no other women knock on your door at odd hours?" she teased with a grin.

Nick didn't answer but let his hand affectionately trail her shoulders as he crossed to the door.

"Sorry to interrupt, Capitán, but this is important." Juancho's dark eyes edged past Nick's shoulder to glimpse Alex sitting at the breakfast table, her hair still wet from the shower.

"Sure, Juancho. I'm just late getting started. What's up?"

The two men huddled as information was exchanged. Alex strained to hear their words but their voices were too low. She almost slid out of the chair in her efforts and was tempted to simply join them. Then she realized their discussion might not concern the search for Jenni at all. Maybe they were planning another airlift of exotic birds. Or something worse!

Juancho left abruptly, without even acknowledging Alex's presence. Tactful, she thought. Wonder how many times he's found Nick with a woman who obviously spent the night.

When Nick rejoined her, his expression was serious. "Father Ramón called with an identification of the man in the photo."

Alex's eyes grew round. "He actually knew from half a face? How—"

Nick's eyes halted her.

"I know, don't ask," Alex reiterated. "So what do we do with a name?"

"Juancho and I feel it's time to include the *policía* in the investigation. He's going to talk to our contacts in the local police department about the information we have. The photos. The identification. The abduction in progress. We have a suspect and a crime. We now have proof of a missing child."

"Do you think they'll help us find her now?"

"They should be more willing, with the new evidence."

"Nick, this is amazing! I'm so excited! We're actually getting close!"

"Take it easy, Alex. The hard part isn't over yet."

"Oh, God! We're on the verge of finding her! What could possibly go wrong? What do we do now?"

"That's the hard part. We don't do a damn thing. We wait."

"It's been two whole weeks, Nick! How much longer?"

"I told you this waiting wouldn't be easy. Alex, every cop in this city is looking for the guy. It just takes time. He'll slip up. It'll happen. And when it does, we have our man. Our link."

"What about our child?" She looked at him quickly, then turned away. "I didn't mean it to sound like that. I meant, in the meantime, what's happening to Jenni?"

Nick's hands clasped gently on her shoulders and caressed her down the length of her arms. "Alex, try to hang in there. It shouldn't be too much longer. And you have to keep telling yourself she's okay."

"Not too much longer," she repeated, motioning futilely to the stacks of boxes and piles of clothes laying across her bed. "That's what I thought two weeks ago. Now, here I am moving in with you. I thought—"

Nick turned her around and held her close. "Never mind what you thought. Living with me won't be so bad. I don't snore. And I make a damn good cup of coffee."

"Oh, it's not that, Nick. You know I . . . want to be with you. It's just that this search is so frustrating. I'm afraid I won't be such a great companion. Plus, there isn't much for me to do to keep occupied, now that my job has been dissolved."

"Maybe we can find something for you around the office."

She chuckled. "What? Driving getaway?"

"Now, Alex, don't be snide. Don't you trust me yet? I was thinking more of secretarial stuff, like answering the phone and—"

"And brandishing a mop wherever it's needed?"

"There you go, again. Maybe you could help build the tour business, like helping us with advertising . . . we really haven't tried very hard to push it."

"No," she scoffed. "You've been too busy transporting strange cargoes at night."

"That reminds me, we'd better hurry with this packing. Juancho should be back with the van any minute to take another load." He kissed her nose then decided on a lingering merger of their lips.

"Nick?" she asked hesitantly when he finally lifted his head. "You aren't doing anything to delay the search just so . . . so we can be together, are you?"

His eyes grew penetratingly hard. "I swear I would never do that, Alex. I want to find her almost as much as you do. I want . . . you both."

Alex smiled faintly, wondering if it was possible. What would happen to them in the end? Would she lose Nick when she found Jenni? The chugging of a motor out front jarred the uncomfortably quiet moment. "There's Juancho. We'd better get busy."

She moved away from his embrace but Nick took her hand. "I know this probably sounds crazy to you, but after all this time, I feel like I know this little girl. I know about her birth, about her life here, how much she means to you. I've seen her pictures, the happy ones as well as the traumatic ones. Jenni is real to me, Alex, not just a name. I want you to know I will do everything in my power to get her back."

Sudden tears welled up in Alex's eyes. At that moment she knew he really cared, knew she loved him deeply for caring. "Thank you, Nick. . . ." She swallowed hard.

"*Perdóna, Capitán,* but this is something you should know!" Juancho stood breathlessly in the doorway, having let himself into the house. He motioned frantically to both of them. "We'll get this stuff later! Come on down to the station! *La policía* have arrested the man who took Jenni!"

CHAPTER TWELVE

Alex's meager belongings, consisting of several boxes of books and teaching supplies, sat piled in the corner. Her clothes were squeezed into Nick's already too small closet. But no one paid attention to the crowded conditions. For hours, Nick's kitchen had served as a quarter for hot coffee and heated debates. The vote was two against one, and Alex couldn't hold her own until Juancho left for dinner with his family. With Juancho gone, Alex managed to score some points as she and Nick continued to argue. However, it was a toss up as to who won the battle and lost the war.

"Now that we know where she is, let's go get her!" Alex's arms flailed the air helplessly. "Juancho doesn't have to go. He can stay here and keep the business going." She stopped short of saying which business. The helicopter tours or the *other.*

"We only know she's been sent out of Hermosillo, probably traveling northward," Nick corrected.

Alex pointed a finger as if catching a flaw in his

reasoning. "We know she's with a couple, a man and woman posing as a family. Hell, Nick, there are just so many roads crossing that region of Mexico. And we can figure she's bound for the Valencia-Jessup border."

"We *think* she is," Nick inserted.

"Nick, he *said*—"

"Dammit, Alex, you can't believe every word of a criminal who would be willing to sell kids on the black market. He would also sing any song the cops wanted to hear in order to sweeten his case."

Alex sank into a chair and propped her elbows on the table. "Then do you believe anything he said in his confession?" she asked earnestly. "That he was actually the one who took Jenni? That he left her at his sister's house, and she took care of Jenni until he made his connections?"

Nick poured each of them fresh coffee and answered thoughtfully. "You have to sort through every word in a pressure confession like this. Yes, I definitely believe he's the man in the photos who snatched Jenni at the scene of the accident . . . and it's possible that he took her to his sister's, or it could have been his girlfriend's. Remember, *sister* sounds better." He paused for a sip of coffee and let his eyes travel to hers before continuing.

"But I hope you noticed that he insisted the child was alone and unattended and that *he thought* she was abandoned. He very cleverly didn't comment when questioned about the obvious fact that Jenni was clean and well-cared for.

Nor did he give a reason for not turning her over to the police. He was very wily."

"In that identification lineup he reminded me of José, the one in Guaymas who wanted to sell us the baby," Alex muttered. "It was easy to despise him."

"Yes, I can understand that."

"So what do you propose to do, Nick? Wait some more?"

He nodded. "Yep, 'fraid so. It'll prevent us from going off on a wild goose chase to Jessup when she might have been taken to Yuma."

"You could fly us there in no time, Nick," she pleaded. "Anyway, the man said there was a connection at Jessup. I feel sure that's where they've gone! It makes the most sense."

"It's the entire chain of connections we're interested in, Alex."

"It's Jenni I'm interested in, Nick!" Alex countered hotly. "To hell with the stupid chain. To hell with all the others! I just want my little Jenni back!"

"Take it easy, Alex. We'll get her. In due time."

Alex glared angrily at Nick. He was maddeningly calm when she wanted to jump through her skin! Now they had something to do, a direction, yet Nick was content to wait here. She simply couldn't understand it. "I'm tired of waiting. Your 'due time' isn't soon enough for me. Jenni is heading for Jessup—"

"Maybe!"

"Maybe," she conceded. "And you want to sit here and wait until the Customs officers call."

Nick leaned toward her, his lips tightly drawn beneath his mustache. His tone was tense. "Alex, I'm trying to convince you how important it is for this scene to play itself through all the way to the end. The way the police have explained it, in order to catch everyone involved in this ring, it's crucial that it be allowed to run its course."

"Why?" Alex asked, aghast. "What the hell are you talking about, anyway?"

Nick realized he was damn close to telling her far too much, and changed his tone. "Alex, just because Jenni left the city with a couple posing as husband and wife doesn't mean she'll complete the journey in their care."

"It doesn't? Sounds like a good way to hide to me. They could take a whole carload of kids across the border and no one would bother to ask about them."

"Well, perhaps it is, but these people may change their M–O in the middle of the trip. It's logical."

"M–O? You sound like you've been watching too many cop shows."

"Then you know that's a military term meaning method of operation for commiting a crime. People use many ingenious methods to cross the border. Sometimes they stow away in special compartments in trucks or vans. They might pose as a family visiting relatives or impersonate American *touristas*. There are various ways to make Jenni difficult to spot, even with Customs looking for her."

"I never thought of that." Alex scooted anxiously to the edge of her seat. "Nick, they wouldn't harm her, would they?"

"No, not after taking care of her all this time. It isn't likely. They might give her a mild sedative to make her sleep. In fact, they might take the most obvious, least noticed route. Just walk across."

"You mean, slip across the fence somewhere remote?"

"No. I mean walk across at a checkpoint with a sleeping child in their arms. Or disguise her in some way like dressing her as a boy. That's why I don't want us to waste our time going there. We'd never be able to find her."

Alex drew herself up and her indigo eyes flashed like blue diamonds. "I don't know about you, Nick Diamond, but I'd recognize her in any disguise. If I came close to Jenni, I'd know her, and most importantly, she would know me."

"I'm sure you would, Alex," Nick granted. "That could be damn dangerous for both of you. But what if you don't get that close? What if she's already passed through the border and is on her way? What if—"

Alex interrupted angrily, "What if we wait too long and she's sold up the chain, or whatever you call it, and becomes lost somewhere in the States? What if she's sent to Maine or Montana and just disappears? They've done it before, apparently. They could do it again, while we wait in Hermosillo! That's what this whole thing is about, isn't it, Nick? Creating a chain that disappears

209

and is immune to the law because the children are adopted legally!"

"So far they've evaded capture, but believe me, it won't happen this time. Jenni won't disappear."

Nick seemed so sure of himself, Alex wanted to lash out at him in her frustration. "How do you know?"

"Trust me."

"Trust you? Ha! Nick, I've tried to trust you through all this and there are still questions you refuse to answer. It's damn hard to believe that you'll be able to prevent Jenni from getting away when we're still sitting right here in Hermosillo! What can you possibly do to stop it?"

Nick's voice was a quiet contrast to hers. "I know, Alex. It's a lot to ask."

"Then don't ask it."

"I must," he answered simply.

"Well, with no more explanation than that, it's too much!" She turned away and walked to the kitchen window. Her eyes, glazed with emotion, passed over the shacks in her line of view. She sought the strength and beauty of the mountains in the distance.

Nick approached Alex and stood close without touching her. She was an emotional powder keg right now and he wasn't sure how to deal with her. He wanted to reassure her. Maybe he should tell her, explain what was happening. How much would keep her satisfied? "Alex, I can tell you this much. We're keeping close contact with Customs. As soon as they know something, they'll notify us."

She swallowed hard and took a deep, shaky breath. "What will they do with Jenni when they find her? Take her into custody? She'll be alone and scared. I want to be with her during that time."

"And I want you to be. I'll fly you there the minute we know something for sure."

"You will?" Alex felt like jelly inside. She was anxious, excited, nervous, bursting with every emotion that could prevent her from thinking straight. Maybe he was right. They should wait.

"You know, this arguing is getting us nowhere."

"The way I look at it, sitting here in your kitchen in Hermosillo drinking coffee is getting us nowhere. Meantime, Jenni is heading for the States."

"Look, Alex, you hired me to do a job. That act required trusting me, a complete stranger. Now we're far from strangers. We've come this close to getting her. Trust me a little longer." His hands rested on her shoulders, allowing warmth to radiate from his body to hers.

"Hired you?" She turned to face him and his arms still encircled her shoulders. "Nick, you never let me hire you. You never cashed that check."

He grinned, slightly off-center. "Well, the intent was there, but other things got in the way. Like wanting to help you. Like caring about you

211

and Jenni. Like the urgency to find her and break the back of this human black-market scheme."

Like love? Alex wondered. "Like us, Nick?"

"From the first, I was interested in this case . . . in you, Alex."

"In the case? Why—"

Nick's dark eyes flickered. He couldn't let her know now. They were too near the end, too close to the culmination of all this work. "You're a beautiful woman, Alex. You intrigued me the first time I saw you. And I . . . wanted you, even then. But I promised myself restraint. It just wasn't enough. We belong together. Let me hold you, Alex. Come here. . . ."

Near tears, she melted in his arms. Frantically, Alex crushed herself against his firm-muscled chest, inhaling his masculine scent, absorbing his solid strength. "Nick, I don't think I can be strong much longer."

"Let me be your strength, Alex. I'll be with you . . . all the way to the end."

"Then what?" She muffled the words, not daring to consider the answer.

Apparently, neither could Nick. "Don't think about that now. Just let me love you."

She clung weakly to him and he lifted her and carried her gallantly to the bed. He undressed her with delicate zephyrlike movements. His lavish kisses followed each garment until waves of desire rippled through her, rising slowly higher with each silky touch. They made love with a gentleness she'd never before experienced, a sensuous elegance, a ritual beauty in the uniting of two bodies. Eventually Alex and Nick merged as two languid mountain streams that join at a fork. There was a gathering of speed and force until the rapid rush when the wild river crashed into the mighty ocean at journey's end. Then they lay in each other's arms as if washed up on a beach after a raging storm.

"What's going to happen to us, Nick?"

"We'll think about that later. There'll be plenty of time."

"My life is in such an upheaval right now. I feel like it's all piled over there in the corner of your apartment. I don't know where I'll be tomorrow, or next week. It's an unsettling feeling."

"I understand, Alex. I never know either. Maybe it's time for . . ."

Alex puzzled over his answer and waited for him to finish. But he didn't. For once, she didn't ask him to explain. In due time, when he was ready, he would tell her. Alex marveled at her patience. Maybe she was too tired to pursue it. Or was this the beginning of her trusting him? Perhaps. She wanted to trust him, oh, God, how she yearned for that kind of blind confidence. She wanted them to be together in the end. And Jenni? Like he'd said earlier, she wanted them both. Was that too much to ask?

"Nick, we didn't have dinner and I'm hungry."

"That's a good sign," he mused. "How would you like one of my fabulous omelets?"

"We've had that twice this week."

"You complaining?"

"Well, your menu is quite limited."

"What would you like to cook, señorita?"

She paused and laughed. "An omelet sounds wonderful."

Nick slid into jeans and proceeded to practice his culinary arts ruggedly bare-chested. Alex wrapped herself in his discarded shirt. It came down to the middle of her thighs and was perfect for fixing her contribution to their late-night meal—the toast. They had finished eating and were starting to wash dishes when they heard a knock.

"Juancho again? This is getting to be a habit," Alex snapped. One I don't like, she thought, but, maybe it's about Jenni.

"Something's up." Nick darted to the door. His conversation with Juancho was brief and staccatolike. This time, Alex moved closer and listened.

". . . contact from *lobo azul*. This one's in the other direction. Pick-up at Yuma tonight. *Vamos!* Right now!"

"What is it this time? Guns?"

"*Quien sabe?* Who knows?"

"Damn! Just when this deal with the kid's coming down!"

As Juancho moved away from the door, Alex could see his shadowy form. He was dressed strangely, all in black.

Nick turned into the kitchen, looking grim and giving orders. "Make us some coffee, will you, Alex? Here's the thermos." He set the huge container on the counter and disappeared immediately into the bedroom.

Alex followed him, privately rebeling at the orders. "Nick, what's going on? Is it Jenni?"

"No! The coffee, please! We're in a hurry!" He began peeling his jeans down his firm hips and muscular thighs, ignoring her presence and her questions.

Alex returned to the kitchen and proceeded with her assigned chore, her agitation growing by the minute. She slammed the coffee pot onto the stove and flipped the flame on beneath it. This was worse than serving as a getaway car driver! Worse than being secretary to a nonexistent business! *Make coffee for us and sit home and wait. WAIT!* She could scream for waiting!

When Nick reappeared he, too, wore very dark clothing. His jeans were jet black and hugged his legs snuggly; his shirt was navy and hung loose over his waist.

"Nick, are you going to explain—"

His hard, dark eyes halted her. His face was taut and angular, his expression closed. What was he thinking? Feeling? He looked the same, but this was a different Nick, one she didn't know and didn't really like.

This wasn't the man who made sweet, tender love to her, who cared for her feelings and the well-being of a child he'd never seen. Here was a man for hire, a man willing to do the dangerous, the illegal—whatever was necessary to make a buck. From deep inside her being, Alex wanted to cry out. What kind of man was this she loved?

"I'll explain as much as I can. As much as you

215

need to know," he said vaguely. His stone face said *Don't ask any more questions.*

She nodded, not sure she could do that but realizing it was all Nick was willing to give.

"Juancho and I have some business tonight. I won't be back for at least twelve hours, maybe a little longer. Here are the keys to the van. I want you to have a vehicle in case . . . in case anything happens and you need it." He tossed the keys on the table.

"What about Jenni?"

"Get some rest tonight, Alex. Nothing will happen before tomorrow, anyway. Maybe later."

"But what if it does?" Alex didn't think she could wait until tomorrow for something to happen.

"Wait for me."

"Wait?" Her nostrils flared. "What if . . ." she paused and finished hoarsely, "you aren't here. What if you don't come back?"

"Then someone else will notify you."

She lifted her chin and wanted to grate *Who, the coroner?* Instead, she murmured, "Nick, I'm scared."

"Don't be." He moved quickly to take her in his arms, holding her close. "I wish I could tell you more."

Alex clasped her arms tightly around his waist, pressing her face to his chest as if to detect the real Nick beneath those strange clothes. Her hands met on the hard, metal object tucked into his belt. "Nick! What the hell is that?" But she knew.

216

He tore her arms away and kissed her roughly.

"What are you doing with a gun?" She breathed the question, not really wanting to hear the answer.

"No questions, remember? I'll see you tomorrow." He winked then moved toward the cabinet. "Coffee ready?"

She grabbed his arm but he jerked away and began to pour the boiling black brew into the tall thermos. "Nick, I don't know what you're up to but it's dangerous if you've got a gun! It isn't worth the risk. Nothing is! No amount of money is worth risking your life, Nick, and I don't want you to do this."

He continued to ignore her and tightened the lid on the thermos. He started across the room and she latched onto his arm again. "Nick, don't go! Please!"

Her frantic begging did no good. He reached for the door.

"Nick, I . . . I love you."

He stopped and looked at her for a long second. "I'll be back tomorrow, Alex. Believe it. Just trust me."

Then he was gone, a tall, dark shadow joining a bulkier one. They drove away quickly and disappeared into the night.

Alex stared at the black emptiness long after Juancho's car vanished. Her mind raced with questions—unanswered questions.

Alex shivered inside Nick's shirt and hugged her arms, trying to draw some warmth from his garment, but she couldn't. The view of him dressed in black haunted her. She wondered which was real: the cold, hard Nick, the man for hire; or the gentle, compassionate man with whom she had fallen in love.

What was he doing tonight? If he and Juancho were smuggling, it was something serious. More so than exotic birds. Something serious enough to require a gun. And that meant the *others,* whoever they were, also had guns! Then it occurred to her that whatever Nick was involved in was more important than the search for Jenni. He was willing to leave her stranded midstream, waiting for the Customs officials to call. And because of her devotion to him, her *trust,* Alex sat here, waiting. Doing nothing. Just waiting. It wasn't enough.

Nick didn't care for her. He couldn't! Even though he claimed he did, Alex was convinced he wouldn't have left her like this if he loved her. He'd said they were keeping in close contact with Customs, but if neither he nor Juancho was here, how could they do that? He also said he'd be with her to the end. And where was he this minute? Not with her!

Alex looked out the window. Five hundred miles beyond the horizon was the Mexican border . . . and Jessup. And perhaps Jenni. Her eyes dropped to the gray van parked below the window. Suddenly, she knew what she must do.

Quickly, she tore off his shirt. After a shower she dressed and threw some extra clothes into a small suitcase. While she finished washing dishes, she made a full pot of coffee for herself and searched out another thermos. She grabbed a package of corn tortillas and cheddar cheese from the refrigerator. It would be a long trip across Mexico, and she prayed the rattletrap van would make it.

Digging into her purse, she found a pen and tore off the end of a brown paper bag in the kitchen. The note was brief. It said all she needed to say: mostly, good-bye.

Alex paused beside the pile of boxes that represented her worldly possessions. She studied the boxes for a minute then began to dig furiously in one of them. Soon she retrieved the small item and looked at it with a grim smile of satisfaction. She closed Nick's apartment door with Jenni's well-loved, frayed teddy bear tucked under her arm.

CHAPTER THIRTEEN

Nick halted and leaned heavily on Juancho. The two men stared at the empty place where the gray van was always parked. "Damn! She's gone!"

"Maybe she took a ride, Capitán."

"Yeah, all the way to Jessup."

"To Jessup? You think she will interfere with the project? Should we stop her? I can call—"

"No, I don't think that's necessary. She'll be too late. The kid's already on her way. I'm almost sure of it." Nick spoke with difficulty and halted to take a raspy breath. "Anyway, it's something Alex had to do. She's damn stubborn, Juancho."

"Ayee, that *mujer* has a mind of her own! Where will she go if she can't find *la niña?*"

"Hell, Juancho, who knows what that woman will do next? Maybe she'll go to Phoenix, to Carol's." Nick gasped as a wave of pain racked his body.

"Come on, Capitán. You're bleeding pretty bad."

Juancho draped a strong arm around Nick's ribs and all but carried him up the stairs. Depositing the wounded man on the edge of the bed, he quickly checked the apartment. He found the note on the table, and trying to avert his eyes from the scribbled words, handed it to *El Capitán.*

Nick read Alex's quickly scribbled words and let it flutter weakly to the floor. "Damn!" His bloodshot eyes had lost their sharp quality. "I don't know how to keep her, Juancho."

"Do you want to?"

"Hell, yes! God knows why, but I do!"

"We'll find her, Capitán. And bring her back."

"Oh, yeah? How? Tie her hand and foot?" He coughed a couple of dry hacks. "Juancho, I'm in big trouble." Nick sank back on the bed and was immediately engulfed in a pool of blood.

Juancho was never sure if Nick meant he was in trouble because he was losing blood or because this spirited woman with a temptress's blue eyes had left him. He had suspected all along that those indigo eyes of hers spelled danger for *El Capitán.*

The moon was a half lemon slice hanging by its tip, illuminating the otherwise black Mexican sky. Its glow was the only light she saw for hours, and it served to lure Alex toward her goal. She stopped twice for gas, saying a prayer each time that the van's fractious engine would restart. It did.

She nibbled cheese and tortillas, drank the devil's-brew coffee, and drove. Drove like a bat out of hell. She was a crusader fighting a holy war

—her own. By dawn she pulled into the border checkpoint at Valencia, the Mexican border town at Arizona's remote southeastern corner.

She was directed inside a tiny green-and-glass building. "I'm Alexis Julian and I'm the one looking for a child who's being brought across the border illegally. I understand the Hermosillo police alerted you about her. This is the child." She shoved her papers across the desk along with a photo of Jenni.

The uniformed Customs officer looked curiously at her, then at her papers.

"Jenni was taken illegally in Hermosillo," Alex continued anxiously. "We think she's to be sold for adoption in the States. That's why we're looking for her here. She was supposed to be taken across this border yesterday, possibly even the day before. Did you find her?"

"Uno momento, señorita." The man took her papers and conferred in rapid-fire Spanish with another officer. Then both men joined her, as if to serve as a united front. "We have found no such child, señorita."

"But surely she's been taken across by now! I . . . I just want to see her, to stay with her. I won't interfere with your investigation or anything. You see, she's been stolen from her home and family. Her mother was killed and I'm all she has left!" Alex felt the swell of panic mushrooming inside her breast and she struggled to stay in control of her emotions.

The men gave her sympathetic looks, but

there was no recognition in their eyes. "I'm sorry, señorita. We have not seen this child."

Alex edged forward on her seat and leaned one arm on the officer's desk. "But you don't understand, sir. You *must* find her for me. They're going to sell her for adoption in the States. We have to stop them—right here—before they can take her any farther!" Alex tapped the desk with conviction.

The men exchanged harried glances, then one spoke. *"Señorita, por favor,* we have found no child these last two days. That is all I can tell you at this time." The finality of his tone told her he wouldn't tell her anything more.

Alex felt as though she had just been slapped. Could she believe them? Damn! Maybe she should ha waited for Nick after all! His forcefulness attracted attention. Got action. Hers merely elicited sympathetic stares.

No! She was here and here she would stay!

"Then maybe they haven't brought Jenni through yet," she deduced aloud. "Do you mind if I wait?"

The officers exchanged glances again, and wordlessly decided she could do no harm. Better to humor her. *"Si, claro, señorita.* You may wait in here." They directed her to a small, square, glassed room where she had visual access to the string of cars lining up to cross the border into Arizona. In the distance, on the American side, she could see the twin smokestacks of the old Phelps-Dodge smeltering plant.

She waited. And waited. Three hours. Four. It

was hot in the little booth. She dozed on the hard bench for a few minutes and awakened with a start, horrified that perhaps she had missed Jenni. She rushed out to ask the officer in charge if a small child had been discovered. He shook his head. Dejectedly, Alex took her seat again.

The realization came slowly. Finally Alex knew in her heart that Jenni had already been transported across the border. It was too late to question how such a thing could have happened when the customs officers were supposed to be watching for this child. It just did. Nick was right. There were ways.

With a resigned sigh, Alex gathered her paper cups, thanked the officers for their kindness, and drove the van across the border into Jessup. *Jessup!* Oh, God, how she had argued with Nick about coming to this place. Now that she was here, it was a letdown. Somehow she had expected more excitement, but what she found was a dusty, rather lifeless little border town, and she felt as bedraggled as the place appeared.

Now what? Where should she start to look for Jenni? Would the baby still be with the connection, the woman who served as the first American link of the chain, as Nick called it? God, how she wished Nick was here! He would know what to do. He would know how to find this woman. Alex drove around the town, which consisted of several blocks of half-dying businesses and small residential pockets. The highway led past McDonald's, the old copper smeltering plant, and the junior college. That was it.

She turned around and drove back into town. Parking on an empty corner, Alex entered the county building. Perhaps the Child Welfare Department could give her the information she needed. Fifteen minutes later Alex stepped back out into the blazing noon heat. No knowledge of the missing child. And they certainly had no knowledge of an illegal baby ring. So now what?

She squinted in the near-blinding brightness and an incongruous sign on the building across the street caught her eye. The shape of a huge cowboy boot, outlined in neon lights, blinked and rocked. COWBOY BAR, it read.

A bar. Of course! You could find out all sorts of information about a town in the bar, Alex decided with a blossom of hope. You could even find out about illegal connections. It was in a cantina that she and Nick had met the man with the baby for sale in Guaymas! Without another thought about the propriety or possible danger of a lone woman entering a strange bar in a strange town, Alex crossed the street and sallied inside, under the flashing boot.

The immediate blackness of the room surprised her. It took a full minute for her blinded eyes to be able to discern walls, tables, chairs, the bar, and five pairs of masculine eyes staring at her. Suddenly she felt naked, as those eyes disrobed her, and she burned with embarrassment and indignation at their blatant ogling. Every one, to a man, gave her a full assessment in the time she stood like a zombie, waiting for her eyes to adjust to the dimmed lights.

Oh, dear God! What am I doing here? Is it a mistake to be here without Nick? I know what they're thinking! I can see it in their eager faces. Will I be able to walk out of here? Maybe I shouldn't walk in! But someone here knows the baby connection. I'm sure of it!

She proceeded cautiously to the bar, where three of the men sat at the other end, talking to the bartender. On her approach their conversations stopped, and the only sound was the twanging country record playing on the old-fashioned jukebox in the corner. Alex leaned on the bar and the bartender ambled over with a welcoming smile.

"What can I fix for you?"

"I'm not here for a drink, thank you," she conceded with a nervous smile. "I need some information. I wonder if you could tell me, uh, if you know a woman who, uh, deals with babies from Mexico. You know, like . . . has them for adoption."

The bartender leaned forward and asked in a low voice, "You pregnant? Want to sell it? Good money for healthy babies, I hear tell."

"No—I, uh, I'm looking for a baby." Alex felt a disturbing heat building around her neck. This was not going to be easy.

"You lookin' to buy?" He eyed her warily and suddenly Alex realized that she was on the edge of illegal turf and playing a dangerous game. She'd damn sure better play their game well or she could be in deep trouble, and with no one to help her out of it, since no one knew where she was.

She shrugged nonchalantly. "Maybe."

He motioned to a man who sat at a corner table by himself, drinking a can of Tecate, a brand of Mexican beer. "Homer's been here longer than I have. Knows more people. Maybe he can tell ya."

Alex's heart pounded as she made her way to Homer's table, disquieted that she would have to repeat her story to this tough-looking man. She tried to ignore the bawdy comments that accompanied her brief journey across the room.

"Hey there, cutie!"

"Mmm, *bonita!*"

"*Guera, chula!* Blondie!"

By the time she reached Homer's table, Alex was aquiver inside. Never had she been subject to such a demeaning situation, and yet she couldn't stop now. Blandly, she watched Homer lick a dab of salt from his thumb's web, gulp a shot of tequila, and follow it with a long swig of Tecate. Boilermaker! Alex stifled a shudder.

"*Siéntese, por favor, chula,*" he directed in Spanish.

Alex decided right away she would not converse in Spanish. After all, she was an American looking to buy. "Thank you. I'll be brief, Homer. I'm looking to buy a baby. Mexican. I understand you know where I can get one."

He assessed her with droopy bloodshot eyes. "Maybe you married?" His gaze dropped to her ringless left hand.

Quickly deducing that a married couple with

plenty of money had a better chance at this, she nodded. "Uh, yes. But I took the rings off, for safety. The diamonds, you know."

"Put them back on. Looks better," he directed. "Where is your husband?"

"He had business in California. A big real estate deal that he just couldn't miss."

"You from California?"

"Uh, well, we have a home there. Palm Springs. But also in Scottsdale, and West Palm. That's in Florida. I hate the Springs this time of year. There is absolutely no one there. And I get so lonesome. You see, I can't have any children. I've been to doctors all over the country and they told me to forget it and just to adopt one. But adoptions take so much time. And Sterling, that's my husband, Sterling, he's been turned down by two agencies already. You see, Sterling's older and, well, you know how picky those places can be." She paused to see how she was doing.

Homer took advantage of the time to take another swig of beer.

Alex cleared her throat. "So Sterling said, honey, if you want a baby, you just go right over there and get one. So here I am." Alex hushed and smiled expectantly, hoping with all her might that she was convincing.

Homer considered her lengthy explanation while he slowly finished off the Tecate. "Go to *la farmacia.* Couple a blocks over. Tell the druggist you're lookin' for a baby."

At that point Alex realized she would have to repeat her story, maybe several times, before she

228

reached the end of the trail. "Thank you, Homer." Discreetly, she slipped a ten dollar bill beneath his beer can. "Have another drink or two on Sterling. He'll be so grateful."

She exited as quickly as she could amid catcalls of "Don't leave so soon, pretty baby!" and "Come on back and let me treat! Then you can treat!"

Alex slipped into the old van and drove to a remote part of town. Damn, she wished she'd kept that wedding ring Nick had given her in Guaymas! She changed into some fresh clothes in the back of the van, rearranged all her papers, and tucked away everything connecting her to living in Mexico. Then she walked the distance back into town, stopping along the way at a pawn shop. When she entered the small pharmacy with a used ring on her finger, Alex hoped she resembled a married woman intent on finding a child.

The druggist was even more thorough in his questioning than Homer had been. He asked for identification, and Alex whipped out her dated Arizona driver's license. He examined it then compared her with the photo. "It's expired. A year ago," he observed.

Alex feigned surprise. "Why, how in the world could that have happened? Oh, I know! My husband took me to the Bahamas for my birthday last year! We stayed two months and it was so wonderful. I guess I just forgot to renew my license on my birthday. Gosh, I'm glad you found it before the police did." She tucked the little card back into her purse. "Well, can you direct me to the place that has the babies?"

The druggist's eyes were gray-cold and wary. "You will have to talk to Consuela. She'll make the arrangements. She runs the café down the street. Tell her you're looking for an original Cabbage Patch Doll. She'll know what you want."

Alex tried to hide her excitement. Maybe she was nearing the end of this chase and wouldn't have to tell her story many more times. "Cabbage Patch Doll? Okay. Thank you very much."

Alex walked to the café, buoyed by hope. When she entered the small eatery, there wasn't a soul in sight. She took a side table and could hear an afternoon soap opera on a T.V. in the back room. A very large, buxom woman approached, and Alex ordered a glass of tea. When the woman set the glass before her, Alex asked, "Are you Consuela?"

The woman nodded.

"Consuela, I'm Alex Julian. I talked to the druggist a few minutes ago and he sent me here. You see, I'm looking for an original Cabbage Patch Doll. He said you could help me."

"I might. Let me check." She disappeared and returned about fifteen minutes later. "Come with me, please."

Alex wasn't prepared for the complete search Consuela inflicted on her, including sorting through her purse and patting down each leg. She was glad she'd hidden her passport and other information proving her years of living and working in Mexico in the van.

"Sorry for the inconvenience, señora, but we have to make sure. You understand."

"Of course," Alex nodded, trying to act calm. "Can you tell me now where I might find one of these, uh, dolls?"

"Someone will come after you and take you there. In about an hour."

"An hour?" Alex felt a definite weariness from lack of food and sleep. The escalating temperature outside wasn't helping any, either. Another hour in this heat, and she might collapse on the spot.

"You could always have something to eat," Consuela grinned.

Alex ate a plate of fiery enchiladas and drank two glasses of tea while she waited. She deposited a generous tip on the Formica-topped table and decided that Consuela wasn't so dumb. Maybe she kept everyone waiting so they'd have time to eat at her place.

Eventually Alex was led to the back alley to board the vehicle that would take her to the babies. She looked at the cream-colored pickup truck and its camper on the back with sudden trepidation. Should she get in? Hell, it was too late to back out now. The driver motioned for her to ride in the camper part.

As Alex climbed into the rear section, her eyes caught a huge platform truck with wooden stakes on the sides. It was the kind used for transporting vegetables, and probably hauled them up from Mexico to Consuela's café and other area restaurants. *And that wasn't all the vegetable truck hauled!*

Alex sat in the semidark camper, barely able to contain herself! *That's* how they brought them across the border! The "Cabbage Patch Dolls" were Mexican babies hidden beneath crates of vegetables and fruit, delivered on a regular basis to the restaurants of Jessup. Sometimes the haul contained a baby; sometimes not! How ingenius! How cold and calculating! Wait until Nick heard that! He would be so proud of her—if he didn't kill her for taking off without him.

They rode around for a considerable period of time, and Alex knew the driver was trying to confuse her. Nothing in Jessup was this far away, unless they were driving all the way to Tucson. The camper windows had been painted black, so she couldn't see anything outside and had no idea where they were. Just when Alex thought she would swelter in the heat, the truck stopped and someone opened the back door for her. Fresh, hot air had never felt so good!

She approached the modest house as if she could care less where it was located. In fact, she took meticulous mental notes of the scrubby foliage in the almost-flat landscape. She was determined that all this effort would not go to waste.

Alex introduced herself to the heavyset woman who came to the door.

"I'm Margaret Hannah," the woman returned, pale blue eyes assessing Alex warily. After a moment's pause, she nodded. "Come on in. I've been waitin' for ya."

So this was the American link. Quite obviously, the American connection wasn't merely one person keeping a houseful of babies but an involved chain of people right here in sleepy little Jessup. Alex couldn't help wondering where the chain went from here. Although this Margaret Hannah was a pleasant-faced woman with slightly graying hair, her expression was guarded, her pale blue eyes severe.

"Would ya like a glass of tea before we get started? Ya look awfully hot. That truck," she shook her head, "is like an oven this time a year."

"No, thank you. I'd like to go ahead and see the babies." Alex grew excited at the prospect of seeing Jenni. She'd been through so much today, she'd almost forgotten that Jenni might be right here in this house, at this very minute!

"Sure," Margaret agreed shortly. "Well, come on. I've only got three right now." She lumbered down the hall and Alex trotted after her. "Two boys and a girl. Do ya care which?"

"Uh, the girl." Alex tried not to sound to anxious.

"Some don't, ya know. They're so desperate for a kid, they'll take either kind. But others're real particular. Like you." She ended pointedly and halted beside an open doorway.

Alex almost stumbled in her haste to enter the room. An infant of about three months napped in the gentle breeze of a ceiling fan. "Is this it? The only girl?" Disappointment was clear in her tone.

"Shh, don't wake her up," Margaret cautioned and jerked Alex back into the hall. "Yep, this is the only one."

"But this just can't be all you have!" Alex pushed past Margaret and looked in every room. There were only two other babies, both napping, both male.

Margaret motioned to the baby girl. "What's wrong with this one? She's perfectly healthy. Good strong back. Real good reflexes."

Alex looked frantically into Margaret's stodgy face. Suddenly she felt all alone, a possible victim in the hands of Margaret Hannah. "Why, nothing. That's a fine baby. It's just that . . . well, I had hoped for one a little older."

"When they're this young, ya can train 'em from the start."

"T-train? Yes, well, maybe you're right. But I'd still like to think it over a little. I really should consult my husband too." A nervous heat spread up Alex's back and she had the distinct feeling she'd better get the hell out of here. And fast. She began walking in slow, ambling steps toward the door. "You see, my husband is a little old-fashioned. He doesn't let me make decisions without him. Not final ones that involve money."

"Or kids?" Margaret raised thin eyebrows.

"Oh, yes, especially involving kids," Alex agreed readily, hoping Margaret believed her.

"If ya want her, ya'd better say so. Sometimes these babies go through here pretty fast."

"Yes, I understand. But you'll have more, too, won't you?"

Margaret cast her a cutting look. "Look lady, this ain't no department store. Who knows if we'll have more? They might be all boys. The babies that come through here are homeless. Nobody wants 'em. We find families for 'em. When they leave here, they've got homes to go to. There's always somebody out there that wants 'em."

"Enough to pay good money for them," Alex finished dourly.

"Sure do," Margaret nodded emphatically. "There's always money exchanged in the adoption of children."

"Now, how do I get back in touch, if my husband agrees to this. Do I need to go back in town to the druggist?"

"Do you think you could find your way back here?"

"Well, no," Alex hedged.

"Then ya go back through the same people. Sometimes things change, y'know."

"Okay." Alex forced a smile. "I imagine I'll see you soon, Ms. Hannah, but I really should be getting back now." She was beginning to see the potential danger of her precarious situation. No one knew where she was. Anything could happen to her now and no one would know. Oh, would Nick be furious with her!

Alex had been so overwhelmed by the singular idea of finding Jenni at this house that she hadn't thought through all the angles. Now her one aim was to get out of here safely. She was so nervous, and her palms so slick, shaking hands with Margaret Hannah was out of the question. She eased out the door and muttered a hasty farewell.

Margaret loomed in the doorway watching, not smiling, just observing with those pale blue eyes.

Alex stifled a shudder and clamored into the back of the camper. Sitting alone in the darkness she fought stinging tears. No Jenni. No Nick. Just Alex alone and not knowing where to turn.

The drive back into town didn't take as long. Perhaps the driver felt she had been sufficiently confused. Alex was released on the street in front of the café and began the long trudge back to the edge of town where she'd parked the rattletrap van. Her all-night chase, her wild and rambling lies, her waiting, had been futile. Still no Jenni. But she had come close, damn close. Alex just knew it. Maybe if she had arrived a day or two earlier, or if Nick had flown her up as she'd begged him to do, they would have been in time to catch the child. Maybe.

Finally, Alex stumbled up to the van as the sun was dropping fast behind the Mexican horizon.

She continued her journey, not stopping until she reached her final destination. It was dark when she knocked on the Phoenix residence.

"Alex, what a wonderful surprise!"

"My God, Carol, you're a sight for sore eyes! Do you mind hugging a tramp?"

The two old friends grabbed each other, hugging and laughing and crying all at once.

CHAPTER FOURTEEN

Alex's first thoughts the next morning were of Nick. She could see his dark form hovering over her, his dark eyes crinkling at the edges when he smiled, his teeth flashing white against the tan of his skin. She could feel his cool kiss, the feather strokes of his mustache on her lips, and the warmth of his body stretched out against hers.

She squeezed the pillow and murmured his name. *Trust me,* he said. But she hadn't. She had disregarded his advice. As she grew more awake, Nick's image faded, and Alex realized he really wasn't with her. He wasn't here because she'd left him in Mexico. She'd defied him to go on a wild goose chase by herself.

To find her precious Jenni!

Alex sat up in bed with a start. Now, she had neither of the two people she loved! She'd left Nick and had no idea where to look for Jenni.

After a quick shower Alex threw on some jeans and a shirt and joined her long-time friend Carol, in the kitchen.

"Well, I was beginning to think you were going to sleep all day!" Carol embraced her warmly.

"It's so good to see you and be back in familiar territory! Back in this country," Alex admitted with a smile.

"Have a cup of coffee and a seat," Carol instructed. "You have a lot of explaining to do, lady!"

"I swear, Carol, you have the most marvelous bed in the world! And the most generous spirit!" Alex poured herself a cup of coffee, climbed onto a curved bamboo stool, and leaned on the counter bar that separated the small kitchen from the dining area. "How can I ever thank you?"

Carol shrugged and smiled. "What else could I do, when my dearest friend appears at my doorstep, looking like some bedraggled waif? You must have been absolutely beat, Alex! You fell asleep before I could give you the bowl of soup and glass of wine you requested."

"Did I? I don't even remember."

"There wasn't much conversation last night. How about a grilled cheese sandwich? I'm in the process of fixing myself one for lunch." Carol flipped the browned sandwich that sizzled in a skillet.

"Is it lunch time already? I did hibernate, didn't I? It's been a long time since I've had a plain cheese sandwich, without corn tortillas on the side!" Alex chuckled and sipped at her coffee. "Matter of fact, a good ol' American grilled cheese sandwich sounds great! I may even give in to french fries later today. It's been ages since I've had them."

"I considered fixing enchiladas to make you feel at home."

"No, thanks!" Alex laughed. "I've had my fill of Mexican food for a while."

"Does that mean you're here to stay?" Carol lifted her eyebrows.

"Um-hum. The job's over for good."

"What about Jenni?"

"No luck there, either." Alex shook her head. "Oh, it's a long story, Carol."

"And I want to hear every word, but I'm puzzled. Your last letter said you weren't leaving Mexico until you and this Nick—" Carol halted with a small laugh. "I'm getting ahead, aren't I? Far be it from me to rush you Alex, but I am dying to know what happened. Have some more coffee, eat a little, then tell me everything, starting with that . . . that strange-looking van in my driveway!"

Alex laughed at the image of the half-rusted gray van now parked in the neat, middle-class Phoenix neighborhood. "It is bad, isn't it?"

"Even worse in the light of day."

"It moves," Alex avowed with a touch of respect. "It brought me all the way from Hermosillo, Mexico. Via Jessup, Arizona."

Carol frowned and set a steaming grilled cheese sandwich before Alex. "Jessup? Are you crazy? That's a little out of your way, isn't it?"

"By a few hundred miles." Alex smiled ruefully. "I drove all night. You won't believe what yesterday was like."

"Try me," Carol advised with a wry smile.

"I've known you a long time, Alex Julian, and I know you're capable of most anything you set your head to."

With small moments of loving laughter to punctuate the piercing emotion, Alex related her entire story. When she'd finished, Carol said, "Alex, forgive me, but what you did in Jessup is one of the dumbest things you've ever done! Do you know how dangerous that was? Why, they could have done anything to you, dumped you off in the desert, and no one would have known to look for you! Nobody knew where you were!"

"Yep, I know. But Carol, try to understand my desperation. I was so close to finding her too."

"I'm trying to understand that, but you can't throw away all caution in order to accomplish this. Why, I'm surprised at you. You've never been so—"

"Daring?" Alex finished dryly.

"Yes, or reckless or imprudent."

"Well, I was desperate, Carol. I lied to find out the information I needed, and I would have gladly paid any fee they set if Jenni had been there. I would've paid it and walked away and never breathed a word to anyone about their illegal activities. That's how desperate I was—still am, I guess." She paused to let out a long sigh. "Are you shocked that I would say such a thing?"

"Yes," Carol conceded. "I understood that you had hired someone to find Jenni. Someone to take these personal risks for you."

"Nick? Ha! He has his own illegal games to play!"

"Alex, I thought—"

"Well, you thought wrong!" Alex responded irritably. She rose and paced the floor, talking as she went. "Nick is too busy to care about us. He has some kind of operation in Mexico involving a helicopter and hauling strange cargoes around. Illegal contraband is his game. Lots of money in that one. Oh, for a while he was interested in finding Jenni for me, but now I realize that he was only interested in me."

"Is that so bad?"

"Yes, because Jenni is very important to me. At the end, Nick and his partner went rushing off in the middle of the night, right when we were waiting to hear news of Jenni being transported across the border! The man accused of taking her told the police they were heading for Jessup. But would Nick fly me up there? Hell, no! He had other business. That's why I left—because Nick wouldn't help any more."

"What were his reasons for not flying to Jessup?"

Alex shrugged. "He said we couldn't find her, that it was better to wait until the Customs agents called, saying they had her in custody. He kept talking about the chain of connections and a ring and going all the way to the end. I knew if we did that, we'd lose track of her in the States. And see? She's already gone! God only knows where Jenni is at this moment!"

Carol poured them more coffee and asked

thoughtfully, "Is it possible that Nick was right? After all, you didn't find her in Jessup."

"No, he— Oh, I don't know! I don't know who's right! And at this point I don't care. I just know he refused to help anymore."

"Alex, sometimes it's best to wait things out."

"Are you defending Nick?" Alex snapped incredulously. "You don't know anything about this."

"No. I'm just trying to look at it from all angles, as an observer. He had to have reasons for his decisions."

"He did? Well, let me give them to you!" Alex pressed her fist against her mouth for a long minute, feeling the pain all the way to her heart. Her words, though, were bitter.

"What we had in Mexico was a fling, an affair. Just as simple as that. Only I—stupid fool that I am—I fell head over heels in love with him! So you were right about that, Carol. But I made the fatal mistake of telling him I was in love. When I did that, whatever we had fell apart. Scared him off. Plus, he stopped looking for Jenni. I should have kept my mouth shut. Obviously I'm no good at these games. When I go to bed with someone, I'm serious about him, and when I'm in love with someone, I tell him."

"Do you still feel that way?"

Alex smiled sadly. "Do I still love him? Of course. One miserable day can't change that. But I realize now that it's completely one-sided. Don't they say there's a thin line between loving

242

and hating? Maybe I'll slip over that line one day. It'll make it easier."

"Do you *know* he doesn't love you?"

Alex nodded silently. "A man like Nick—a man for hire—can't love."

"I wish you'd give yourself some time to think about this. Now is not a good time to make sweeping statements, especially about love. You're still too distraught over Jenni and all you've been through in the last twenty-four hours."

"I don't need more time for Nick but I feel that I'm running out of time for Jenni." She paced again, pausing to take a deep breath and think. "All right, so I messed up the relationship with Nick. Assuming he was right, maybe he knew what he was talking about when he wanted me to wait for Jenni to be found. And I've screwed that up too."

"He may be tracing her down right now, Alex."

"Boy, you're sure giving him a lot of credit, Carol. You just don't seem to understand. Nick was only looking for Jenni as a way to get to me. He's actually involved in some type of criminal activity."

"I simply find it hard to believe you'd become entangled with someone like that, Alex. Tell me more about this Nick."

"Well, he's tall, a little too rugged to be called handsome. Dark hair and mustache. He has a wonderful take-charge attitude that appealed to me in the beginning. I thought he would find

Jenni when the police failed. I believed he could do anything. Foolish notion. Too idealistic."

"You needed help," Carol added, "and had to have confidence in someone. I can understand that."

"Nick and Juancho, his partner, make quite a pair," Alex volunteered with a shy smile. "Between the two of them, you would think they could accomplish anything! Juancho is shorter but built like a brick wall. He has a fabulous Pancho Villa mustache, out to here." She motioned to each side of her face. "And curly on the tips. They remind me of two black panthers on the prowl. Dangerous."

Carol observed the hint of admiration in Alex's voice whenever she spoke of Nick. She obviously had strong feelings for the man but whether they were love, Carol wasn't sure. "I wouldn't give up on Nick yet, Alex. You still have to go back sometime and move your things out of his apartment. Maybe you could talk to him then. Get some answers to your questions about his activities."

Alex shook her head stubbornly. "I'll be better off never seeing Nick Diamond again, and I'm afraid I'll never see Jenni, either. My one consolation is that Margaret Hannah, the woman who keeps the babies in Jessup said Jenni would be sent to a good home. She'll be loved—" Alex halted, a catch in her voice at the thought.

"Now you're talking like you're defeated!"

"Well?" Alex shrugged. "I've lost them both. I don't know where to turn. I've reached a dead-end, Carol."

"Sometimes what looks like the end is really the beginning, Alex. Don't give up yet. There is someone here in Phoenix who is in a position to help you. He works for the governor's office now and would be perfectly delighted to assist you in any way he could. He knows a lot of people, has lots of connections."

Alex's eyes widened. "Not Jack Kingsley!"

"Yes, Jack. He would like nothing better than to help you, Alex."

"Oh, no he wouldn't, Carol! He came to see me in Mexico and I, well . . . let's just say I sent him away angry. Uh-uh! I couldn't possibly!"

"Then you're a fool." Carol folded her arms and spoke candidly. "Jack could help you. He has the inside track on details that most people never know. Including crime."

"I just couldn't, Carol!"

"Depends on how desperate you are to find Jenni." Carol cleared their plates off the counter with a flick of her wrist. "The governor's office has assigned a task force to solve children's problems in this state. Additional money has been appropriated for delinquents, runaways, abused and abandoned kids."

"Mexican kids?"

"You're a citizen of this state, Alex. If you made the request, I'm sure he'd listen. I happen to know that Jack is attending a benefit banquet tonight for the Children's Home. It's a fancy affair, black-tie and all, written up in all the papers."

"Come on, Carol," Alex pleaded. "I told you, we parted on less than friendly terms."

"A knock-down, drag-out?"

"No, but—"

"For you, Alex, Jack would do anything. Still. Trust me. He'll be at the Hilton. The gala starts at eight." Carol left the carrot dangling and turned to load the dishwasher.

Trust me. Alex could hear Nick's beseeching tone. *Trust me. Trust me.* Perhaps, if she had trusted him, she wouldn't be facing a dead-end today.

That night, shortly after nine, Alex trotted down the thick-carpeted hall of the Hilton. By waiting until the attendees had been served dinner, she managed to slip into the entrance. Compared to some of her recent escapades this had been quite simple. No lies required. She located the correct banquet hall and decided to wait in the ladies' room until the orchestra started and she could mingle easily with the guests. They were playing "The Impossible Dream" when she decided to make her move. Hope that isn't appropriate, she mused as she sighted her target.

"May I have this dance, sir?"

Jack Kingsley's face showed his complete surprise when he saw Alex. She looked stunning in a deep teal-blue cocktail dress with a sequined bodice. Her blond hair was piled glamorously on her head with a loose tendril or two for softness. A curving side slit revealed just enough thigh to be daring. The dress fit so well, one would never guess she'd borrowed it from Carol.

"Well, do I have to drag you onto the dancefloor or are you going to stand there staring all night?"

"Forgive me, Alex. I'm just so surprised to see you here." Immediately, he took her in his arms and whirled her around the floor. "Hey, you're a knockout in that color. My God, woman, you take my breath away!"

"Does that mean you aren't going to throw me out on my ear for crashing your party?"

"I have other ideas for your ears, babe." He leaned forward and nibbled her left one tenderly. "I thought I left you in Mexico to stay."

"I thought you left angry."

He pursed his lips. "Not angry, Alex. Disappointed."

"Good." She smiled mysteriously. "Maybe an apology will make up for the disappointment." As they danced, Alex admitted how very handsome Jack was with his blond hair stylishly cut. He was impeccably dressed in black tux and cummerbund. He was smooth enough to say the right things every time. It occurred to her that he was being groomed for an eventual state position—perhaps even the governorship—and all she had to do to reestablish their wrecked relationship was say the word. She could do worse.

Yet all she could think of tonight was how he could help her find Jenni.

"Are you in town to stay? Looking for a job?"

She nodded. "Possibly. Right now, though, I'm still looking for Jenni."

"You haven't given up that futile chase?"

She stiffened. "No. The situation has changed since you were in Mexico. We have reason to believe that she was brought into this country, and yet, the trail seems to have stopped at Jessup."

They continued to dance and the band played "You've Lost That Lovin' Feeling." It's true, Alex thought. The only feeling between them was a strained friendship. Nothing stronger.

"Alex, I don't know if it's possible to trace her."

"It is, Jack," she said with conviction. "If you know the right people. And if those people have the right connections."

"People like me? Are you considering using me, Alex?"

She smiled gently. "You know how politics works, Jack. You scratch my back, I'll scratch yours."

"I never thought I'd hear you say that." He shook his head in mock dismay.

You've never seen me desperate, she thought. "Why, Jack, don't tell me that people don't approach you daily for favors. Wouldn't you consider my request, for old time's sake?"

He sighed. "Alex, babe, you know I'd do anything in the world to help you. Honestly, though, I don't think—"

"Listen to me, Jack." Her soft voice hardened slightly. "This isn't the usual political favor that will lean toward big business or overlook a legal violation. This is a very personal matter that will directly affect the life of a very little girl, and mine."

"When you put it that way, how can I refuse? You should know, Alex, I'm as soft-hearted as they come."

She smiled warmly. He said all the right things; now they were getting somewhere. "Jack, there's a group of people, a ring, bringing babies up from Mexico through connections in Arizona."

"Alex, we've all heard those rumors, but no one has been able to substantiate them."

"I can."

"What?" He shifted closer and the orchestra began to play another song. They continued to move together, more by rote than actually dancing. "How?"

"I've been through the system. I can tell you the procedure. I know people, places, names. I could direct you to the very house that keeps the babies until they're sold. I can tell you the method used to slip them over the border."

Her words were shocking. Jack eyed her warily for a moment. "You're serious, aren't you, Alex?"

Her eyes met his like cold steel. "Never been more serious in my life."

"Come over here and let's talk, babe." He led her to a private table and ordered them each a glass of white wine. "Now, tell me everything. When did you find out about this information? And how?"

Alex briefly outlined her experiences the day before in Jessup, carefully omitting names, places, and her vegetable-truck theory for illegally transporting the babies. "Details will be forthcoming if you'll help me, Jack. Please, don't turn me away."

"Is this a form of blackmail, Alex?"

"Call it whatever you like. I have valuable information. In the right hands, it could create quite a stir, and expose international corruption."

"You know I'd like to be the one responsible," Jack admitted. Rubbing the back of his hand thoughtfully over his chin, he considered her story and the accompanying plea. "This will take a little time, but if you can tell me what you claim to know, we can blow this case wide open. It'll have media exposure, the works."

"I only care about finding Jenni."

Without a pause, he concurred. "Yeah, sure, and we'll find Jenni. I'll need some time, maybe a couple of hours. I'll have to contact certain people who aren't in this room tonight. Then you and I need to be able to talk someplace private."

She nodded. "Make it tonight, Jack. We're losing time. Where?"

"Tonight?" He lifted his handsome head so that their eyes met. "My place?" The implication was obvious in his questioning gaze.

She hesitated, knowing what he was asking. *Once more, for old time's sake.* The game was getting tougher for novices to play. Novices like her. How much pride was she willing to swallow for the sake of finding Jenni? Alex's eyes flickered and she forced a confident, "Sure, Jack."

He reached into his pocket and discreetly handed her a key. "I live in a different place now,

Alex. I'll call the doorman and tell him to expect you. You go on over. Make yourself at home. Fix yourself a drink and watch T.V. I'll meet you there in a couple of hours." He jotted the address on his business card, and excused himself.

Alex gazed bleakly at the card. *Okay, kid. You're playing in the big leagues now. Even with old friends, the stakes are high.*

CHAPTER FIFTEEN

Alex felt strange letting herself into Jack's luxurious apartment. She left her purse on the dining table and wandered around his exclusive abode. It was a far cry from the modest place they'd shared when they were both teachers. Of course, his present salary probably exceeded their combined incomes of three years ago. She remembered when they pooled pennies at the end of the month to have enough for a movie.

She entered the bedroom, a spacious room in cool blue tones with subtle, Southwestern accessories. She stared at the king-sized bed and tried to imagine making love to Jack again. That's what he expected, didn't he? But could she? *Impossible*, was her first thought. *Unlikely . . . difficult . . . oh, hell, what am I doing here?*

Alex considered leaving without her information. But where else would she go for help? Using the elegant French phone on the bedside table, she called Carol, saying she probably wouldn't return tonight. And yes, Jack had agreed to help.

There were no questions, no judgmental comments from her friend. Just a tender warning. "Alex, please be careful."

"Sure, Carol."

Alex walked back through the house and slumped on the curved sectional sofa which seemed to go forever around the room. Lifting the small remote-control device, she turned on the T.V. and changed to a dozen channels with the flick of one finger. Such convenience, she thought. And I've just returned from a country that struggles to feed its children.

After a while the waiting grew monotonous and she searched out a pen and paper. Scribbling as fast as she could, Alex filled the page in no time. When finished, she folded it, stuffed it into her purse, then ambled over to the bar. She poured herself a little glass of wine then settled down to late-night T.V. and more waiting. She'd rushed out of Mexico to escape this infernal waiting. For hours she'd waited at the border, waited at Consuela's cafe, waited in the back of the camper. Now here she was, waiting again.

She couldn't help wondering if she would have been better off to wait for Nick. Thoughts of him flooded her, and she could almost see his strong image. She missed his boyish smile, his ability to reassure her, his love. Where was he tonight? What was he doing? Like her, seeking company elsewhere?

Oh, Nick, how could I do this to you? You are really the only man I love. But what a way to prove it! She covered her face with her hands, trying to blot out the guilt that overwhelmed her. She fell asleep curled against plush pillows, dreaming of Nick.

"Is this any way to greet your lover?"

Alex started awake, Nick's name on the tip of her tongue. She opened sleepy eyes to Jack's handsome countenance. "Oh, Jack. Hi."

"Hey, babe, the least you could do is fake enthusiasm to see me." He kissed her nose and walked across the room. "How about a drink?" He rammed a finger into his tie to loosen it.

"No, thanks, Jack. I had some wine. That's probably why I fell asleep." Maybe she should imbibe, after all, she thought. This might be an evening she would want to blot out of her memory. The sound of ice clinking against a glass told her Jack was fixing a drink for himself. She almost said, *Make mine a double*, but something on T.V. caught her eye.

An old Charles Bronson movie was on, and she was struck by the similarities between the rugged movie star and Nick. Not in looks, especially, for Nick was taller, not as leathery, and better looking. Still, Nick did have that scar on his cheek, giving him an appealing ruggedness. The two men moved their bodies alike in an ambling gait, maneuvering broad shoulders as well as long legs. They were both men of action; both had a wide-legged masculine stance that caught a woman's eye. Neither were slick or smooth, but both possessed a take-charge attitude. She stared at the screen, spellbound. Why hadn't she trusted Nick to remain in charge of the search for Jenni? If she had, she wouldn't be here tonight.

"Your undivided attention would be appreciated."

"What? Oh, Nick—Jack, sorry," she fumbled inanely. "I was just . . . the movie reminded me of something." She pushed the off button, blacking the screen. "What did you find out?"

"Not much. We'll have to pool our resources to break this case open." He paused to take a sip of double Scotch and to remove his tie. "But I'm convinced, if your information is accurate, we can find that kid for you, Alex." His tux jacket joined the tie across the back of a chair.

"If my information is accurate?" she snapped, now fully awake and leery of what article of clothing he would remove next. "Of course it is! I've been through it! I know every exacting detail. By God, Jack, you promised! Don't try to back out now!"

"All right, all right, Alex. Take it easy." Jack slipped the first two shirt buttons open, to reveal sexy chest curls, and joined her on the sofa. His fingers dug into his shirt pocket. "Tonight what I managed to come up with is a lawyer's name. This man works out of a legitimate office in Ohio. It's been rumored for years that he's involved with such shady deals as this, but no one has been able to pin anything on him. Now, maybe we can."

Alex's hand shook with excitement as she took the slip of paper from Jack's hand. This name meant the possible end of the long search for Jenni. "Jack, how can I thank you? This is wonderful. It's something positive. A link."

255

"Well, as I said, it's a start in the right direction. My opinion is that by working with the FBI, we'll be able to track her down for you. Whether you'll want to keep her at that time, is another question."

"Oh, no, Jack. There's no question about that. I want her!" Alex rose and walked to the sleek mahogany dining table. Digging inside her purse, she pulled out the yellow sheet of legal-sized paper, filled from bottom to top. She handed it to Jack. "Here's my part of the bargain." The verbalized part, she thought miserably.

Jack took the paper and scanned it. Listed were the names of the bar, the pharmacy, druggist, restaurant, codeword, methods of travel—everything Alex could remember about her day in Jessup.

A certain light filled his eyes as he read. "My God, Alex! I can't believe it! You are amazing! Cabbage Patch Dolls! This is . . . this is just great, babe!" He took her in his arms and pulled her close for a kiss. The act of placing his lips on hers elicited no response from Alex, neither inviting warmth nor cool rejection. Nothing. She remained still, compliant and passive, willing to play the game out to its conclusion. After all, she'd made a deal.

Jack broke free from the kiss and stepped away. "It's all right, Alex. Obviously, this has been a hectic week for you. Go on home and get some rest. I'll work on this tomorrow and we'll get on this case first thing Monday morning."

Her eyes widened. "Jack?"

He nodded and winked. "For old time's sake, babe. Go on."

Relief flooded her entire being and Alex tried not to show the joy she felt. Instead, she just smiled.

"It doesn't take a genius to see that it's over between us, Alex. I'm sorry, but it's true."

"I hope we can still be friends, Jack."

"Of course we will. Why, with this information you've given me, I'll be at the top of the governor's list. It'll boost my career tremendously, Alex. I'm grateful to you, babe. I'll always remember it. And when this is all settled and you're ready for a job, let me know. I'll get you something exciting, anywhere in the state."

"Thanks, Jack." Impulsively, Alex stepped forward and kissed his cheek.

"Hey," he grinned. "That's more warmth than I've felt from you all night!"

She grinned back. "If this leads to finding Jenni, you ain't seen nothin' yet! I'm afraid I'll be hugging everybody in sight!"

"I hope I'm around when that happens."

"I won't forget all you've done, Jack." She smiled wistfully, picked up her purse, and headed for the door.

"Hey, Alex, do you think I should take you home? This is pretty hot information. It might not be safe for you to be out alone."

"Don't be ridiculous, Jack. What could possibly happen? I'm just parked on the corner under a light, and I only have to go a few miles to Carol's house."

"You staying with your old friend, Carol Weymeyer? I remember her from ASU. Well, okay." Although he nodded, there was a reluctance in his voice.

"Thanks, Jack. For everything."

"See you Monday."

Alex's heart sang with joy as she rode the elevator down six floors. Her thoughts turned unavoidably to Nick and she wished with all her might she hadn't left him in Mexico. She wished she could share this moment with him. When all this was over, maybe she'd go back to Hermosillo as Carol suggested and demand some answers. By then, maybe she would know her own heart.

Within moments of leaving the secure building where Jack lived, Alex knew she was being followed.

CHAPTER SIXTEEN

Alex could hear him, sense him, feel his ominous power, before she actually saw him. She glanced quickly over one shoulder and caught sight of a hulking form moving along the semilighted sidewalk. He wore a suit and a fedora pulled down over his eyes. And he was massive.

She considered running back to Jack's secure building but her follower was too close now and stood between her and the building. She could scream, but there was no one on the street after midnight. Her best bet was to dash for the van parked at the corner. It seemed a mile away.

Just as Alex broke into a sprint, she heard her name called. "Alex! Wait!"

But she didn't. Adrenaline pumped through her veins, supplying a surge of fright-engendered energy that spurred her on.

Suddenly, steely arms clamped around hers, pinning them to her sides. Alex fought like a wildcat. "Let go of me!" She kicked. "You brute!" She twisted in his grip. "Turn me loose! Help!" she screamed.

"Señorita, please! Shut up!"

Alex froze stock-still. She recognized that voice, the distinctive Mexican accent!

"Alex, it's Juancho!" he grated against her ear.

She slumped against him, faint from relief and gushing adrenaline. "Juancho? You scared the hell out of me!"

"Sorry, señorita." He pushed her into the van and slid his considerable bulk in the driver's seat. "Didn't mean to scare you. I tried to get your attention to identify myself and I didn't want to attract the attention of others."

"Then you shouldn't have grabbed me like that." Alex pressed a hand to her pounding heart.

"I see that now," he admitted with a wry smile. Some fighter, this woman of Nick's, he thought.

She leaned over to get a closer look at him. "Why are you wearing that ridiculous suit and hat, Juancho? And where is your magnificent *mustache?*"

He grinned proudly. "This is my new disguise. Don't I look respectable in a three-piece suit? We had to get out of Mexico quick. Too hot! Now we're waiting for things to cool down."

"Juancho, I don't understand. Do you mean—"

"Nick will explain." He started the van and proceeded through town.

"Nick? He's here? In Phoenix?" Her racing heart almost lurched into her throat.

"Yes. He wants to see you, señorita."

"He does? I'm surprised. I thought he'd be furious because I took off without telling him, and in his van."

Juancho nodded. "He was."

"What's he doing here in Phoenix?"

"I told you, Alex. It got too hot in Mexico. And he wanted to find you before . . . before you did anything else."

"What do you mean, it's too hot in Mexico? And how did you find me here?"

"Through Carol Weymeyer."

"How did you know about her? Did you follow me there?"

"No. We knew about her in Mexico. Through your letters."

"You intercepted my mail?" Alex bellowed indignantly. "How dare you!"

He shrugged. "In the line of duty, of course."

"Duty? What duty?" she demanded, furious at the invasion of her privacy.

"Nick will explain," he said again.

Alex stewed quietly for a moment, trying to gain control of her anger and decide what warranted the intrusion of one's mail. "You've been following me tonight, Juancho?"

"Yes."

"Why?"

"For Nick."

"Then you know where I went? And why?" She realized it didn't look good that she had emerged from Jack's apartment.

"You went to the Hilton and talked to Jack Kingsley, aide to the governor," Juancho droned. "Later, you met him at his apartment."

"It isn't the way it looks, Juancho. He's an old friend."

"And lover."

"Not any longer. All that is in the past."

Juancho shrugged ponderous shoulders. "It doesn't matter to me, señorita."

"I know how you work, Juancho. You report everything to Nick. And I want to set the record straight. Jack gave me some valuable information tonight that will be helpful in the search for Jenni. I have the name of a lawyer in Ohio who takes these kids and sells them to desperate couples. Then he legalizes this whole sordid business. He may even know where Jenni is at this very minute!"

Juancho pulled to a stop in front of a modest motel. "Nick will be interested to hear this."

"He's in there?" she asked incredulously, and suddenly felt reluctant. "Are you sure he wants to see me? After . . . everything?"

"Yes. Very much."

"Juancho?" She looked at him hesitantly. "I . . . I don't know if I want to go in there. You see, I . . . that is, I don't think I should start something again that can't be finished."

"He insists on seeing you, señorita. You must go. . . ." Juancho paused. He didn't want to sound too emphatic with this strong-willed lady but he remembered Nick's ranting and raving about Alex on the entire trip from Hermosillo, how he'd fluctuated between insane worry and vicious anger that she would put herself in such dangerous situations. Oh, yes, *El Capitán* was sick . . . in the heart. And she definitely would see him if Juancho had to force the issue.

"Juancho, maybe I shouldn't—" Alex was torn.

262

Perhaps she should put some distance between herself and this man she hadn't trusted. She knew she couldn't trust herself to stay out of his arms if she saw him again.

The burly Mexican man sighed. There was no way he could tell Nick she had refused to see him. He would be a wild man! *Por favor, señorita.* Go in there. He is injured."

"Injured? Hurt? How?"

"He was shot."

"Shot?" The image of Nick clutching his ribs and staggering down a narrow Mexican street flashed through her head. "I knew it! Those who live by the gun, die by it! I knew he was doing dangerous stuff. That's what you get when you're involved with illegal activities! Oh, damn, Juancho! Here I am rattling on—how is he?"

"He'll be okay. Just a shoulder wound. But he's weak."

"You're right. I should see him. I want to give him a piece of my mind."

Juancho held out the key. "Two-seventeen. Upstairs."

Alex snatched the key and flew up the outside staircase. She stopped for a moment to lean over the rail and call "Thank you, Juancho!"

She waved and Juancho ducked. Damn woman! Despite all his careful efforts to remain incognito, to hide the injured Nick and slip this woman in to see him, she now blew any cover he thought he had! Juancho immediately moved the van to an obscure location and continued his vigilance. Tomorrow they would be gone and he could sleep.

Alex burst into the room. The two days since they'd seen each other seemed like two years. Emotions flashed in their eyes—fury, irritation, passion, love—who could know which was dominant in that split second? Certainly not Alex. Maybe she felt all of those and more. Her indigo eyes flared then caressed Nick's entire length as he lay stretched out on the bed. She wanted to touch him, all of him but stood there drinking in his masculinity, just staring. He sat shirtless, leaning almost casually against the headboard of the bed, the white bandage on his shoulder contrasting with his bronzed skin. Her eyes went to that bandage and she swallowed hard. Damn him, anyway! How could he get himself so hurt? It was crazy, but that injury made her mad!

"Nick—"

Nick's alert dark eyes darted over Alex. Her blond hair spilled rebelliously from the pompadour, her sequined dress was twisted and somewhat frumpy. God! She was a beauty! He sighed and the breath seemed to come from deep within his soul. After all his fretting and worrying, here she was, safe and all in one gorgeous piece. He wanted to grab her and cuddle her gently and spank her, at the same time! They began speaking, but not to each other.

"Alex—"

"Nick, how did this happen?"

"Alex, I have been worried sick about you. Why did you leave like that? I told you to wait."

"You shaved your mustache! Just like Juancho! Why?"

"I had to see you tonight, Alex. Had to know that you were safe."

"Did you have to follow me? Scare me half to death? Inspect my mail?"

"That was a damn-fool thing you did, leaving by yourself."

"How can you say *I'm* foolish? Look at you! All shot up!"

"Traveling alone across Mexico is bad enough. But getting involved with that ring in Jessup was dumb!"

"Speaking of dumb, if you hadn't been involved with illegal smuggling, you never would have gotten shot!"

"Alex, those people are dangerous. And now that you've seen them and can identify them, you're in even greater danger."

"So we can hide out together? Is that what you're suggesting?" She smiled devilishly. "You should have seen me in action, Nick. You, of all people, would have been proud. I had a pretty good story going with them. I can lie almost as good as you can."

"I've never been so scared in my life! I should have gone after you! Made you come back! Dammit, woman, when you got into that camper, I almost came unglued!"

She looked at him askance. "How did you know that?"

"I was watching your every move!"

"How?"

"I just was."

"Oh, so the devil has ways and means! If you were watching, why didn't you come on out and help me? I needed a fake husband anyway. I had to invent a story about where he was and why he wasn't with me. Pretty good, too, if I do say so myself."

"That's the problem. You were doing so well by yourself, the decision was made to let you continue. Anyway, we'd never been all the way through their system, like you were. But that doesn't mean I was at ease with you getting so close to them. You were in too much danger."

"How could you let me go through all that hell? You knew Jenni wasn't there."

"It wasn't entirely my decision." His eyes softened. "But now we have them, Alex. Every stop you made. It's all on film."

"Nick, I don't know what you're talking about. Why would you take pictures?"

"That's the trouble. We've been talking too much. Come here, Alex." He paused and his voice lowered. "I want to touch you . . . to feel you close to me." He reached out his right arm.

Drawn by a power greater than her own common sense, Alex slid next to him on the bed. She ran her hand across the sizzling skin of his bare chest, relishing the soft curls nestling between the rounded muscles. She followed the dark trail down to his navel. "Oh, Nick, I've missed you so. This illegal stuff you're mixed up with has to stop! I love you too much to stand back and watch you risk your neck like this. What if you'd been caught? Or killed?"

His lips caressed her cheek and found her eager, pouting lips. "I think I am caught, *mi vida.* In your loving trap." His near-savage kiss halted further conversation. Nick's longing for her was wild, untamed, and she could feel it. Even with one arm in a sling, he managed to snare her, body and soul. There was nothing weak about his ardor.

Alex responded with unrestrained eagerness, clasping him to her, pressing herself to his bareness, running a stockinged toe along his leg. She yearned to feel his heated flesh next to hers, burned for his passion, hungered for his love.

"I want you now, Alex. Need you." His hands touched her through the dress, and she felt as though she had on a suit of armor.

She craved to have his skin in direct contact with hers. "Oh, yes, Nick. I want to feel you next to me. I want you to be a part of me!" Her hands dug feverishly at his snap and zipper.

She helped him scoot the jeans down, then slithered out of her sequined dress and dropped it to the floor. She hovered over him, bathing him with kisses and murmuring words of passion and love. She watched with feminine delight and anticipation as his maleness burgeoned before her eyes. Oh, how she loved this renegade.

Awash with the renewed flush of love, Alex caressed every inch of her injured scoundrel. Nick only had to lay back and respond to her fevered kisses and erotic caresses, and respond he did. Neon lights flickering outside reflected on her shimmering softness as she moved over him. Her breasts were firm and round, luscious ecru globes, the valley between them beaded with moisture. Her hips undulated sensuously, driving him crazy with their arousing promise.

With an impassioned thrust, she forged them together. The impact left them both breathless for a moment and they lay very still, relishing the mingling of their bodies, the merging of their souls. Alex raised herself and began rocking with the ancient dance of love, methodically increasing the tempo of the choreography until, with a sharp cry, the crescendo crumbled all around them.

Finally, with a small stirring of flesh against flesh, the dance ended. Alex slid her slick body beside Nick's, still clinging to him, reluctant to relinquish her hold. Yet she no longer clasped him in her feminine warmth, no longer felt his masculine strength inside her. It was a feeling of definite emptiness.

"Nick, I can't deny my love for you. It goes beyond anything I can control."

"Alex, *mi vida*, you set me on fire."

"I want to love you, Nick, but not like this. Injured. Hiding from the law in some motel on the edge of town."

"Alex, my sweet, naive darling. Don't you know whose side I'm on by now? I'm with you, always have been."

"Nick, I'm no good at this Bonnie and Clyde stuff. It's good for jokes, but not in real life. I can't stand the thought of you hiding out or risking your neck. I want you safe with me."

"I'm not hiding from the law, Alex." He chuckled low. "I'm trying to lay low in case some of my recent clients hold a grudge."

"What do you mean? They're after you from Mexico?"

"Maybe. You never know, when you've been playing both sides against the middle, like we have."

"Both sides? You mean you haven't been doing anything illegal?" She puzzled over his words. "But the birds—that was illegal. That had to be, especially with have. Furthermore, why are we here, if he ing out?"

"I can see I have a lot of explaining to do."

"Apparently, you do."

In the darkness of the motel room, with his good arm securely around Alex's bare form, Nick began: "For your safety, I couldn't tell you much. Juancho and I are working as undercover agents for a special force of our joint governments. Junacho, for the Mexican *Federales;* I, for the U.S. Federal Government. We infiltrated smuggling rings to detect various schemes. Both countries are losing millions of dollars each year in contraband. We attempted to put a stop to it. But, damn, I'm afraid it's like a finger in the dike. Now our sting operation is finished."

Strangely, Alex started to laugh. She felt slightly delirious, even giddy in her relief. "I don't know whether to be angry that you didn't

trust me enough to tell me or completely relieved that I haven't fallen in love with an outlaw
trying to hide from the law."

"It wasn't a matter of trust, Alex. I was instructed to tell no one. Juancho was even forbidden to tell his wife details, only that it was important. It's difficult when your business supersedes
your personal life. I could only hope that some
day you'd understand why I wasn't totally honest
with you. I felt helpless when I could see you
slipping away from me. There wasn't a damn
thing I could do about it, either. Nothing short of
believe me, I considered it."
strain me now." She nuzzled his
teasingly. "In spite of everything, Nick, I
did trust you. Because I loved you so. Now, I love
you even more."

He caressed her lips with his, tenderly relishing their taste. "I love you, too, Alex. . . ." He
admitted it gruffly, almost reluctantly, then
pressed their bodies together, seeking complete
absolution in the closeness.

"Hold me, Nick. Don't ever let me go."

"All night long," he mumbled sleepily, and
kissed her hair.

"Not just tonight. Forever."

"Forever."

"Nick? I want . . ." Her finger erotically
traced his upper lip.

"Tomorrow, darling."

"Nick, I want you to let your mustache grow
back again."

"Later, darling. Go to sleep."

Alex smiled happily and drifted in contentment. Her beloved had returned to her. For how long, she didn't know, but right now she didn't care. She only knew he was here with her, and had vowed his love. To Alex, his love was all that mattered. She memorized the gruff way he said it. *I love you . . . Alex . . .*

They were awakened early the next morning by a loud pounding. Nick rose stiffly and spoke earnestly to Juancho through a small opening in the door. With a grateful nod, he accepted two steaming cups of coffee. He took a deep breath and turned back to the still-snoozing Alex. An increased flow of adrenaline pumped in his veins. The flush of excitement accelerated his brain. His blood quickened. The wheels were in motion. The whole thing was coming down! The circus tent would fold today!

"Get up, Alex. Here's coffee. We have a busy day ahead!"

"What time is it?" she groaned through kiss-swollen lips and buried her face in the pillow.

He set the coffee cups on the bedside table and braced an arm on either side of her. "Alex." His voice was unusually gentle. "Turn over. I have something very important to tell you."

She lay perfectly still and mumbled, "Tell me you love me, Nick. And that we won't go on meeting like this in motels."

"I love you, Alex. I promise we won't continue to meet in cheap motels. Now, come on . . . I think we've found Jenni."

Alex's heart froze. A chill ran through her en-

271

tire body, followed by a flash of fire. There was a touch of exhilaration, a moment of depression. Her flesh went hot then cold. Her feelings soared then plummeted. Suddenly she wanted to cry out, to shout for joy.

She'd been through this expectancy and building of hopes so many times before, she steeled herself. The pain of disappointment was doubled, *tripled*, when anticipation was high. She refused to believe it, to build up false expectations. Yet Nick had never said those words: *I think we've found her.*

She flipped over, her indigo eyes round and full. "Nick?"

He nodded silently. "We think she's in Ohio."

"Ohio?" *Was it possible?* Alex swallowed hard and closed her eyes, trying to force back the gush of hot tears that burned the insides of her lids. "You . . . you've found her?" Did she dare believe it?

"I'll explain the details on the plane. We have an early flight to catch. We need to get you some decent clothes. A sequined dress is a little too much for the occasion." His tone was gently cajoling, urging.

Alex scooted up to a sitting position. She felt paralyzed by a strange combination of optimism and dread fear.

Nick shoved a cup of coffee into her hands with tight-lipped orders. "Drink. And hurry."

"Nick, I'm scared. Oh, God, I'm scared."

His voice took on a strict matter-of-factness. "Alex, get a hold on yourself. We need you to

272

identify the child if it's Jenni, and to press charges. You are the crucial person who will break this ring up. We're going to nail them, from the scumbag who picked Jenni up off the street in Mexico to the lawyer who provides legal adoptions to innocent couples. Now, come on!"

He propelled Alex through the motions of a shower, then Juancho drove them to Carol's for a change of clothes. The meeting between Carol and Nick was disappointingly brief. However, they both understood there were more important things to do today.

As they rushed out the door, Carol rem~~~~~ Alex, "Let me know what happens. Pl~~~~ And the guns. me. I'll be waiting to hear from y~~~~ ~~~~ with this injury you

Alex turned back to her ~~~~ ~~~~ ~~~~ not hid- ~~~~ ith this ~~~~ will. Thanks."

"Good luck," Carol whispered hoarsely. Sudden tears sprang to her eyes as she watched the rickety gray van drive away.

As they approached Sky Harbor Airport, Alex dug frantically in the back of the van. Finally she found her prize, the item she'd dragged all the way from Mexico for this very moment.

Almost in a daze, she kissed Juancho's ruddy cheek. "Thanks, Juancho, for everything."

"Bring back *la niña, señorita.*"

She nodded, unable to answer.

Nick hurried her down the concourse just as the loudspeaker was announcing their flight number. Alex boarded the plane with a frayed but well-loved teddy bear tucked under one arm.

CHAPTER SEVENTEEN

The low drone of the jet's engines was strangely comforting. *Closer and closer,* Alex kept repeating.

"How did you get this lawyer's name?"

Alex handed the slip of paper to Nick. "From Jack Kingsley. He said this lawyer in Ohio had been suspected of shady dealing for a number of years but they couldn't pin anything on him."

"Now they can," Nick muttered sardonically. "With your testimony, Alex, they can put him and the entire ring away." Nick folded the paper and stuffed it in his pocket. "Away for good."

Alex pondered for a moment. "Including Margaret?"

"Who's Margaret?"

"Margaret Hannah. The woman who keeps the babies in Jessup."

"Oh, yes. Definitely. Her too."

"Nick, she . . . she believes she is doing the right thing, finding a loving home for these kids."

"Is she?"

Alex took a deep breath. "I don't know. She

doesn't mistreat the kids. She takes care of them."

"The law doesn't have a heart, Alex," Nick affirmed stoutly. "It's against the law to steal babies and sell them."

"I know. But she didn't actually steal them herself."

"She's an accomplice, Alex." He sounded tough and unyielding.

"Yes, I realize that." Alex studied Nick's face. Now, without the mustache, the scar on his cheek stood out more clearly and she wondered how he got it. His eyes were steady and alert. But she still couldn't read anything there. He was trained not to reveal feelings. Was he also trained not to feel emotions? "Nick, is it all happening today? On a Sunday?"

"Depends." He left unsaid the deciding factor —*if Jenni was found.* "Otherwise, it could be tomorrow or the next day."

"Then you knew about the lawyer all along?"

"Sure. He's on our list of suspects. But as Jack said, until now we didn't have anything that would stick, or anyone to file charges. You see, it's difficult if not downright impossible for a poor Mexican woman to pursue her missing child into the States. Now, with you to press charges, Alex, we'll slam them all behind bars until they're old and gray."

"If you knew about this lawyer, my talk with Jack was for nothing." And my risk, she thought.

"Not really. It always helps to have a politician on your side."

"Nick, I don't know if he's on our side, but he knows everything about this case. He knows about Jenni being taken in Mexico, about Teresa, and I gave him every detail of what happened in Jessup. Even names, places, all about the Cabbage Patch Dolls."

"That's okay, Alex. We'll contact Arizona state officials as soon as we land. I'm sure we'll have their complete cooperation on this. We don't want anything done there until arrests have been made here. We're after the head honchos of the ring. After that, everyone else will fall into place. The rest are just pawns, anyway."

"Nick, if . . . that is, could you make sure the Arizona investigation includes Jack? Since he knows all about the ring in Jessup, and in a way, had a hand in helping to find Jenni, he should participate in bringing the accused to justice. Don't you think so?"

Nick glanced warily at her but didn't say anything.

"Please, Nick. Jack's an old friend and I promised him. Of course, I had no idea this would happen today. I thought he would have to do it."

"An old friend, huh?"

"*Just* an old friend, Nick. I feel I owe him this, for old time's sake."

Nick answered tightly, "Sure, Alex. As long as this is all you owe him."

"It is." She slid her hand into Nick's and murmured softly, "I love you, and I'm very glad you're with me this time. The waiting has been hard, but alone, it's hell. I'm nervous about what this day will bring . . . or won't."

He leaned over and kissed her serious lips. "Put a smile on that beautiful face, my darling. This is going to be a happy day, and we're going to see it through, together."

Her lips quivered into a faint smile, and she gripped his hand tightly. The plane started its descent over Columbus, Ohio.

The next hour was a blur in Alex's memory. It was funny how she remembered specifics of the accident that took Teresa's life. Colors, smells, individual faces. But today her focus was toward events to come, on one little brown-faced child.

FBI agents in three-piece suits with walkie-talkies attached to their belts and, she was sure, guns hidden beneath their armpits, met the plane. Introductions were made but names flew immediately out of Alex's head. She was whisked through the airport into a waiting car, and escorted through the city. Since it was Sunday, traffic was light and they zipped along at a rapid clip. Alex was sure they were exceeding speed limits but guessed the FBI could do that when they were on a hot trail.

She should be excited, she thought, but other emotions took precedence; mostly fear. What if . . .

She sat stiffly in the backseat, looking neither right nor left, not caring where they were going. She didn't need to memorize this trip. Nick was here. She spoke very little and clutched the frayed teddy bear. Alex was acutely aware of

Nick's presence, of his concern for her, of his love. It was a strong feeling, like warm vibes, and it gave her strength to keep on with this frustrating chase. She prayed this time it wouldn't be futile.

Finally the car pulled to a stop before a house. It was a typical house, a place in suburbia with neighbors and a car parked in the driveway. Alex wondered if the neighbors had any idea what was going on here. Two more cars pulled up behind them. Suddenly FBI agents with walkie-talkies drawn were everywhere. It's like a movie, Alex mused, feeling almost as if she were detached from the action and watching the scene on an ultra-wide screen.

But she was very much a part of the action in this scenario. She was ushered up the front steps and events whirled faster than ever. Flashes of badges . . . startled cries . . . the drone of rights being read. Alex moved past the doorway —was shoved past, actually—and began a room to room search.

This place, unlike the quiet one at Jessup, was a busy hub of activity and noise. A T.V. blared a game show to no audience in the den. Someone in the kitchen was diligently filling a row of baby bottles with formula, and a radio played rock music in the corner.

Several women who obviously took care of the children scurried out, possibly trying to escape. Didn't they know the exits would be blocked? Alex's heart pounded as she recalled Jenni's small cherubic face.

"There's a bedroom in here." Nick motioned and led the way.

She practically ran into the room but halted with a sharp gasp. Two infants had been sleeping, but with the noise of the invasion, their naps were disturbed. One raised his head, took one look at Alex and Nick, and began to cry. That prompted the other one to join in the wailing.

Alex grew frantic. "Oh, God, Nick! She isn't here!"

"Let's look upstairs."

Alex bounded up the staircase and reached the second floor ahead of Nick. Someone pushed past her, causing her to drop the teddy bear. She ignored it. *Where? Where is she?* "Jenni! Jenni!"

There were other infants in the upstairs bedrooms, and several toddlers in another room. As Alex rushed from one room to another, she left a trail of upset and crying children. *Brown eyes! Brown eyes! Where are you?*

It seemed that every child in the place was screaming. Then the cacophony died away and Alex heard only one.

Only one small voice shrilled above all the rest. *"Mamacita! Mamacita!"*

"Jenni!"

Wildly, Alex grabbed the child up in her arms, squeezing her small body, laughing and crying at the same time. They swirled around and around, dancing in a circle. All the miserable days and sleepless nights and weeks of searching were compressed into that one magic moment of hearing Jenni squeal with laughter.

279

"Mamacita! Mamacita!"

Nick watched the scene for a moment then turned away, embarrassed by the rush of emotion he felt. No one saw him wipe away the unbidden tears that formed in his golden-flecked panther's eyes. If Alex had been watching him at that moment, she would have known he hadn't lost touch with his feelings. And she would have seen the love clearly written on his usually stoic face.

Tough and ruthless as he was, Nick had never experienced such absolute joy nor felt such deep gratitude as he did while watching Alex whirling the dark curly-haired child in her arms. His feelings for the two were cemented forever in that moment.

When Alex calmed down, she turned an ecstatic, tear-stained face to Nick. "Come here. I want you to meet Jenni."

The child kept her chubby arms tightly around Alex's neck, but lifted her head to gaze curiously at the large man who stood there, clumsily holding a frayed teddy bear.

"Jenni, this is Nick. He helped me find you today. Can you say 'Hello, Nick'?"

Jenni gazed steadily, silently at him, then her dark eyes dropped to the familiar teddy bear he held.

Nick smiled and offered her the toy. "Is this yours, Jenni? He's been looking for you a long time. And so have we. Thank God you're safe. Would you like to hug him? He's pretty lonesome."

Her little brown hand tentatively reached out for the teddy. Jenni clutched the bear tightly and snuggled it next to her heart. "My bear," she said possessively. Then she looked up into Nick's soft, tawny eyes. *"Gracias,* Nick."

"De nada," he mumbled, thinking he might melt on the spot. He touched her chubby golden cheek affectionately, and she bashfully ducked her head against Alex's shoulder.

He spoke gently to Jenni but his words were directed to Alex. "You'd better get used to having me around, Jenni, because I expect to be your adoptive father, if I can persuade your adoptive mother to marry me."

"Nick!" Alex exclaimed, startled. They had never discussed what would happen when they found Jenni.

"Sorry, I didn't have time to plan all this with you, Alex. But I can see this little kid needs a father."

"Not half as much as I need a husband," she said softly, with a happy smile.

"Is that a proposal?"

She nodded, her eyes glistening with fresh tears.

"I accept," he murmured. "I thought you'd never ask." He kissed her lips until a small chubby hand pushed his face away.

"My *mamacita!*"

He glared at the little girl and said teasingly, "So you want to play possessive, huh? We'll see who wins this game. Don't forget, I'm the biggest, kid."

281

Alex laughed, still somewhat giddy. "You said it! You're the biggest kid!"

He wiggled his eyebrows. "She gets the teddy bear at night and, *mamacita*, I get you!"

Alex smiled warmly, tears still evident in her indigo eyes. "Nick, thank you for not giving up on her . . . on us."

"I wouldn't have missed this moment for anything in the world, Alex. Now both of you have me in your clutches, which is exactly where I want to be. Come on. We have a date with the local police and the FBI. You have some identifying to do. File some charges. Sign papers. Then we can go home."

"Where's home, Nick?"

"First, I figure we'll have to return to Hermosillo to start proceedings to adopt Jenni legally."

"While we're there, do you think Padre Ramón would be willing to perform a wedding?"

"I think he would be glad to make all this legal . . ." Nick smiled as they started downstairs. "And to give this child some parents. Then we'd both better consider settling down. After all, we're a family now. I'm tired of apartments and moving around and living out of boxes. It's time we had a house."

"And a decent car!" Alex laughed. "My, my, how domesticated you've become in just the last few minutes, Mr. Diamond."

"See what you do to me, woman? I won't be satisfied until you're Mrs. Diamond. There'll be no more holding back on love, Alex . . . for the three of us." His lips sought hers again and his long arms embraced both Alex and Jenni.

This time, the little girl hugged him back.

Hermosillo, Mexico
June

Dear Carol,

Nick and I were married last week. Juancho and my friend Rosemary were our witnesses. I'm sorry you missed the wedding but I'm sure it's one Padre Ramón will always remember. It was very emotional, but not for the usual reasons.

Jenni was a darling little flower girl but she wet her pants halfway through the ceremony and was so embarrassed she cried the rest of the time. We had to shout our "I do's" above her wailing! Family life is a wonderful challenge, huh?

The adoption will take some time, but our lawyer sees no problem. Meanwhile, Nick and I are having a honeymoon for three! Thank God for Rosemary and her husband Sam. They've been baby-sitting with Jenni to give us a little privacy. Believe me, though, we can't stand to let her out of our sight for long, now that we finally have her back!

We'll be seeing you soon when we move to Phoenix. Nick has sworn off guns. He'll do FBI recruitment and special forces training sessions for both state and federal governments. I've always wanted to run my own pre-school and now seems to be a good time to do it. After all, I am a wife and mother now. And I've never been happier!

Love,
Alex

You can reserve October's Candlelights <u>before</u> they're published!

♥ You'll have copies set aside for *you* the instant they come off press.

♥ You'll save yourself precious shopping time by arranging for *home delivery*.

♥ You'll feel proud and efficient about organizing a system that *guarantees* delivery.

♥ You'll avoid the disappointment of not finding *every* title you want and need.

ECSTASY SUPREMES $2.75 each

☐ 93 ISLAND OF DESIRE, Antoinette Hale 14146-X-15
☐ 94 AN ANGEL'S SHARE, Heather Graham 10350-9-30
☐ 95 DANGEROUS INTERLUDE, Emily Elliott 11659-7-28
☐ 96 CHOICES AND CHANCES, Linda Vail 11196-X-44

ECSTASY ROMANCES $2.25 each

☐ 370 SO MUCH TO GIVE, Sheila Paulos 18190-9-11
☐ 371 HAND IN HAND, Edith Delatush 13417-X-27
☐ 372 NEVER LOVE A COWBOY, Andrea St. John . 16280-7-24
☐ 373 SUMMER STARS, Alexis Hill Jordon 18352-9-23
☐ 374 GLITTERING PROMISES, Anna Hudson 12861-7-53
☐ 375 TOKEN OF LOVE, Joan Grove 18715-X-17
☐ 376 SOUTHERN FIRE, Jo Calloway 18170-4-15
☐ 377 THE TROUBLE WITH MAGIC, Megan Lane . . 18779-6-10

At your local bookstore or use this handy coupon for ordering:

DELL READERS SERVICE—DEPT. BR782A
P.O. BOX 1000, PINE BROOK, N.J. 07058

Please send me the above title(s). I am enclosing $_____ (please add 75¢ per copy to cover postage and handling). Send check or money order—no cash or CODs. Please allow 3-4 weeks for shipment.
<u>CANADIAN ORDERS:</u> please submit in U.S. dollars.

Ms./Mrs./Mr._____

Address_____

City/State_____ Zip _____

JAYNE CASTLE

excites and delights you with tales of adventure and romance

____TRADING SECRETS

  Sabrina had wanted only a casual vacation fling with the rugged Matt. But the extraordinary pull between them made that impossible. So did her growing relationship with his son—and her daring attempt to save the boy's life.
19053-3-15 $3.50

____DOUBLE DEALING

  Jayne Castle sweeps you into the corporate world of multimillion dollar real estate schemes and the very private world of executive lovers. Mixing business with pleasure, they made *passion* their bottom line.
12121-3-18 $3.95

Rebels and outcasts, they fled halfway across the earth to settle the harsh Australian wastelands. Decades later—ennobled by love and strengthened by tragedy—they had transformed a wilderness into fertile land. And themselves into

The Australians

WILLIAM STUART LONG

THE EXILES, #1	12374-7-12	$3.95
THE SETTLERS, #2	17929-7-45	$3.95
THE TRAITORS, #3	18131-3-21	$3.95
THE EXPLORERS, #4	12391-7-11	$3.50
THE ADVENTURERS, #5	10330-4-40	$3.95
THE COLONISTS, #6	11342-3-21	$3.95

All-new Candlelight Newsletter

An exceptional, *free* offer awaits readers of Dell's incomparable Candlelight Ecstasy and Supreme Romances.

Subscribe to our all-new CANDLELIGHT NEWSLETTER and you will receive—at absolutely no cost to you—exciting, exclusive information about today's finest romance novels and novelists. You'll be part of a select group to receive sneak previews of upcoming Candlelight Romances, well in advance of publication.

You'll also go behind the scenes to "meet" our Ecstasy and Supreme authors, learning firsthand where they get their ideas and how they made it to the top. News of author appearances and events will be detailed, as well. And contributions from the Candlelight editor will give you the inside scoop on how she makes her decisions about what to publish—and how *you* can try your hand at writing an Ecstasy or Supreme.

You'll find all this and more in Dell's CANDLELIGHT NEWSLETTER. And best of all, *it costs you nothing*. That's right! It's Dell's way of thanking our loyal Candlelight readers and of adding another dimension to your reading enjoyment.

Just fill out the coupon below, return it to us, and look forward to receiving the first of many CANDLELIGHT NEWS-LETTERS—overflowing with the kind of excitement that only enhances our romances!

DELL READERS SERVICE—DEPT. BR782E
P.O. BOX 1000, PINE BROOK, N.J. 07058

Name_____

Address_____

City_____

State_____ Zip_____